BANSHEE

BANSHEE

Rachel DeWoskin

dottir
press
NEW YORK CITY

Published in 2019 by Dottir Press
33 Fifth Avenue
New York, NY 10003

Dottirpress.com

The excerpt from the poem "Acts of God" by Heather McHugh first
appeared in *Hinge & Sign: Selected Poems* (Wesleyan University Press, 2011)
and is used with the permission of the author.

First printing June 2019
Design and Production by Drew Stevens

Trade Distribution through Consortium Book Sales and Distribution,
www.cbsd.com.

Library of Congress Cataloging-in-Publication Data is available for
this title.
ISBN 978-1-948340-10-6 (hardcover)
ISBN 978-1-948340-11-3 (paperback)

For Zayd,
who understands everything
from the most granular to the most profound,
including the wildest reaches of fiction.

CHAPTER ONE

THE FLESH BLEW OFF HER BONES
underground. That's how the waxy anchorman put it;
you could feel his lips loving to make the shape of the
word *blew*. The reason they knew? They'd had to exhume
her. He sighed, going for horror, but conveying pleasure,
maybe not accidentally.

I was sitting in front of the TV that afternoon—three
days ago—on an orange chair in the waiting room of a
clinic for breasts, so I happened to be turning questions
of tissue over in my mind anyway. In some chambers, the
idea of this poor dead girl's body exploding and being
dug back up seemed like more than I could stand, the
last click in a game of thought roulette. I waited for the
release of a bullet that might knock me flat. But in other
chambers, it felt acceptable, predictable, a revelation
that I, as a sane adult, should be able to tolerate.

I imagined the anchorman, that plastic action figure,
digging her up with bare hands himself, a spray of dirt
and decay blowing into his open mouth. My husband
had dated the now-wife of the anchorman in college (a
coincidence), and so I imagined her, too, married to the
salacious half-rhymer of *blew* and *exhume*. She had to listen to his voice and watch his face stretch into approxi-
mations of human expressions every night at dinner. Did

graphics run underneath him as he brushed his blinding teeth? Did she suspect him of the perversions I did? Or know his actual ones? Maybe she shared them.

It wouldn't have surprised me. One disappointing aspect of middle age was how few perversions remained shocking. I did feel a jolt, though, at learning that in addition to dying and liquefying, we also explode after being buried.

A NURSE CALLED my name, "Samantha Baxter," and I leapt up, nodding like a doll on a dashboard, and followed obediently. A light-green hall became a light-green room on the right. The nurse weighed me, then stunned my arm with a pressure cuff and said, with her eyes cast down sorrowfully, that my blood pressure was elevated.

"I'm not surprised," I told her.

"No," she said, staring as if trying to determine whether I was slow, joking, or both. "I mean, it's significant. The doctor will have to retake it later."

She handed me the usual life-sized paper towel I was to wrap around my waist with a plastic ribbon and turned to go.

"Please put this on, open to the front."

I shed my jeans and shirt, folding them into a miniature stack on the light-green chair before placing my bra and socks in my purse. I lined my ankle boots up, not wanting to appear unruly. I learned when my mother was diagnosed with breast cancer twenty years ago that I shared the gene that predisposed us to particular cancerous outcomes. It had letters but no name, and sounded to me like bric-a-brac, some country kitchen pattern on a quilt. I had been diligent about climbing into magnetic tubes for MRIs and making my breasts go horizontal in mammogram machines. From the moment I learned about the gene, someone had his or her hands up my shirt constantly. Meanwhile, a chorus of advice rose around me about prophylactic surgeries, but those seemed strange and medieval to me when I was young and spry and busy having, nursing, and raising my daughter. So I kept vigilant until now, when, as it turns out, I wasn't vigilant enough and I should've done the prophylactic lopping when I had the chance. Because now it doesn't look like it will be prophylactic anymore. Now I'm in some trouble. But just for the sake of honoring my own risky former self, I let myself be happily catapulted back to a time when even the word *prophylactic* suggested a tiny raincoat of pure, impending fun.

The nurse returned and took my blood pressure again. I stayed quiet, knowing it wasn't going to matter who took my blood pressure where or when. Goat, boat, mouse, house, here, there, anywhere. Something was building in me like applause or lava, about to shoot out of my head—a sound? A bolt of sci-fi light? Actual brain matter or blood? I felt as bubbly and unpredictable as a cartoon. I found it tricky to calibrate my blood's panic when its container was in peril.

My body knew it was in danger; every cell in me, including the Judases who were dividing, replicating, partying, knew this next news would be bad. That what we—all the parts of me—were waiting to discover was a question of margins. How dire? Catastrophic? What story would I be telling Charles at dinner—a hopeful version, a euphemistic one? Or telling Leah, if I took that wild route instead?

Leah! See? I was already contemplating it before I got the full impact of the diagnosis. Maybe this whole can-cerpalooza is no excuse.

A "spot of calcification" had shown up on my most recent MRI. The deceptively maternal-seeming Dr. A was the one who told me this, holding my slide onto one of those backlit boxes I'd only seen in movies before. She flicked a switch and pressed the picture of tissue up onto that box of light, her broken nail pointing out a spot of white. She spit slightly when she said the word "dense" in her incredible sentence, "because your breast tissue is especially dense"—all those slobbery and disgusting *s*'s crowding out the verb, the nouns, the actual meaning of the sentence. I never heard what the clause modified, or understood what this especial denseness foretold.

Instead, I watched her spray of spit like a shadow puppet show across the lit slide, wondering whether the white spot was a presence or an absence, a small pearl in a dark sea of tissue or something removed by a mini hole punch. Either way, corrosive cells were coursing through my marrow.

Even before that appallingly alliterative appointment or the one three days ago, when I heard about the dead girl and my own body's prospects veered toward worse, I had stopped watching television shows that only featured women either naked or dead. That sounds like a pretty low bar, but it eliminated everything. It excluded espe-cially whatever my husband loved, including the pilot episode of a detective show he and the rest of the world were particularly rapturous about. The only character in whose story I could invest my energy was a corpse, hogtied to a tree before the series even got started. How luxurious would it be to find myself among the chorus of men in cop costumes circling that bloodless, naked body, taking notes, aroused, distressed? Furrowing my brow with the concentration of the artificially living, I would vow to avenge whatever also-man had done this heinous thing, all while untying the girl and stretching her out on the grass.

It was less fun, even as a viewer, to identify with the decaying victim. At least for me. And probably every other woman watching.

My husband, Charles, joked good-naturedly with our many friends—also good-natured—about how fussy I was. He had to screen anything we were going to watch together to make sure there was at least one female character who was clothed, alive, and competent enough to speak reasonable sentences.

He found almost no shows suitable for a tyrant like me, although he liked what he called the "Baxter test" and seemed to cherish the task of pre-screening and eliminating anything sci-fi, macho, politically reprehensible, or indifferent to the perspectives of women. We had very little time for television anyway. He was helping corporations defend themselves against whatever litigious clients or environmentalists sued, and I was teaching poetry.

I was alone in the waiting room when I heard about the body. This was right before my body divided into versions I had to work to keep separate, before I betrayed

Charles in a fury worthy of some tragic Greek character. Before I made a devastating choice right at the end of my life. Except my choice was tawdry and banal. And even now, it's only been a few days since I made it, like I said, so I don't know if it's the end of my life and won't until at least a few weeks from now. Maybe my mind has begun to take over, marching my body straight out of my own life, even as I try to save that body, that life. What's the difference between a body and a life?

After watching the news in the waiting room, I sat on the paper-wrapped table, wrapped in paper myself. Dr. A came pounding in, and right away she said, "I'm afraid I've spoken to the pathologist, and the tumor we found on the MRI and biopsied in the core biopsy did, in fact, turn out to be malignant."

Dr. A is a big waster of syllables. There's nothing lyrical or efficient about the way she speaks. The sound of blood rose up around and inside me when I heard the word *malignant*. I wished Charles had come with me, could hear the rest of whatever she said, could ask reasonable questions, could try—as he was wont to do—to statistic me back to the good kind of oblivion, the kind where we pretended numbers were in our favor.

During the core biopsy she mentioned, someone in a lab coat and surgical mask had drilled a screwdriver so deep into my body that I'd had the sense it might impale me, nail me straight to the table. My entire side had remained purple for two weeks, making a carnival mask out of the bruise against the dire pale skin on the rest of me.

Now Dr. A was yammering away about de- and recon-structing, asking questions to which apparently nei-ther of us had answers: Which parts of my skin would they spare? How close to my chest wall would they have to scrape their scalpels, dig with trowels? I never knew chests had walls. I thought of the date again, November 1st. A calendar fell open in my mind: How long would it take me to get over whatever horrors awaited me here? Should I wish the time away, or would these weeks be my final romp on the planet?

Dr. A was explaining that she would do the surgery. She said, "I take the tissue," and when I didn't respond, added, "I do the removal."

"Do" seemed an odd word to me, spinning into all of its forms, due, dew, doo-wop.

I asked, "All of it?"

"All of what?"

"My tissue."

"We try to get as much of the breast tissue as we can. Of course, we can't be certain we've gotten all of it. Some cells may remain."

Some cells sell seashells. Maybe I'd write a tongue twister or a limerick. *There was once a woman with cancer / who frolicked and*—well, what rhyme, *answer? Dancer? Prancer. Enhancer. Breast enhancer?* Oh my God. Okay, so maybe—*There once was a woman with breasts. Whose doctor put both to the tests. She spared her some nipples, but*—*triples, stipples,* ooh, how about a subtle internal rhyme, *dimples? Leaving the cutest of dimples?*

Dr. A was talking and talking.

Pay attention, I reminded myself. Yes, yes, I gestured with my bobblehead while she said the words, "Depending on what we find, we would either cut under your breasts or across them." I imagined the knife. A box cutter? A steak knife? How much like a regular thing did it look? Incision here, incision there. She began to draw on the paper table, and I watched. She drew grimaces, one underneath a blob; the other straight across its twin blob. I had an almost overpowering urge to color in the drawings, hear the metrical, waxy click of crayons on paper.

Would the incisions end up hidden under my breasts, or straight across them—real badges of damage? I wasn't certain which I preferred, to what extent I'd want to hide that this had ever happened. If I survived. And might my preference also depend on how long I survived? Maybe I'd wish to mask the experience in the short term, but then want my body to bear the marks of it later.

In any case, I didn't know how or want to discuss this aspect with Dr. A, armed as she invariably was with a barbed comment veiled as care. The first time I met her, before she'd examined me and done the slideshow of my dense tissue and calcification, she'd said (in front of Charles), "Well, since you have implants, you're at least familiar with parts of the process, should you choose mastectomy and reconstruction."

I had not had plastic surgery, was not familiar, stopped breathing because I was so stunned by this remark. On what basis had she concluded this? Something in my chart?

"I don't have implants, I—" I said, shaking in my sweater. It sounded like I was lying.

"Well," she said, glancing and clucking at me, "You have very large breasts, then, for your frame."

Absolutely incredulous, I responded, "Yeah? Well, all this can be yours."

And Charles had the audacity to shoot me a look.

IT STILL AMAZES me, which I guess doesn't mean that much, since it happened only three weeks ago. But is it possible for a breast surgeon to say to someone who has a genetic certainty of getting cancer, and is about to learn there's a spot of calcification on her especially-dense-very-large breast scans, "Well, since you have implants," without knowing whether that's true? It seems impossible to me, even now, after it happened. That night, Charles gently implied that if I were less abrasive and crazy, my conversations would go awry less often, less reliably. I railed back at him that it was her fault, said I hadn't done anything to prompt her idiotic comment about the surgery she'd assumed I'd had. I said, *how dare she?* I didn't want her as a surgeon; how could anyone who said such insane and inappropriate things to her patients be a reasonable doctor?

Charles calmly recycled the word "reasonable;" she was the best breast surgeon in the state, I should "be reasonable," it wasn't important to like her, we just needed her to save my life was all. As long as we could count on her to do her job, it hardly mattered whether she was "likable." I shut his voice out. I teach poetry, like I said, and I don't let my students use the word "likable" when describing the work they read or write. I don't care whether characters—or even people, really—are "likable." Can they just not be unbearably tedious?

But here, I clung to the word, because it seemed to me that if a surgeon was that insensitive, she lacked the capacity to care about my life enough to save it. I considered giving her a copy of my first collection of poems, many of them about bodies, but I haven't yet. She doesn't strike me as a reader of poetry. And if she is cleverer than I think, and understands the embedded criticism or even the title, *Temporary Conditions* (which now seems like a joke), will her understanding make her more likely to leave something dangerous inside me? To scrape less close to my chest wall? Save me less?

"Let's schedule a nipple-sparing mastectomy for as soon as we can."

"Oh, okay, yes." Nipple-sparing! I saw a double "r" instead of just one, *sparring*, not *sparing*, nipples in fencing costumes, jabbing at each other. From there I got *sparking*, nipples with flashing metal tassels, chips of flame flying. Dr. A was staring at me. She could tell something, but I didn't know what.

"Do you have any questions?" She sighed, maybe bracing herself for whatever unpredictable social fireball I might lob at her next. She struck me as the sort of doctor who resented being asked anything at all. She was already halfway out the exam room door, and who could blame her? She got to escape each of us and our miserable fear and questions over and over in that lime-green hallway, and then at the end of each day.

Look how normal I was, though! I wanted to prove her

wrong, to make this conversation okay. After all, there was still one day left before I gave up pleasing anyone ever. I asked, "How long is the recovery? I mean, before I'm okay?"

She dared to look bored by this. What had she been expecting? Hoping for?

Then she asked, "Do you mean how you look? Or how you feel?"

Ah, so Dr. A thought I cared too much about what I looked like. I had felt the vicious undercurrent of this judgment every time she spoke, from the aggressively frumpy pedestal of her own cancer-free body.

"How I *feel*, obviously," I defended myself. "When I can be up and about, when I can *teach*." See, I'm smart!

"Well." She surveyed me, made some vague and slurring sounds about *two weeks*, *three weeks*, *depends*, blah blah, *drains*, oh, and *fluid*. Fluid? She clapped a black folder shut fast—what doctor carries a black folder? — and left. She was a Disney villain. About to save my life. Or not.

"Thank you!" I cried out, hoping to inspire love in her, make her want to rescue me.

She glanced back over her shoulder, a lemon look on her face. "I'm going to send you over to Dr. B, our plastic surgeon now. He can discuss reconstruction options with you."

The door clicked. I was alone, free of her. I stripped off the paper towel, folded it, and put it in my purse because I didn't want to open the dead-gown bin. Then I slowly and carefully returned my body to its own clothing— inappropriately tight jeans, a silver T-shirt, a scarf, and bronze ankle boots. It was, I guessed, my hideous, visible vanity that made Dr. A so scornful of me.

I walked from Dr. A's office to Dr. B's office across the hall, zig-zagging to avoid the quickest route between any A and B and looking dizzily at the other women sitting in the waiting room. One in three of them would, at some point, find herself where I was. I felt such gutting sorrow at that fact that I swayed and sat, nauseated with our collective misery, as fearful for a moment for those strangers as I was for myself. Back in another orange chair, I realized the news was still on, a different anchorman now, his voice eerily similar to the first one's.

"According to the autopsy reports, whoever killed the seventeen-year-old high school senior peeled off her skin. *Meticulously*," he reported.

Meticulously? How did they know? And did they discover the peeling after she had already decayed? How was that possible? Forensics? What did they do, test the dirt and bone and skin cells? What skin cells? And how, from such testing, could they get *peeling*, let alone *meticulously*? Something involuntary and metrical inside me was leading me from subjects of the flesh to other subjects of the flesh, as if my mind and I were bouncing down enjambed lines. I landed on my own skin, being peeled away, tissue taken from underneath, replaced with what? Something plastic, something lasting.

Once I was in Dr. B's office, he drew pictures of breasts, too, teardrops versus perfectly round planets. They were lovely; he was a much better artist than Dr. A, which I guessed made sense. He was wearing a lavender bow tie and looked meticulous. Oh, his waxy, prettily ageless face! Had he done his own work? Put himself half to sleep and reconstructed his neck, back-spaced wrinkles off the page of his face? And when he peeled people's skin back (mine, for example), when he worked on our faces or breasts or whatever construction site needed injecting, stretching, or implanting, did he move "meticulously?" His hands looked precise and graceful, instruments of poetic care. I imagined them coming into contact with my skin, tracing lines down my body, tickling my back, playing "X marks the spot" and then burrowing under my skin, into the blood and tissue—or absence of tissue—beneath.

When I stopped thinking about his clothes and fingers and the cartoon breasts he'd drawn, I realized we had moved on and the words coming out of his mouth were "fat grafting" and "grades of silicone." He had asked me something, something about where he'd farm fat from elsewhere on my body and which of the various gummy shapes he was pointing to on his desk I'd like him to implant under the muscle wall of my chest.

He looked at me expectantly, as if I might have a response to any of this.

CHAPTER TWO

IT WAS JUST TWO DAYS LATER—
yesterday, November 3rd—that I found myself in a bathtub five floors above University Street, soaping up one of
my graduate students.

I don't mean this as an excuse, since bathing my student was a low I never thought I'd sink to, but I'm certain
that I wouldn't have been there if I hadn't just discovered
that I was literally coming apart. I don't mean "found
myself" in a spiritual sense or to suggest it wasn't by my
own agency that I took—or, well, Leah took—my clothes
off. Or that I didn't leap into the tub voluntarily, basi-
cally singing my consent. I just mean the situation itself
gave me a new perspective from which to view my body,
which was about to be transformed forever. Demoted, I
thought, although I also tried to convince myself I'd be
bionic, perky, invincible. They'd clean the terrors out of
me, and in my improved body, I would also find myself
somebody new.

But fuck the cheerful, hypothetical version of the
facts. Suddenly, for the first time in my nicety life, I'd
prefer to fillet my own heart than sit through another
brunch with Charles's or my colleagues—than ask or be
asked, "What are you working on?"—than cook, write,
sleep, teach, think, do what was right, or remain me. In
fact, I wanted to crack open my own cage of bones and

20

run straight out of myself. Or, failing that, could I just sleep with my student Leah every second until the doctors knocked me out?

This turn was only surprising because I'd been such a polite pleaser and goody-two-shoes until now. But maybe that life was a dishonest dress rehearsal for this, my actual final performance. Or maybe it was simpler than that—this impulse toward recklessness predated my "condition," and I just wanted the wreckage of sex with Leah in the way that drinking too much at a party made you want something you already wanted, and if you drank enough, let you do it. Cancer was letting me do this! Thank you, cancer!

Or maybe my case was, in fact, dire, and therefore forgivable? What if I had very little time left to do anything that took place naked? Or, what if the numbers were off, or I was in that small percent of the bad side of the numbers, the two percent of people who didn't wake up? (I mean, once it happened to you, then the chances were 100 percent, right?) What if I was one of the ones who was going to die on the table, or just after? Then I would have no time to do anything at all, so that was why I had to risk my entire life. Just to identify what that life was.

Or—let's say I do survive this. I might still no longer be myself once I'm housed in an altered body. So how can I count on that later self to do anything that might benefit the me I am right now? In fact, what holds a person together at all? I acted in my own self-interest. So this is an excuse.

And in any case, forgivable or not, this chaos felt worth revving the engines in my blood. The way I saw it,

I was sparking something I might keep, or at least get to remember after Drs. A and B cut the circuits in my brain with anesthesia. After they "did the removal" of my tissue, which Dr. A described to me at the very-large-breast (hereafter referred to as "VLB") appointment as "external." She was reassuring me; the idea was that mastectomies were easy. Maybe among the reasons she seemed to hate me is that I had the gall to ask about the tissue she was lusting to excavate: "External to what?"

And she and Charles had looked at each other, each saying to the other with eyes meeting over me, "See what I have to deal with?"

Charles is the most rational person I've ever met. Our daughter Alexi is nineteen, which—if you love math—means we had her when I was twenty-three, which—surprise, surprise—means my pregnancy was probably an accident. Which makes us seem wilder than we ever were.

I hate math. When I see numbers, a dusty velvet curtain drops over my mind and I can't think. By the time she was in fourth grade, I had to study for hours just to help Alexi with her fractions and least common whatever, multiples? I was intent on not allowing her to believe that women are worse at math, so I rallied. I also made Charles or the repairmen we hired work at night or while Alexi was at school when they fixed things, so I could say I'd fixed them. And I learned the basics, could unscrew a pipe, find what was wrong with the washing machine or dishwasher, turn on the digital TVs, etc. So, I lied until it was true, in other words. Ish.

It's true that when Charles and I got married, we were

young and knocked up. But Alexi was only an accident in the sense that we hadn't planned to have a baby *at that moment*. We'd had a lot of rollicking sex, and I liked the extreme-sport-unprotected variety—wasn't it enough that I was so monogamous? Plus, I was such a jittery teen-age boy of a person and body; I never really believed I could get pregnant. This body? Morph into something big and earthy and productive? Ha! I had always con-sidered my body a vehicle for pleasure. I didn't have the capacity to imagine it building other people's spines and eyeballs.

Charles always suggested protection—was always sane, thoughtful, "let me get a condom"-ing me, but by the time I met him I was petulant and distracted. I no longer liked to have the plot interrupted, to roll out of the story into the nightstand drawer, rip open a plastic package and find the slippery, vending-machine prize inside, only to have to unroll it and wrap up the present I had just unwrapped. No! So there it was. My lunacy shap-ing the rest of our lives.

And yet—even though it was my love of reckless sex that landed us with tiny Alexi, when I showed Charles the stick with the double lines, he hugged me right off the ground and laughed with happiness. At dinner that night he was pleased and pragmatic; it was just a little earlier than we'd expected but good, now we'd be young, which meant our chances of having a healthy baby were excellent and we'd be fine. He'd always known we were going to stay together forever, what was a few years early on the baby front? Maybe he'd been thrilled that we were getting a jump on middle-age stability.

I told Leah none of this, of course, just put my mouth on her mouth, then her neck, shoulders, breasts, stomach, thighs. I didn't reveal anything about my diagnosis or personal life, because obviously such confidences are inappropriate in a student-teacher relationship.

Here's how yesterday happened: she came to my office hours. And sat in my giant green chair, wearing tight, straight-leg jeans, work boots, and a tee shirt with a tiny rhino icon on the left breast. Was I looking? I'd never really noticed in any sort of real detail what my students looked like, but for some reason she came into clear view. Her hair, short and red, looked like a lit wick, and she said, "Professor Baxter, can I ask you something?"

And whatever she asked was about love poetry, but I didn't hear her. And then she cocked her articulate, angular face to the side and said, "Hey, do you want to come over and chat about this someplace quiet? Someplace—" She looked around slowly at the walls of my office, and I noticed how big her eyes were on her face, how far apart, and I saw the walls she was looking at and suddenly felt trapped, almost consumed by them.

"Well," she laughed, a throaty, boundary-shattering laugh. "Someplace not *here*, anyway. Professor?"

And I said, "Yes," without a pause long enough even to honor what had once been rules I lived by. And she moved her boots in a way that looked like dancing or clicking her heels together. And stood.

More mysterious than my life-dissolving "yes" was how Leah had the bravado to know to invite me to her house. Maybe she was in the habit of getting the things she wanted, which wouldn't be surprising. There was something very strange and appealing about her, her particular toughness, the brave eye contact thing she did, the way she took my clothing off like it and I belonged to her. She was entitled to all her appetites, delicious. And I, an utter stranger to myself, went shy when I tried to unbuckle the belt I hadn't noticed she was wearing. And unzip her jeans. She laughed while I moved them down her hips, slim like a boy's—or what I thought was like a boy's, because I'd been, up until this point, somewhat unimaginative.

Then we were in the tub, because she said, "Let's take a bath. I have a very good tub," and it was true. Old-school, with feet, claws.

In the water, she tried to sit in the back behind me, but I didn't like this idea, wanted her in front of me, so I could see and not be seen. She didn't object too strenuously when I positioned myself, just climbed in and leaned her smooth, straight back against my front. The feeling of her spine, skin, and neck caused me to float above the scene we'd created, taking certain stock: a late-fall day at the equator of my medical experience, three weeks after the initial lump and crisis, three weeks before the surgery. There were slick, sand-colored tiles, Leah, bubbles, hot water, and even a very flattering image of me, a blameless extra in someone else's unforgivably banal, clichéd—well, okay, kind of hot and titillating story.

She turned and looked right at me with her giant, straightforward eyes. I felt shocked, even though it shouldn't have come as a surprise to me, either that I was in this situation or that eye contact might be required at some points during it. The right half of Charles's blond,

familiar face loomed in my mind like a blimp over a sta-
dium, even as I met Leah's gaze. I saw his half-gray unibrow, thought, *I love him*, and grimaced, because even my
thoughts were now badly wrought. And because what
difference did it make if I loved him or not? Nothing
about dutiful or romantic love had prevented me from
leaping into my student's life and frolicking as if I were
either an unmoored teenager myself—or worse, one of
my ancient male colleagues, dragging a beautiful youngster down the drain of my midlife morbidity.

I even thought, well, at least Alexi, our daughter,
was an undergraduate, so she and Leah couldn't really
be considered the same age. What a hideous witch I'd
become! And yet, what *fun*. No wonder this shit was
what men did all the time. Although most of the men I
knew who had gone this route seemed to have been in
positions of greater power than I felt I was in, somehow.
Was I an old man? A powerful professor of poetry taking
advantage of my vulnerable student? It didn't feel that
way. Slipping down an existential cliff, I began to make
small, repetitive circles on Leah's hip. Leah, the redhead
whose poems and papers, although unexceptional, had
made my stomach lurch.

Leah was laughing, and I was glad. I told myself that
this was fun for her, fun in the way things are fun when
you're young and have no sense of consequences. She
turned the water back on with a sleek foot, and a jet of
heat spread up my calves. I closed my eyes and rested
my head on an inflatable neck pillow secured to the tub's
back ledge.

How much time did Leah spend bathing? She was the

one who'd suggested getting in, so maybe she diligently read my assignments while half-submerged: *Beowulf* with lavender sea salts, Thomas Hardy as the water turned gray, Elizabeth Bishop while Leah loofa-ed. Now she leaned even more fully back into me, letting her knees fall against the sides of the tub. Her red hair, although short, haloed out in the water, suddenly less spiky. I wondered what she put in it, how she combed it to make it look so prickly when dry. Now it had become soft strands.

I moved my hand from her stomach up first, onto the landscape of her breasts, trailing bubbles over her nipples, then moving my fingers down under the water to her rib cage and stomach, flat and hard. And even so, the next image arrived in my mind: a set of stacking bath dolls I once bought for Alexi, rubber renditions of Russian nesting dolls, but with hair—who thought that was a good idea for a bath toy? Water remained between them no matter how long they dried or how vigorously I scrubbed, so mold grew all over them like disfiguring birthmarks or cancers.

I said, "Leah," out loud, reality trumping the mottled dolls momentarily.

"Yeah?"

I had nothing. The next image was me, dead, Charles and the forensics team finding my blue body here in the tub, bloated as a carnival doll. The dead star of a show I wouldn't be willing to watch.

"Sam?" she asked.

Um. *Sam?* I got that I couldn't really expect her to call me Professor Baxter in this context, but I would have preferred *Samantha* at least, as if those two additional syllables could help correct for some of this.

"Hello? You okay?"

"I'm fine, Leah. I was just making sure you're still here." I liked her name, *Leah*. It reminded me of Star Wars, something quirky and sci-fi, otherworldly. Like her.

I GATHERED MORE bubbles from the surface of the water and rubbed them into the slight dip of Leah's hip bone, felt them disappear, felt the jut of her hips for as long as I could stand not to move my fingers down, slowly. As I traced the shape of her, sliding my fingers between her open legs, a bunch of disconnected nouns surged back: first, the sidewalk we'd just walked down on University Street came at me—pavement squares, a parking meter, wheels, the curb rolling like punctuation. Parentheses. Leah's skin. All outside matter was merging dangerously with inside.

Leah was rubbery, the warm water dissolving whatever was left of my clear thinking, early boundaries. She moved like a mermaid, wiggling against me. I was counting, holding my breath, whatever used to be selective about my permeability vanishing. I was borderless, without outlines, and therefore no longer myself. Convenient, because then I could keep moving my fingers, feeling the steam rise around us as Leah slid around and the tub filled.

The bubbles rose above its edge and oozed over, onto Leah's (face it, Sam), angry-emoji-shaped bathmat. The nouns came back, and I had the sense I'd often had lately—that I was literally asleep, dreaming atop our green sheets, a set sent by Charles's mother, geraniums bloom-ing across them. That I might wake up any moment with his arm draped over me, or his foot tangled around my ankle.

Even as I tried to focus on Leah's sea creature-y sig-nals, I thought of sheets Charles and I had shared, how for nineteen years I'd washed and stretched the sets out again and again over the tight corners of a series of mat-tresses that seemed suddenly like an ill-conceived art installation. What if I lined up every mattress we'd ever slept on? I could bounce from bed to bed and maybe make it across the entire planet.

"Don't stop," Leah whispered, arching her back and pressing into my hand, moving harder against it. I didn't increase the pressure of my fingers, just kept a soft, con-sistent movement inside and outside of her, letting Leah move against me until she made a cricket sound in the back of her throat, a chirping signal of pleasure almost painful. Then she relaxed into the water, laughing. "Okay, now you can stop."

That sound! My life dissolved like an old-fashioned slideshow catching fire. Each image melted and curled: Charles's hands, knotted, arms tight and sinewy, cradling his head on a pillow. He'd slept like that when we were young, holding his own face as if it were a baby, and then later—after we'd lived in two cities and three apartments—holding one of my arms, as though he'd exchanged his head for it. From there, the slope was dangerous; he began to fall asleep with any part of himself wrapped around or holding or lying directly on part of me: an arm, leg, foot, shoulder on my shoulder, sometimes even his head on my chest. It was a weight and tangle I thought kept me awake, except I must have fallen asleep each night, because I'd wake later having glided out from under Charles into my own cool space.

Here were Charles's size thirteen feet. Here, the fallen tree shapes his legs made under the quilt. Here, his chest rising, falling, breathing. Here was Alexi, toddling up the first porch step, a clean diaper on her head like a little barrister wig. My mother, coming out of the door of her house onto the porch, clapping.

And in the treacherous eye of my mind, here was Alexi again, this time in a cap and gown, grinning sideways at her best friend, Siobhan, ignoring my camera. Alexi, with the tattoo high on her collarbone, a tiny lightning bolt that signified some secret between her and Siobhan, one she never revealed to me, and which I could hardly hold against her now, no matter what it was. Alexi never looked directly into a camera, but always sideways— always away from whoever wanted to capture her, maybe especially me. Or maybe she was like me, cagey, fast, distractible. Here—kill me—was Charles's mother, visible from across a stretch of golf-able lawn, raising the pale drink in her hand up to meet her angry mouth.

Leah turned over and flattened herself on top of me. She looked down as if deciding something, then put a hand on my stomach before climbing out of the tub, careful not to crush me. She stepped onto a damp pile of clothes on the floor: her jeans and belt, a black tank top, infinitesimally small and complicated underpants.

"You want a cheese sandwich?"

In order to have wanted a cheese sandwich less, I

would have had to be dead already. I imagined cutting a sandwich in half for Alexi, the insides oozing out. I imagined knives. How do doctors get knives under human skin? Do they peel the skin back and then scrape the tissue out? Does skin peel away in a pure sheet? Doesn't it tear? Scrunch up? Bleed? What happens to the blood? Do they suck it away with one of those loud tubes like water from the back of my open mouth at the dentist?

I didn't move or speak. The water was cooling creepily.

"Stay there," Leah said. "I'll bring it. I don't want you to go hungry at my house."

I imagined a sandwich floating in the bath with me. Leah dropped the towel to the floor and walked naked out of the room. My stomach fluttered with multiple wings. Desire—how far would it take me? It had certainly taken a statistically meaningful number of my colleagues into affairs, and, in at least two recent cases (including that of the former dean of arts and sciences, who left his wife for a male adjunct), new states. Some it drove straight into the ground. The original chair of our department had a heart attack twelve years ago, after which we all learned he'd been sleeping with our three best graduate students that year. Maybe not the worst way to go. At the time, I was thirty, the newest hire. I'd considered him to be an absolute fossil, ready for death, was only shocked he even had it in him. He was probably fifty.

Did Leah consider me the oldest person ever? She didn't seem awed, if so. I turned the hot water back on and reviewed our encounter so far. When we'd arrived at her house, she'd asked whether I wanted a drink, either mature for her age or an actual grown-up. I'd been confused by the question; it seemed so clear to me that we'd called off all the rules that her polite, "What can I get you?" seemed almost a parody, so old-fashioned as to be off.

"Oh," I'd said, stunned quiet either by her youth or by my own, running behind me, catching up, knocking me over in this strange, possibly gross moment.

"Um, I'll have whatever you're having." I never said *um*. Until now.

And neither did Leah, even now, because that was when she'd said, "I'm having *you*," and pulled me to her without ceremony. My mind caught fire and burned blank.

Charles was so critical of faithlessness and those with pathetic morals that riling him up used to give me an illicit charge. In the beginning, we both liked it—he found it funny and scandalous to hear what gossip I could concoct, and not only about sex, but also about human behavior in general.

Later, even though he was less enthusiastic, I still liked to provoke him with dirty, presumptuous, and judgmental stories, but maybe there was some tragic or poetic logic to my compulsion. In any case, the gossip seemed crueler and less frivolous now that I was either already or about to be the object of it. Charles never even hovered near a tempting flame himself; he was genuinely above such antics. His father James often said, usually apropos of nothing, "Human beings are morons. No one ever lost money overestimating the stupidity of other people," and, "The world operates at a C-minus level."

He meant those without the exclusive blessing of his

genetics, of course, including me—he'd always counted me among the humans who collectively brought down the universe's GPA. A disastrous match for his son. Of course, now he had incontestable evidence that he was right: not only was I illness-prone, but I was also a faithless disappointment to Charles. If I died, either on the table or because they couldn't cure whatever poison was in my cells, then he'd be even more right. He preferred being right to anything else and was, frankly, selfish enough to enjoy this latest victory, even if it came at the cost of his own son's marriage and happiness. Not that marriage and happiness are the same.

Now I heard Leah's feet slip and pad along the kitchen floor, heard the fridge door open, hot splash of butter hit the skillet. I looked down at myself in the now-cool water. My hips, bluish skin, the slip of my belly, cheating legs.

I stood, dizzy, and put a hand on the wall, grabbing a discarded towel and wrapping it around my waist. I wiped the mirror above the sink and saw myself surrounded by the fog like a tacky school photo, misty with me in the middle, my stupid face wet with steam. My skin was tight, mouth expressionless and familiar—the bottom lip so full it suggested pouting, the upper one thin enough to contradict it and give me some sternness I'd once been grateful for, but now just made me look old. And predatory. I opened the cabinet to punish myself: mini o.b. tampons, a little glass bowl of rings for her belly button, which I'd noticed in the bath had a small silver object in it. And endless ChapSticks and round tubs of lip gloss, which surprised me. She didn't seem the type.

Someone my daughter's age. It was a good thing I don't believe in God, because otherwise I'd be high on the list for smiting. Charles and I used to gossip about the trolls who drank the youth of students and then either abandoned stunned wives or traded entire lives of actual thinking and living for epic sessions of couples therapy. I always thought counseling was talking that happened at the expense of living, that if you had to discuss your relationship all the time, you probably weren't busy or happy enough having it. Hence, Charles and I never went to couples therapy, although I guess I didn't really get to keep gloating about that now.

And as for the gossiping, it was really just me. I gossiped while Charles furrowed his face and cleared his throat occasionally to demonstrate that he hadn't died of boredom or judgmental-ness.

I peered out into Leah's hallway, steeling myself against additional innocence: beige plastic bins everywhere, likely for everything from toiletries to paperclips. There were socks strewn about, cheap throw rugs, pillows on a futon. A futon! Until this, I hadn't had sex on a futon in fifteen years. When I said so, Leah joked that maybe this was my version of buying a new car and fucking my secretary, which would be funnier if it weren't so obvious.

"Where's my convertible, then?" I asked, trying to flirt. "And where's my secretary?"

"You're an academic," she replied, tartly. "You have too much irony and too little money for a real mid-life crisis. And I'm your secretary."

I felt defensive then, because I wasn't the type to force

my TAs to do secretarial tasks. I didn't even have a TA; I taught poetry to twelve students. But *if* I had one. And I had plenty of money, too, although there was no reason my students would suspect that. I didn't come to class dripping with jewels, in spite of Charles's wealth. We exuded quiet evidence of the care that comes with expensive food, exercise, potions for the skin, good medicine. My clothes also probably cost more than their simplicity suggested, but none of that was recognizable to young eyes.

I wondered if Charles had it in him to punish me with money. I doubted it somehow. He'd always been generous about sharing everything, and in any case, he preferred moral judgment and remaining blameless himself. He'd be kind about cash, whether by continuing to allow me access to our shared bank accounts or in alimony payments, if we ever actually formalized the utter ruin of our lives. Especially since I was sick. Maybe he wouldn't punish me at all, would just let me have this. Our marriage wasn't in crisis, I don't think—I just got sick and wanted to burn the world down. Still want to burn the world down. Or the parts of it that are trapping me, anyway.

I stood in the hallway. A line of photos on canvas: Leah and somebody, probably her mother, an anemic-looking blonde. What did her mother think of her lovely, boyish girl? I pushed the question from my mind. Here were Leah and another girl in sunglasses, the other girl in a small bikini, Leah in some kind of short wetsuit, a giant body of water behind them. Next, Leah holding a baby I assumed was someone else's. I knew nothing about her family or life and hoped not to learn much.

How little could I hear and say, and still keep her close and naked? Or was she keeping me? She'd driven the day. Who even was I? I stood staring at a nail hole in Leah's wall, just under the bottom edge of the canvas print of her and the baby; she'd probably tried to hide it with that photo but hung it just slightly too high. I itched to fix it.

And in that moment, it came to me: I would tell no one about my surgery. Just like I'd say nothing about Leah, obviously. I wouldn't tell the department that I might be dying, would teach my way through the entire thing while averting my eyes. If I needed additional treatment, chemotherapy, radiation, poison they would have to pump into whatever was left of me after, I'd cross the question of whether to admit any of that later. I felt ecstatic relief. If I didn't tell anyone, then maybe none of this would have happened.

I just had to get to and through the surgery, and then it would be Thanksgiving. Alexi would be home. We would eat pies and strip my drains and then hopefully by the following week, I would prop myself up and teach. Fake my way through until it was true that I was fine. I felt, for the first time since the diagnosis, like I would be alive someday, on the other side of this.

Of course, if that was true, what the hell was I doing in a towel in my student's hallway?

"Sam?" Leah peered her head into the hallway, hair in small, wet lines that looked drawn onto her face. "Hey. So. Your sandwich awaits you."

I thought, if I told no one that I was sick, then when it was over, it would be over and gone. Although—what was the line in that Heather McHugh poem about the hurricane, or was it a tornado? Anyway, the line happens after the storm:

It was over for maybe minutes.
Then it was never over.

Maybe this would be like that, never over, even once it ended.

"Coming," I told Leah. I walked down the hallway, absurdly still in a towel, then doubled back to the bathroom and put my clothes on. I thought, while I was at not telling anyone about my illness, I also wouldn't leave Charles. There was no reason to get divorced unless someone wanted to remarry, right? Although—I guess he would, actually.

Because that's what men do, I thought, they remarry.

Maybe Leah and I should get married in white dresses, Leah with nothing under hers—no bra, no tank top, no underpants. We'd hold hands down an aisle and kiss in front of an audience of horrified relatives: Charles and his parents; Alexi, home from college; my mother, Sophia, slack-jawed; and who else? Oh my God. My older brother Hank and his wife, Sarah, and how about the students from my poetry seminar this semester? I'd assign them to write occasional poems and then appear myself, clutching a Sappho collection. I'd still be bandaged in my strapless gown, wound drains hanging like balloons from a car: *Just married!* Two drains on each side, blood collecting in their plastic bulbs. Someone would have to "strip" the drains and measure their fluid. Maybe I'd be able to do it myself. Would Charles still be willing, after this? Or

I could twist Leah's imagination for the rest of her life by asking her to do it: *Hello, sexy fling, would you mind measuring the gore pouring from my wounds?*

I had a sickening jolt of considering what the others in my class might think at Leah's and my imaginary wedding. Or if they saw me now. What I myself might think of this if I saw me now—in other words, if my mind were still intact.

There were twelve graduate students in my workshop, all talented, one genuinely on her way to being a writer. I'd always prided myself on knowing who the stars were long before it was obvious to the world. It wasn't always the ones whose writing was the most polished or gleaming, or even those—to my dismay when I was young—who worked the hardest or read the most. Once, it was a girl who consistently wore pants that rode below her pelvic bone. Every time she stood up, she flashed the entire class a band of waxed skin and I wondered, where do my responsibilities begin and end? Why had her mother not taught her to wear underpants? Or had she, and this was a rebellion? Was it obliviousness?

There was a quality about my best writers that was difficult to define—enormous talent and curiosity, yes, but also willingness. Maybe that makes me sound like a narcissist who, in addition to seducing my student in spite of having a loyal, diligent husband of nineteen years, also tries to turn young writers into other Samanthas. (Some wanted that, in fact—read *Temporary Conditions* when they were young and then showed up in this nowhere land of a university town to find me because they think my work helped form—or could help form—theirs).

But I've never wanted students who wrote my work. I've hardly even wanted to write it myself.

What I mean by "willing" is that they had to be able to discover what kinds of poems they could actually make, which required a willingness to recognize and acknowledge when they hadn't figured out yet what they were capable of doing. Most people lack various components of this ability: some can't tell in anyone's work what's successful and what isn't. Others are blind only to their own work's strengths and failures. Some can tell what's wrong but haven't learned to fix it. Not to mention the next requirement, which is to be open to making those poems you can make well, all while keeping enough variety and experimentation not to become an imitator of your own work—a problem I consider "being Jack Nicholson," even though more than one student has pointed out to me that being Jack Nicholson would be awesome.

"But you know what I mean," I say when that happens. "He just plays himself over and over."

And they stare like a group of surprised deer, anxious to flee but unsure in which direction.

In the kitchenette, Leah stood at the counter, pouring orange juice into glasses embossed with cows. She was still naked, her stomach flat and stacked with muscles. I wondered if she ran, jumped, crunched. She pushed a round blue plate across the counter toward me.

"Don't say I never wined and dined you," she said. "Here, I'll even get you a napkin." She grinned at me, and I thought she was signaling that she was both too young to be believed and also wisely aware of how young she was or maybe seemed to me. I remember when I was young, having the constant irritated sense that I knew how little I knew. I reminded myself not to be a wise old woman now—why couldn't I just revert to my younger self with Leah so we could enjoy each other?

She bent to open a drawer and pulled out a paper towel, so unselfconscious that I wondered what it felt like to be her. Maybe weightless. Her small, un-jeopardized breasts appeared immortal. She was still smiling, assembling this meal for me. Leah was a good person, composed of all the qualities I lacked. She was easily, fully human. And her poems, like her papers, were always oddly off the mark, but this made the fallible beauty in them somehow more compelling. And she was starkly unpretentious, a rarity in the workshop.

I looked down at the food, desperately flat on the plate. Leah was watching me. She came around to where I stood and stood behind me, put her hands on my hips, and slid them up and down like she was measuring something. I lifted the sandwich off the plate and took a bite. The cheddar was chalky and under-melted, the bread thick with congealed butter. I tried to avoid chewing, swallowed the doughy glob, and coughed out, "Thank you."

"You're welcome," she said. "Can I get you something to drink now? I mean, to go with the sandwich?"

I felt like flinging all caution to the wind, and anyway, how was I going to get this sandwich down? I said, "Whiskey."

"Oh, um, I have beer—is that okay?" Now she sounded shy, defeated. She hadn't had the thing I'd asked for.

"Of course," I said, even though I hate beer. It makes me feel like someone has pumped me full of air and hops and wheat or barley or whatever it's made of. Plus, the smell. Like the woods at night, burning dirt.

She handed me a beer in a bottle, yellow as a urine sample.

"Aren't you having one?" I asked, buying time, wondering where I could hide both the beer and the sandwich, collecting unwanted treasures from Leah.

"I don't drink," she said. "Bad history."

I didn't ask, didn't want to know, just took a long, thirsty sip of the beer. It tasted better than I remembered beer tasting, although I thought suddenly that this was one of those beach beers, and she was supposed to have stuffed a slice of lime into its neck, right?

"I'll be right back," she told me, as if we were buddies on a field trip. Then she went to get dressed and I quickly wrapped the tragic sandwich in the paper towel and buried it in Leah's beige trashcan, under melted candles, an empty bottle of cucumber lotion, and containers that had once contained pre-washed baby kale. I poured the bright beer down her sink.

My phone came alive then, buzzing in the back pocket of my jeans: Alexi. Her name ignited the new combination of fear and longing I felt every time I thought of my family. I hadn't told her yet. *We* hadn't told her yet. And now would I compound the announcement of my mortality with the one of my infidelity? "Your childhood was good—you're welcome. But now that you're nineteen, I have cancer and I'm sleeping with one of my students, who is barely older than you are, and dreaming of leaving your father for the first time in nineteen years of either being happy or deadening my fantasy life."

Because I need more actual life for a minute, in case I die either of cancer or of some unpredictable disaster or complication during surgery three weeks from now.

Hard to imagine a way to put that euphemistically. I didn't pick up.

CHAPTER THREE

LEAH SAID SHE WAS GOING TO go spend the next day at the park, that I should join her. The park was a long strip that ran through our tiny university town like a green vein. She wanted to sit outside together and read, maybe eat something, a picnic? She asked the last word with one thin eyebrow arched, her big eyes sparkling with something devious. Tomorrow. Would we see each other tomorrow?

The thought of a picnic with her was a tourniquet around my heart, so I said I had errands to run, things to prepare. I left her place in the early evening, drove my car down the newly throbbing streets. Pulling into Charles's and my driveway, I felt like I was driving over all the years underneath this one, every day I'd driven home, every conversation he and I had ever had, every other me I'd ever been.

Never having cheated before, I hadn't realized what an instant accelerant sex is for disorientation and guilt.

Out of the car, I walked by plants I'd once cared about, up the stone walkway to our imposing, pretentious front door—what assholes lived here? —and turned my key in the lock. A metal taste spread to the back of my mouth, as if I'd licked a bloody knife. I set my purse on the in/out table, kicked my shoes off, and walked into my own kitchen. The young me watched the old me and thought—seriously, it's come to this? Who are you?

"Sam?"

Charles was home. My name in his voice sounded familiar and just, brought back the delicious horror of hearing it in Leah's voice.

"Yeah, it's me," I said, my fake words clanging around, the taste of Leah and impending lies on my lips.

He walked out into the foyer to find me, looking like a sleepy hunter, someone who has stayed awake all night in a blind, watching for deer. Except I was the deer, and he wanted to save me instead of killing me.

As he came close and hugged me, I said, "I feel very strange and tired."

"Do you want to lie down?" he asked, but even though we'd known each other for what now felt like our entire epic lives, I couldn't decode this. Was it a proposition, and if so, of what sort? Was he offering to lie down with me? Was it a romantic offer? An exhausted one?

"I want to watch a nature show," I said.

He nodded, and I saw myself as if I were a character in a story in which Charles was the protagonist. He said, "How does *The Blue Planet* sound?"

"Good."

"I have a call, so I can't watch with you, but I'll set it up. Do you want something to drink, Sam? Tea? Coffee? Water?"

I deserved to perish from my own thirst. If I was going to quench whatever the desire for Leah was, then maybe I should desiccate my body by ignoring its other more mundane drives. "No thanks," I said. "Thank you, though. I'm fine." Too many words, lined up unnaturally.

As we headed to the couch, Charles asked, uncharacteristically, "Were you at school?"

"Um"—I was now formally a person who said *um*—"yes."

The lie bounced around the room between us, like one of those horrible Orbeez Alexi used to grow in bowls of water. They were hard beads until they absorbed the stagnant water and then they became juicy, bouncing little gelatinous balls that fell all over the house and rolled everywhere but also smashed into clumps of a kind of disturbing Jello when stepped on.

I sat on the couch and Charles used one of our seventeen remotes to turn on an endless menu. He scrolled and typed through to *The Blue Planet* and waves came on the TV. I felt nauseated, seasick.

"Can I have *The Great British Baking Show* instead, please?" I asked, and he scrolled again, and as soon as the hosts were bawdily joking about bread boxes, I felt instantly better. Cured, bright, happy.

"Thanks, honey."

He sat for a minute more. "Sam?"

"Yeah?"

"Can we talk about what's happening? Are you—"

Poor Charles. He wanted, I knew, to ask if I was insane, having a nervous breakdown, going to be okay. He wanted to send me somewhere to get whatever help I needed, but he knew better than to ask if I was crazy, in case I either was or wasn't, and flipped into a mad rage at having been confronted.

"I'm fine," I said. "Just anxious. I just need a little space."

I knew immediately that this had come out wrong. He seemed to reel.

"Space—space from what, Sam?"

"You know, from this—from our—from, I don't know. I need to think this surgery through before it happens."

"Of course. Let's think it through together. Are you saying you want space from our—" Here he paused, because he was incredulous. "—marriage?"

My face was on fire. Were we actually having this conversation? I tried to backpedal, but needed to go forward with it, too. Otherwise, how would I justify what was already underway?

"Not just that," I said. "From everything. I need to float up above my life for a second to get through this."

"Which means watching *British Baking* during the day? Which means not teaching? Which means what, Sam?"

Fucking my student.

It means fucking my student, and never being polite or apologizing again. It means shedding every rule like itchy lizard skin, suffocating all the people I love most, you included, and freeing myself. Then putting back on only the ideas and habits I believe deserve to be worn.

"It just means I need a minute to think through who I am, in case this is the end."

He took my right foot in his hand and set it on his lap like a pet. "Oh, Sam. I'm sorry you're suffering, honey. And I get how scary this is. It's a nightmare. But there's no reason to make it worse than it is. This is not 'the end,'

46

no one dies on the table. It's not a catastrophic diagnosis. The surgery and treatment are common and well-tolerated. Look at your mom—she's doing fine, all these years later. You'll be fine too. Please try not to exaggerate the danger. You're torturing yourself."

I took my foot back. I didn't want to be told I'd be fine.

"I think I need to go for a walk, actually," I said, and I turned off *The Great British Baking Show*, even as the meringues were being whipped in the glass bowls, even as the bakers were talking about the necessity of adding the sugar spoonful by spoonful.

Even as the blood sausage was being wrapped in fatty pastry.

"A walk is a good idea. Do you want company?"

"No thanks," I said. "I'm just going to clear my mind."

"Of course. Go easy on yourself, honey," Charles said, and he let me go. I walked through the park until the sky darkened, knowing I would walk through it again in the light with Leah. Tomorrow.

THAT NIGHT I slept alone. When I went to bed, Charles was in his study, and then he never came to bed. I woke up alone, showered, dressed, and headed out our backdoor toward the park, dialing Leah's number. She picked up, and her "hello" was low, maybe because she was asleep, or maybe because she didn't know who was calling.

"It's me," I said in a very sexy voice, because I couldn't sign up for either *Sam* or *Professor Baxter*. "I'm done at home. You still free for a picnic?"

"Oh, wow, okay," she whispered. Her voice stayed low, so maybe that was just what she sounded like on the phone. "I'll get ready now. We can meet at the bench next to the sundial."

Something about the way she said that—without asking where I'd like to meet, without checking—made me feel like she was standing over me. With a whip.

The hills were scattered with a complicated mess of leaves. It was unusually warm, even in the morning—a sign of impending global disaster, but which meant I didn't have to be cooped up either in Leah's embarrassing apartment or in our house. Instead, I could skip across nature, an innocent, infatuated, middle-aged teenager.

As I walked toward the hill, I wondered about women who left their spouses. And then what, rented apartments? How boring and unbearable. An apartment seemed like the opposite of an affair. Not to mention, I couldn't possibly leave Charles because 1) I loved him, and 2) then what, I would wheel myself from the hospital to a basket-case tank/bachelorette pad I had rented two days after being diagnosed with cancer?

That sounded mentally ill, even to me. The mere thought of looking for this grim potential apartment seemed a task so insurmountable and final, it required me to crawl into whatever bed was closest, likely Leah's. Looking at apartments always made me feel not only mortal, but also deflated in the present tense—like, why even bother living if a drafty, dust-covered (or worse, object-filled) space is all it comes to? I'd fly around the room at the very thought and then land flat on the floor, a balloon weeks after the party.

Even without the sad bachelorette tank, if I moved out, I would have to tell Alexi what was happening, and that was obviously impossible. I wanted her to get through her finals first. No wonder men who had affairs kept them secret and tried to have it every possible way at once. How convenient it would be to stay married to Charles, live in our house, and recover or die from whatever illnesses ravage me, while also pretending I was twenty and loving whoever else I wanted to on the side, feeling reckless again as I careened into antiquity and death.

I suspected from Charles's gentle, unfinished, "Are you—" that he was worried I was having a breakdown. That he didn't know about Leah. He knew something was happening, but not precisely what or with whom. To his great credit, he didn't ask that, even after I said I needed space. For Charles, the larger picture was always possible. He's never been petty, but he wasn't correct about the breakdown narrative. My mind was lucid. I didn't blame him; all of our friends who'd been left had accused the deserters of being mentally ill. How else was it tolerable to be the victim of such a choice? Especially when you were as famously blameless as Charles?

It wasn't him, it was me. I just wanted to leave him for a while, even though he was almost as perfect a person as he considered himself to be. This particular brand of certainty reminded me of what I experienced when I decided to marry him. I'd known I wanted it—but forever? For a while? For how long?

Maybe this would all turn out to have been an absolute bloodbath, but even that possibility—that there were reveals left that I couldn't see, outcomes I couldn't guess at, thrilled me. I remember when I was thirteen, I read "soap opera" and didn't know what it meant, because I'd always thought the words—which I'd only heard up until then—were "soap bopper." This had seemed, at the time, both terrible and exciting. I knew I'd had something deeply wrong, and understanding that indicated to me that there might still be other discoveries that awaited me. It's not a great example, but I was reminded walking away from our house that getting something wrong often felt right.

If I had turned around, I would still have been able to see our house on Riverview Court. Charles, who studied engineering before becoming a lawyer, designed it and had it built: imposing, modern, made of light, blond wood that looked like his straight, straight hair. The house remained as chilly and unblemished as his family, no matter how many Midwestern seasons it endured. It was a beautiful palace, and when I first moved in, I felt like a Disney princess, promoted from my own ratty life to Charles's lovely kingdom. He was very artsy in those days, hanging paintings and surprising me with throw pillows that complemented the red leather couch he'd chosen.

I found Leah at the sundial, leaning back on the stone bench, her eyes closed. The early sun looked like it might light her pale face on fire, and I wanted to warn her to hide her neck, lest some wild animal bite it. But I sat next to her and she opened her eyes slowly and calmly. "Hey," she said. "Long time no see."

She'd never been one for radical originality, but I laughed agreeably.

"Should we walk?" I asked, thinking that if we saw

anyone—if anyone saw us—well, fine, we were having office hours, a student and her teacher on a stroll through the park. Right?

We headed along the park's path, Leah chirping and chattering about a dream she'd had in which a squirrel leapt out of her tote bag and bit her. I tried to listen, watching young mothers pushing strollers, students in fleece staggering under the weight of their enormous book bags, two readers sitting on backpacks and sipping from thermoses of coffee. A child darted away from his mother and rolled through a pile of leaves and I remembered the story my fourth-grade teacher had told us in a ghoulish whisper, of kids in a pile of leaves being crushed by a car. The driver parked on the pile? Seriously? I guess her point was not to lie in the street even if there was a tempting leaf bed there, but the fact that every time I see toddlers playing in leaves even now, thirty-five years later, I think of *that*? It's an instance of a teacher having a hideous and everlasting impact on her young student. I wonder why it was on my mind.

Leah spread a blanket, pink with leaves and needles remaining in its fibers from days she had already spent in the park, hopefully frolicking with people her own age. She sprawled upon it so earnestly that I wanted to either devour her or be her—if there was even a meaningful distinction between the two.

She rolled onto her stomach to take a book out of her bag and started reading. She was wearing textured tights and a very short cargo skirt, which now rode up her legs. She kicked her feet up and used one hand to hold the book, the other to shade her eyes. Sun filtered through the trees. It did not seem to occur to Leah to smooth her clothing down or cover herself. What was her mother like? I pushed the question from my mind.

The book was Janet Malcolm's biography of Gertrude Stein and Alice B. Toklas, which Leah was loving, maybe because Alice B. was its underdog heroine, a fun shock to the system for anyone who had grown up with the Gertrude-as-protagonist paradigm.

"Listen to this!" Leah said, beginning to read loudly enough that several other picnickers looked over at us. I neither apologized for nor shushed her. She wasn't my child, after all.

Alexi was never like Leah, and neither was I. Leah showed up on the first day of Poetry and Performance wearing a black button-down lumberjack shirt with an olive tank top visible underneath, and the first three books on the syllabus already read. Read carefully. She always stayed three assignments ahead, and I didn't know what exactly she was proving or to whom. Her adoration of Edna St. Vincent Millay and Audre Lorde was so undiluted as to be comical.

Leah's eagerness would have been solely silly if it hadn't been contained by a macho, unapologetic affect— her red hair a threat to the room, about to turn and burn us all down. Her shoulders, wings, arms slim and muscled, eyes absolutely frank. She was a living dare.

When she put *anaphylaxis* in a poem, I was surprised to learn it was hers, that she had allergies, but maybe she knew we'd feel doubt, because she showed us her EpiPen that day in class, tucked in her shirt pocket. Leah's appeal was odd, linked to her way of thinking, and—patronizing though this was—to her way of trying. Leah tried very hard.

"She must have been furious," she said now, meaning Alice Toklas.

"Probably," I said, "but who knows whether more or less than any of the rest of us."

"What does that mean?"

I shrugged, tipping my head back until the sun hurt my eyes. "Just that rage is part of the program," I deflected.

"I'm not really enraged," she said mildly.

Should I have said what I thought, which was "not yet?" I didn't. Instead, I put a hand on her back, before remembering how wildly inappropriate this whole situation was and lifting it off like I'd burned myself.

"Keep your hand there," she demanded, and I put it back.

"Move it down," she said, louder, and I did so fast, wishing she'd say less, or at least speak quietly.

"How about Gertrude Stein not admitting she was Jewish?" I asked, changing the subject as I moved my hand off of her, hoping she wouldn't notice or direct me to put it back.

"Well, I guess you can see why she felt she had to hide it, right?"

"It's unsavory."

"I don't know," she argued, "I think it's forgivable. Can any of us really say we'd have been first in line to announce our Jewishness when it might have gotten us killed? Wanting to survive isn't really selfish or unsavory, is it?"

"Depends on how far you're willing to go, and at whose

53

expense," I said, like a bitter old man. It seemed funny to me that even though Leah's idea was slightly more cynical and less idealistic than mine, her reason for believing it was forgiving and kind. Whereas my impulses were now jaded and rusty.

"I have to stretch," Leah said, twitching on the blanket. She stood then and bent at the waist, and I had a moment of horrific expectation that she might do an entire yoga routine. She reached her arms up to the sky. "Join me," she said, grinning. I wanted to do yoga with Leah in the park about as much as I'd wanted to eat the disastrous cheese sandwich, but I didn't want to be cranky or immobile, so I stood and reached my arms up. I did everything she said, is the truth. Maybe she was the perp and I, the innocent victim.

"Sun salutation," she said.

The only sports I liked were swimming and climbing the sheer faces of cliffs. There was something about the private, single-minded focus of those two activities that allowed me to engage without embarrassment, self-criticism, or pure loathing of the way they made my body feel. I hate teams. I hate sports that involve rules or balls or getting chased or hit or even interrupted in my own pursuits.

Alexi was always athletic, talented, even when she was a baby, kicking her chubby legs furiously. She never had to try hard, but maybe needing to make a bigger effort might have benefited her, given her some necessary experience.

Once, after a volleyball game in which Alexi leapt up to the net and slammed a ball down onto the other team's side, whooping like a superhero, a high school boyfriend of hers said, "You know what you're good at? At being good at things."

Alexi reported this to me at the time, unsure why it made her unhappy. "He meant it as a compliment," she said, "but I don't like it."

"Of course not," I told her. "Because you work hard and he can't see it."

She surveyed me skeptically. "Yeah," she said, "maybe." I looked away, caught. Had Alexi ever had to work hard at anything? And if not, was it because she had enough talent to compensate? Maybe Leah was the daughter I'd never had, the pleaser. Oh my god—reroute your thinking, Sam! Stop imagining them in the same sentence, please.

Leah was embarrassingly planking on the blanket, her body an absolute two-by-four. I did what I always do when asked to plank, which was to collapse and lie on my stomach. I looked at the grass, the billions of blades, the leaves on top of it, and tried to see individual shapes and colors. A bug struggled through a tangle of damp leaves, finally triumphing and finding itself on top. Now what, bug? Sunbathing? What's your goal?

"That's not a plank, Professor Baxter," Leah said. She rolled onto her back and shaded her eyes from the sun.

"I'm observing nature," I told her, my face scalded by shame at my own fancy name and title, dripping as both were with desire and irony.

But now she sounded genuinely curious. "For a poem?"

Ugh. How dark did I want to go? Did I want to say what

I was really thinking, that soon I'd be packed among the dirt, bugs storming my body, flesh blowing off my bones?

"Yes, maybe," I said. "For a poem." Then she touched the small of my back.

Once, when I was in seventh grade, I made a bug collection, and one of the beetles didn't die properly even though I asphyxiated it with nail polish remover before pinning it to the foam board with all its dead colleagues. When I woke in the morning, the hearty beetle was turning slow circles on its pin, its stomach leaking, its eyes black with either life or impending death—I couldn't tell. I put a nail polish remover pad over it so it would be drenched and certain to die, and then I cried all the way to school and all day at school, including during my presentation of the bug collection.

"I remember when I first read 'Button,'" Leah said, her hand still on my back, possessively, I thought. At the mention of my work, nausea rolled me over and trapped me on my back. At least this meant I shed her hand. I imagined kicking my many insect legs while I closed my eyes and hoped Leah would say nothing else about that poem, which had gotten more attention than any of my other work (and which I could hardly stand to remember). Kill me! That pompous motherhood poem—why had I written it?

And why had everyone liked it more than any of the other awful or good poems I wrote? "Button" was a poem about my mother infusing me with everything she was, and my only realizing it once I had a baby and had, in the way we all do, become my own mother. While buttoning Alexi's coat. I outlasted Leah by not saying anything, not even grunting in acknowledgment that she had mentioned the poem.

"It made me think someday I'll be like my mother," she said, shrugging and using the hand that had been traveling down my body only a minute ago to shade her eyes. "And that being like her, I mean, will be okay."

"Oh, wow. Thanks," I said.

I hadn't yet told my mother. I was worried she'd die of seeing me in danger, of having to recalibrate her entire notion of me, the way she'd understood me her whole life, depending on my invincibility for the narrative of her two children to work.

"Sam?"

"Uh huh?"

"Do you have sisters or brothers?"

I so didn't want to be having this conversation. Why was it impossible to avoid intimacy with someone with whom you've had sex? Already here we were, on a picnic, paddling down a river of talk that would likely lead from our siblings to our exes.

How could I redirect this deep talk into a series of meaningless one-night stands with her in a row? Probably not going on a romantic picnic to the park with her would have been a good start. Oh well. "I have a half-brother, from my mother's first marriage."

"Oh," she said, gazing up at me. Was she batting her lashes? "Did you grow up together?"

"Only somewhat." I looked away.

"Are you close?"

I took a long time responding, hoping that would signal my lack of interest in having this conversation. I was looking at the faint view of Leah's underpants under her tights, visible between her legs, up her skirt. I put a hand on her leg again, imagined sliding it straight up her warm thighs in public, then thought better of it—but only by a slim margin. Were my half-brother and I close? Hank, from our mother's first, brief marriage, frail and wounded his whole life, alternately in love with and furious at our mother, both poles informed by his desperate need of her. He married a woman ten years older than him, a curly-haired, outgoing beauty so much like our mother that it almost seemed like an intentional joke. I loved her. I was thirteen when Hank married Sarah, and she was like a second mom, made significantly better by the fact that she wasn't actually my mom. And by the fact that she was the kindest, smartest, most beautiful woman I had ever known.

"Hello?" Leah asked. I was staring at the curve of her on the blanket, resting my hand on her hip.

"We're only sort of close," I said. I didn't ask about her family, just gently squeezed her.

"Well, I'm a twin," she said.

I was as surprised that this hadn't come up in the workshop as I was distressed to know it. I felt I should know nothing about Leah except the way she felt against me, the taste and feel of her—nothing about her family. If I had learned she was a twin in the workshop—when we were discussing Keisha's poem about her sister, for example—that would have felt less obscene. But I had my hand on her ass, my fingers pressing, worrying her clothes away, wishing they'd dissolve and that we were in her bed, on her floor, back in the bath. I wondered dirtily whether Leah and her twin were identical. Would I immediately desire her sister too, if I met her? How much of my wanting Leah was about her body and how much about herself, and again, that question: what was the difference?

"Are you two alike?" I asked.

"No. She's better at everything," Leah said, because she's a child.

"That can't be true," I said.

"Well, it is."

This was the sort of thing my half-brother Hank might say about me. I wondered if the cancer would change or punctuate that idea for him, the theory that I was a thieving, attention-stealing winner who took all. I hadn't told Hank about the cancer, either—how would he be able to bear it if I was the one who was sick for a minute or two? And I couldn't tell Sarah, because she'd suffer knowing I was sick, which I couldn't bear. Sarah was the one I told when I decided I "needed" a bra. I was eleven, and she took me on the secret shopping trip and let me choose. She didn't even embarrass me about my choice: a heavily padded, pink-and-black-leopard-print lace one.

"She's a musical prodigy," Leah was telling me about her twin, who was also, apparently, a straight-A student at Harvard Law, and had been an Olympic-level pole-vaulter during high school and undergrad. Did *she* make the cricket sound in the back of her throat when she came? Would she buck against me the way Leah did? Pin me down?

"It's tough to compete with someone like that," I said

mildly. "Maybe don't approach your sisterhood as a competition?"

Leah rolled her eyes. "Well, except we have to compete for our father's love," she said.

I laughed and she stared at me.

"What's your father like?" she asked, as if we were teenagers falling in love.

"I have no father," I reported truthfully, inexplicably still laughing. "I was conceived in a fit of fleeting passion my mother always described as her 'feminist' rebound after my half-brother's father left them."

Leah's mouth was open. I wanted to put my burning fingers in it and cool them, or put them in the collar of her jacket, open her shirt, press my hands into her chest, her stomach. Instead, I stood up. I didn't care about the thing with my father/no-father; someone else could parse that with Dr. Freud. I had present-tense fish frying here. I hoped she would suggest returning to her apartment, but she saw me stand and said, "I'm hungry," so we walked back to University Street for vegetarian bibimbap—and then to Leah's.

She peeled off her patterned tights in the hallway, taking my hand and placing it under her cargo skirt while looking straight at me. I was disoriented by her confidence, and we tumbled into the place unzipping and pushing and falling. Suddenly in her underpants, Leah looked like a rare creature I'd trapped in a jungle somewhere. She took my arm and tackled me onto her futon.

Ah, her futon. On the surface of that flat mattress she pinned and slid up and down me. Somehow, I thought of Connect Four, the little plastic coins sliding down into their proper places, lining up. She was so young and hard and smooth I couldn't help but wonder for a moment what my body—not bad for a half-dead professor, but still—looked and felt like to her.

Did she see the danger of my age, the slight sag between my breasts and ribcage, the whisper of a C-section scar across my bikini line? What did she make of all the parts of me that made me irrevocably not hers and not available to her? Her tongue was on my stomach, in my belly button, tracing a delicate line down across the scar. Her eyes stayed open, looking up. Was she daring me? I closed my eyes.

When we lay flat across each other later, we were like attached disposable chopsticks. I could taste some outrageous mixture of the two of us and feel all the places she was wet.

"You can stay the night if you like."

That's how she put it, *stay the night*, and I whacked into reality so fast my head hurt as if I'd hit it against concrete.

"Oh, um, no thank you," I said, and the formality and awkwardness prompted me to continue, so I added that I had to prepare to teach the following morning. As I spoke these words about my teaching, they popped and cracked with the sweet absurdity of candy.

Leah diminished the hilarity, though, when she rolled off me and into her own corner of the horrible futon and responded, "I know. I'm in your class, remember?"

"Of course, right. Well, yes, see you tomorrow." I almost called her "dear," but pulled myself together before that happened.

Oh, my silent house, the slip of light under the door

of his study the only evidence that Charles was there. In our bathroom, I took my clothes off, stood in front of our giant mirror, and stared. My breasts were tragic in the flattering light, sagging only the tiniest bit, their general curve still round, skin taut, nipples as transparent pink as they'd been when I was a girl. I liked their slightly tired look, the line suggesting a dramatic contrast between breast and rib cage. Leah had touched them; maybe that was why they had a literary, golden sheen. They looked like characters in a novel. I then had the dissociating sense that I was looking at Leah rather than at myself, and found it comforting.

From now on, I would think only of her breasts, never my own, even when I looked at myself. I would think of her nipples, rising to meet my fingers when I made small circles over, across, and around them. Speaking of which, it didn't matter to me that Leah was a woman, except insofar as she reminded me of something beautiful and important, and I needed to keep stripping naked with her in order not to lose whatever it was forever.

I put on pajama bottoms and a tank top, and climbed into bed with Mina Loy's *Lunar Baedeker*, but my mind fell from the lines over and over, as if they were ropes strung too thin and precarious for me to balance on. I could think of nothing but Leah and illness. Well, and death. And Alexi.

None of this—not the affair, the lying to Alexi, or the being alive—was sustainable. Maybe Leah knew that too, but most likely only I knew for sure. Who knew what Leah knew?

Something. Part of what I missed most about being

young was the way in which youth made it impossible to guess at the limited outcomes of love. Even if you'd been wild, or been burnt, you still had unbroken hope that the potential endings of each story were limitless. It's like the difference between having a secret admirer and finding out who it is. When it's still secret, it feels like everyone—and then when you know who it is, it's just that one person. And that person who actually admires or loves you? The narrow eliminator of all the other possibilities, crusher of hopeful scope.

So, it wasn't going to last, okay, that shouldn't have kept me up, because it was something, at least—for now. And something and nothing were more clearly opposites than I'd ever known them to be, or stark choices anyway.

I heard feet on the stairs—Charles's—and listened as if I were a detective, deduced he'd made it about halfway, and then the sound stopped. Was he standing mid-staircase, frozen? It would have been so unlike him, any gesture of indecision. All the mean bones in me hoped that my horrible behavior had introduced to him the human experience of not being totally certain all the time that you were right, a tiny dose of crazy. At the same time, I wished he would climb into bed and fall asleep with a book on his face. Or wrap an arm around my neck. Our routines shorted out, just like that, after nineteen years of enacting them until I thought we had calcified into their patterns. Were they gone now, those patterns?

Maybe my fear that the universe would rob me of what mattered most was making me destroy what mattered most in advance, a wildly childish breaking-up-with-my-own-life-before-it-could-break-up-with-me. I never did hear Charles make it up or down the rest of the stairs. Would he spend the night stranded mid-staircase?

I turned the light off and listened to the hum of the park outside our window, wind, the crisp leaves snapping finally and falling slowly onto piles of other leaves, a huge dead salad. I tried to put my breasts far outside myself. Some nights, they seemed small, manageable, a wisp that could (and now would) be swept away; other nights, like this one, they seemed to swallow the rest of me, to be a season, something abstract and around me, around us all, impossible to remove by way of surgery or any other means.

Dr. A's words, "No problem, because the tissue is external," joined the nighttime sounds, and I imagined my skin inside-out, the tissue internal to me becoming literally external. I imagined what tissue looked like and felt fear so intense it made me see lights, glittering and spinning in my vision. I closed my eyes, but the constellation remained.

I wanted to watch TV, longed for Amy Schumer, the girls from *Broad City*, Abby and Ilana, or for Samantha Bee. Someone sharp, hit-or-miss maybe, maybe only half-funny even, but always on the side of what was right, a risk-taker.

But now that I was taking risks, I had forfeited the right to entertainment, to watching TV at all. That belonged to Charles, and now if we watched TV together, I would have to confess what was happening. And then it would actually be happening. A throbbing, irrational fury of self-justification rose in my chest; I imagined it solid, knocking on the wall they'd soon scrape.

Men left their wives all the time and shacked up with graduate students—or, in the case of our former dean, other middle-aged men. This anger was replaced almost instantly by twin forces of guilt and freedom: I would be cast out by society forever, or would have to cast myself out.

I saw, in my mind's now-vicious eye, the slides of my breast tissue, all that dark swirl and a single devastating spot of white. Dr. A's words spritzing the light box.

The night came down on me, sheer, cold fear of a sort I hadn't felt since childhood, gasping under the covers at the clear calamity of what *forever* meant. Feeling in it all I'd never see again: spit, light, leaves, a slide, my girl.

I sat up and called my mother.

"What's wrong?" she asked before I'd even said hello.

This would have seemed eerily prescient if she hadn't always answered the phone that way. The only counterpoint to my mother's cheerful firecracker style was her own belief that catastrophe was right around the next bend. I think she believed—in some primal way, a feeling more than an articulated thought—that worrying would stave off actual danger if done diligently, constantly, relentlessly. Like if she could just prevent misery from sneaking up on her, she'd prevent it entirely.

"Well . . . the news from that MRI wasn't excellent, and I—"

"Oh, Sam! What? Is it malignant? Oh my God. I'm coming over. I'm on my way."

"No, Mom! Please don't come. I'm in bed already, I taught all day, and I—"

"What are we going to do? What are they recommend-ing?

"Surgery and then we'll see."

"What surgery? When? Have you scheduled it?"

I couldn't say the word. "It's on the 21st."

"But that's—

Was she going to point out that it would ruin Thanks-giving two days later, on the 23rd? I wanted to provide her an opportunity for further consideration before she did, so I interrupted, "Mom—"

"So *soon*. I was just going to say how soon that is—do they feel it's an emergency?"

"Isn't having cancer that could be spreading through your body always something you want to address sooner rather than later?"

"Oh, Sam. Do they know what stage it is?"

"No."

"Is it in both breasts?"

"No, just the one."

"But you're going to have a bilateral mastectomy, right?"

I squeezed my feet and then released them, made fists and released those too. I tried to shrug my shoulders, which were riding up near my ears.

"Oh, Sam!" my mother said. "I wish this were me again, not you."

My mother had what her doctors called an "insignif-icant" breast cancer twenty-four years ago. At the time, it felt significant to my mother and me. I was desperate for my mom not to die, so terrified when I let myself imagine losing her—which I almost never did—that I blacked out and whacked my head on the floor of our apartment.

And then she was fine. She had her surgeries and didn't need any additional treatment, and slowly the doorway to that hellscape closed and eventually, it seemed like nothing bad could ever happen to us again. I no longer remembered what that fear felt like—until now.

I said, "Thank you, Mom."

"You don't believe me, but I really do."

"I believe you. That's how I'd feel if it were Alexi."

"What can I do?"

"Um, this is fine. You can just talk to me about it."

But then I said goodbye and we hung up. I felt like I'd run out of words. I went outside in my pajamas and stood on the deck, relieved and terrified at how big nighttime had stayed even though I was an adult. What does it mean for human beings to disappear? When our bodies quit their jobs, what happens to our minds? Dickinson was right that the only secret people keep is immortality. I think the reason we can't babble about it and have to keep it secret is that we have no access, can't say what we don't and will never know.

No wonder I was this disoriented by the possibility of my own dying, of even just admitting, acknowledging that we're all dying, sooner than I'd realized.

CHAPTER FOUR

ALEXI KNEW, OF COURSE. KIDS always know everything, a fact we can accept when recalling our own childhoods—the handcuffs in our mothers' pajama drawers, the war-torn (ripped, oh my God, why?) copy of the *Kama Sutra* under other books in the bedside table, the candy and naked photos and weed and old love letters and appalling musical taste they thought were secret from us. Ha. Nothing is really safe from children, not even death, and children aren't safe from anything. But somehow, when we consider our adult selves the protagonists, we forget that.

There was never any chance of keeping my illness a secret from Alexi, no matter what I told or didn't tell her.

Although she left no message after calling when I was at Leah's, I called Alexi back two days later, on the morning of November 5th, sunlight blasting into every bedroom window, screaming a Frank O'Hara kind of joy. I thought of the violent happiness of his poems, streams of consciousness, lines running all the way over the page, crossing into each other, never slowing—imagined orange juice, sight, sunrise, the details of a newspaper headline or a short walk through New York made meaningful.

"Mom, what the hell is happening?" Alexi asked. She had picked up before the first ring finished ringing.

"I'm fine," I said. "Everything's okay."

"What? What do you mean *you're fine*? As opposed to what? Everything's okay, but what, Mom? There's a but, right?"

"Well, they found a little bit of calcification on my MRI—"

"What? What is calcification?"

"It turned out to be a little bit of cancer."

"Oh my God. Is that why you haven't been picking up? I knew it was some fucked up thing. What do you mean a little bit of cancer—what even is that? Is Dad there? Are you okay?"

"Calm down, Alexi," I said. "Of course I'm okay. Dad's at work. I'm about to go teach."

"And then what?"

"Then what what?"

"Are you having chemotherapy? What do they do? Has it spread?"

"I don't know yet. I'm going to have surgery and then we'll see."

"See what? What surgery? Oh my God, Mom."

Here I paused. Each time, the word *mastectomy* made my bones vibrate because of its hybrid quality, its list of hideous words mashed together, some extinct animal covered with enormous pelts of dirty, scratchy hair—a mastodon, I guess, and a WASPy sailing term Charles's father once used in front of me, testing whether I knew it (I did, you dick): a *barque*, which is a boat with three or more masts. A mast is a spar rising from keel or deck. *Dick* and *deck*, okay, so back to the *-ectomy* dissection, lighting inside me the smell of fetal pigs from ninth grade biology. I had stored that formaldehyde in my senses all these years. When I dissected the pig—cleverly named "Cletus" by my adolescent lab partner—I accidentally slipped and dropped its rubbery heart, which bounced on the table in the saddest way. I pretended to find it funny. A kid named Liam, laughing at the black slate desk next to mine, accepted a dare and took a nibble of his pig's liver. It was probably still preserved inside him, twenty-eight years later.

"Mom? Are you there?"

"They're going to take it out is all, sweetie," I said. "And they'll take some lymph nodes to see whether it's likely to be elsewhere, but they don't think so. It's early, they think—small or whatever. The surgery isn't risky. This is their bread and butter; they do these surgeries all the time. I'll be okay."

"A mastectomy? Is that what you're having? How is that not risky?"

Was she thinking of the same terrors as I was? Had I nursed them into her, a DNA-style passing-on of neurosis, à la my ancestors? I had nursed her for two and a half years on demand, could still feel those years, our quiet milk-life, running underneath this year. Some kind of heaviness. Some kind of loss.

And was the reason my own fear seemed so outside the normal human range because my great-grandparents died in gas chambers? Of course, we'd all read that trauma gets passed down, but is that true, even if we diligently hide it? Do you have to know you're fucked to fear it? Or is it in the drink, the milk, even the mama-baby eye contact?

It was unlike Alexi to be so worked up, and I felt irritated at being reminded that having cancer was both alarming and bad news. I could hear her trying not to cry, a swallowing sound, and I thought how I'd never kiss her goodnight in her dorm, how she'd never be my toddler again. I'd never snap her in and out of a romper. This created a vacuum of blood away from my heart and I thought I might black out.

"Yes, there's always some risk, I guess, but it's going to be okay. I promise." Who was I to promise?

She collected herself quickly, put her Charles voice on. "When is this happening?"

"The week before Thanksgiving."

"Jesus, Mom. Why didn't you tell me?"

"I did, honey. This is me telling you."

"I mean when they found it."

"I wanted to know what it was and what was going to happen before I told you. And now we know it's not that big a deal. It's going to be okay, and you have to stay at school, honey. Don't panic. Like I said, the surgery is apparently quite simple." I waited, hoping she would say something, but she was silent. "They say the tissue is external, so it's easier to—"

"External to what?" Ah, girl of my heart; thank you for asking. She was still at least part mine, not 100 percent Charles. Although why did it sound practical and rational when Alexi asked this, whereas when I asked, it was considered irrational feminine lunacy?

"You know, uh—" I said, my fake voice metallic, "—my organs. They don't have to cut near my heart or lungs or anything dangerous."

"But they know it's cancer? That's what they said?"

"Yes, but it probably hasn't spread, so—"

"So they can take it out and you'll be okay?"

"I hope so. They're optimistic."

"I'm coming home."

"No. Don't come home yet. Finish your quarter. You'll be home for Thanksgiving anyway. I'll need you then. I'll be recovering; it'll be cheerful to have you here. Do your work. Stay in New York. I'm a grown-up."

She said, "Since when?"

Once, when Alexi was in sixth grade, she went to camp for a few days. It was the first time I'd gone a single day without speaking to her. Even when I went to far-flung writers' colonies and lived in the woods, I ran miles to find internet or phone service and stood—sometimes with foxes trotting by me—on the phone, hearing her daily rose, thorn, and bud. That five-day camp had felt like a devastating dress rehearsal for this empty nest. I had hated it, waking each day feeling like a depressive (which I'd never been), staring at the ceiling knowing I would not only not see her that day, but also not even hear her voice. It felt like having nothing to look forward to, which made sense, because for me that's what it was. I loved seeing Alexi, loved 3:30 after school, walking her home from the bus or waiting for her later when she was older, listening to her kick her shoes off and toss her backpack into a heap on the floor, hearing about her days, sitting with her and Charles at dinner or just with her when he worked late, watching her twist noodles on her fork or lift a glass of milk to her small beak.

That stupid camp! I was shaken by the confidence of the other mothers—that their children would be

72

returned to them intact, that nothing would be lost by five days without each other. I recognized that the problem was mine.

"Mom? I have to go, Mom. I have studio. I'm so sorry that this—"

"I know, lovely girl. I love you. I'm sorry too. But please don't worry so much."

We hung up. The room buzzed with sunlight. It was apocalyptically hot for November 5th. The piles of leaves appeared to be burning. I slipped into simple black pants, black ankle boots, and a white pressed shirt. I put on pearls and lighter lipstick than usual, and when I looked in the mirror, I saw Charles's mother instead of myself. But I went to teach anyway, drove out of the garage and down tree-lined Maple Drive to Oak, past the park, where I could see myself and Leah sitting on her blanket reading yesterday, as if I were driving across time. My chest tightened as I remembered going back to her apartment. It was a relief to think of her instead of myself or Alexi, so I veered toward the scent of Leah's skin, working to make sure my thinking could be overdriven as much as possible by the sleek feel of her.

I parked outside the Humanities building and clicked in on my boots. I sounded professional, professorial, like an adult. The Police song "Don't Stand So Close to Me" poured back and forth from my mind to my ears. No one was playing it, I reminded myself, it was just inside me, the entire un-ironic 1980s contained in my tissue. How many 1980s lyrics would be scraped away or excised by way of the surgical removal of my breasts?

I opened the door and turned a light on, causing my

beautiful office to hurtle toward me with its green chair, airplane of a desk, and walls of books. The room seemed to be moving, jolting around outside of time, even as I set my bag down and grabbed a folder of student poems. I picked up a pen Charles and Alexi had gotten me for my fortieth birthday, one with a silver feather jutting from its cap, my name engraved on its side. Its real, heavy weight filled me with relief. I could be sensitive, sensible, could still feel what existed.

I walked out and climbed the stairs to my classroom two floors up. A cluster of students at its door disbanded a beat too early and slightly unnaturally as I approached. They knew, I was sure of it! Leah wasn't among them, and I didn't care whether she'd been the one to tell them or whether they'd guessed. I didn't even exactly care that they knew. I just hoped we could talk about poems in class without an undercurrent pulling any of us down.

"Good morning, guys," I said, and even though I had said *good morning, guys* to hundreds of groups of students for what felt like hundreds of years, the words sounded artificial, excessively intimate, casual in a look-ma-no-hands way. Had I always been a show-off, trying too hard in front of youngsters, or was I just painfully tuned in now that I was—what, having an affair with one of them? Was that what this was, an affair? Was there a difference between an affair and sheer fucking? And which one was this, in any case—how tawdry and shallow was my connection to Leah? I'd only been to her apartment twice and there'd been no build-up, just her wide-eyed, badass invitation. Just her mouth, her arms, her neck. It wasn't blameless, but was it irreversible?

I had never even sworn in front of my classes! So, I did have some self-control, because I had a dirty mouth at home but could turn it off while teaching. I never minded when Alexi swore, wanted her to have full use of any vocabulary she might need to convey any feeling she might have. But I did tell her, especially when she was young and sometimes ran through the house shouting, "Jesus Christ, Anfer!" at the cat she had named herself, that she should not say "bad words" at school. She had asked, guilelessly and wisely, "How do I know what are bad words?"

"You can ask me," I said.

"But how do I know what words to ask you if they're bad, Mama?"

Exactly. Who knew? Even I didn't know which words were bad anymore. Maybe now I'd shout all the profanity I'd been bottling up during workshop, another boundary dissolved.

"Hey, Professor Baxter," a student said.

Shit! Fuck! Motherfucker! Just kidding. We all mumbled hello and filed into the small wooden room on the third floor, trees and the tops of other students' heads visible out the windows, the hum of the old radiator our usual soundtrack. I shuffled papers and my students shuffled papers and then the room quieted. We all looked at each other. Leah had come in and was sitting toward the far end of the table, looking down and picking at a cuticle, her lashes casting shadows.

"Hello, everyone," I said, more formal now, hoping to regain something that was almost certainly irretrievably lost. "Let's discuss the Montale and then we'll take a look at Keisha, Sharon, and Roger's revisions. Those of you who read the Arrowsmith translation, let's start with you. What did you think?"

A student named Jin Yi raised her hand. I nodded at her, and she said, "I thought the Xenia sequence—to his wife?—was amazing. Because even though I don't read Italian and I was reading it in translation, I felt like I could hear the other language in the English."

We were off. The next hour elapsed instantly, almost as if we got to go back in time by way of talking about poetry. And I knew, as I always know even when I forget, that teaching—or talking about words, anyway—should be what we prescribe just after a cancer diagnosis, or a divorce, or any physical or emotional suffering.

I had a surge of vindication. If I could be this distracted and engaged, then I had been right to think that talk therapy was a waste of time, at least for me. Talking about myself, or my breasts, or even Leah would have been a significantly less effective way of treating my anxieties over those matters than talking with students about Montale's grief and love for his bug-eyed, vanished wife, about his crazed sunflowers, about the shadows of men on walls.

My gratitude for Montale was matched by the empathy I felt for my students, in all their angst and seriousness, their desperation to write poems as moving as Montale's. I understood this feeling and the fear that accompanied it, a fear of never making anything worthwhile. I spent my own twenties and early thirties trying hard to figure out what poems I could write, my mid-and late thirties writing them, and now that I was gallivanting around town with a girlfriend (and soon wound drains and inflatable breasts), maybe I'd write newly inspired verse.

Or doom myself to a lifetime of caricaturing my own better, earlier work.

Or die, and leave only what I'd made so far, which made me think I could have done better work up until this point. But how? I should probably have invested less time in spackling my lips with makeup and falling off Leah's futon, and more on revising lines of verse.

My students appeared to be spending their time worthily. Keisha's poem, entitled "For My Sister, High Above Our Lives," took me out of myself slightly less than those of the Xenia sequence, but it gave me the chance to redeem myself by keeping our classroom conversation constructive.

Then Leah raised her hand and said, "I admire the metrical precision and double entendre of the lines, 'She went, 5'8", 102, without saying / goodbye.'"

I immediately pictured Leah naked and gyrating on my lap. I said, "Can you say something more about what you mean by metrical precision and double entendre?"

Leah's cheeks lit, surprising me. Everyone looked down. Papers shuffled. *Did* my students know? Or were they simply looking back at the poem? Either way, I should have just said, "Oh, good point," or nodded and called on someone else, but I no longer knew how to do anything that didn't seem horrifically unnatural. Or to read the most basic signs in my own classroom.

In fact, it was kind of exciting. Like entering the mystery version of what used to be my predictable and boring existence. Or being Jane Goodall, observing poetic chimps—including me—in our natural habitat.

"Um," Leah said, "I just mean I think it's an interesting way to thwart the cliché of something—you know, 'going without saying'—to break the line there. Um . . . because I don't think that's where the line break happened in the first version of the poem, right? So that's what I mean about the double entendre, just that the line is literal—I mean, the sister goes, right? She dies or she disappears, literally, and also, it goes without saying that 5'8" and 102 are her height and weight. And it goes without saying that those aren't healthy numbers."

Now I said, "Excellent."

I did not follow up on metrical precision, since there wasn't any, really, and I didn't want to call Leah or Keisha out. Leah didn't speak again during class.

After class I hid in my office and read my students' comments on each other's poems. Roger wrote a poem about anti-miscegenation laws and his grandparents, on which Leah wrote: *The historical research in here rules, and so does the anecdotal material about your own family. But the synthesis of the two isn't quite there yet.* This seemed like a useful note to me, so either she was more astute than I had given her credit for being or else I was dumber suddenly, maybe blinded by affection.

Affection seemed like a useful word. I lik̀ed it, after finding it in my own mind, thought it was mild and appropriate. I told myself, that's what this is, affection for Leah.

When my phone rang, it was the pre-surgery nurses calling to schedule my next appointment, which was a physical designed to determine whether I was hardy enough to survive the surgeries: three of them, at least, the removal of the tissue, then the lymphectomy, where they'd take a sentinel node and try to read it for signs of escaped cancer elsewhere in my body. Then they'd put in the expanders, metal breasts under my skin, designed to stretch it until it was rubbery and generous enough to tolerate the insertion of silicone balloons in another surgery three months from now—one Dr. B affectionately called the "swap," swapping the metal expanders for permanent implants.

The truth is, when I thought about those steps, I felt convulsive, like I might throw up and fall off the edge of my own life. I talked like a sane person to the nurses, all while putting the thoughts of what this really meant deep in my marrow for later, with the smell of the fetal pig and every song lyric Billy Joel ever wrote. Also, my impending heart attack-ack-ack-ack-ack-ack-ack—

A knock set me off like a jump-started engine, panicked I'd be overheard and discovered. I hung up on the pre-op nurse and powered my phone off before calling out, "Come in!" wildly, knowing the door was locked and buying myself time to stagger across my office, rattle the handle, and lie, "Oh, is it locked? Hang on a second."

I opened the door to Sean, my skinniest, nerdiest, most awkward writer, hanging in the doorframe like a strange photo of himself, someone I didn't know.

"Oh, hi, Sean."

I went back and sat, grateful to be mostly hidden by my desk. Sean stayed standing. "Have a seat," I said, looking over at a big, green chair most of my students were happy to sprawl in during office hours.

Sean perched on the very edge, his posture so straight it looked painful. I wondered what it felt like to be him, as I often wondered about Leah. What was it like to have a boy body, to move through the world in something as skinny and crispy as a scarecrow, invulnerable to breast cancer's attacks on that particular soft tissue? Of course, that wasn't fair; men had prostates and all sorts of other soft parts invaded by their own vicious cells—could even get breast cancer, I knew, but it seemed not the same in that moment, somehow.

". . . or even Frost, or Stevens," Sean was saying, but I hadn't heard the beginning because I'd been considering his prostate.

He was waiting now, looking up at me with round brown eyes. I looked up at the light, trying to appear thoughtful rather than lost, but I had dropped the thread of our actual conversation, had no idea what he'd asked. Needle, eye, drip, IV. Something about Wallace Stevens?

"Have you looked at Helen Vendler?" I asked, hoping for some vague-but-possibly-related segue back to his lost asking.

"Oh, um, no, I will." He nodded, all lollipop head on a stick neck. "What of hers should I read?"

"*Wallace Stevens*," I said, worried the title might reveal why I'd thought of it. I went spelunking into my memory for a subtitle and found one. "*Words Chosen Out of Desire*—I think—is the subtitle." I was immediately more embarrassed for having said the word *desire* than I was for realizing only after I'd remembered the words that I'd actually spoken them. Or for any of my other more insidious transgressions. Could Sean see that desire was dismantling me? My face was melting, Indiana-Jones-bad-guy-style; soon all that would be left were the white globes of my eyes, then bones. Then nothing.

"Professor Baxter? Um, about the poem—do you have any advice?"

"Remind me which poem you mean," I said.

"The one I—here." He stood, flushed, and set a piece of paper on my desk. I glanced at it. The first line, bolded and underlined, read, "Neither Jar nor Hill nor This, for Frost, After Stevens." I read it again, incapacitated, either incapable of or unwilling to make sense of it. I could not try as hard as I would have had to to say something that was actually about whatever the poem was about.

"Let me read this tonight and ponder it," I suggested. "I'll get back to you."

"Okay! Thanks!" Sean brightened, as if this was precisely the outcome he'd been hoping for: an extra read of his poem on a week he wasn't workshopping.

As he stood, I was so stricken over my private indifference to him and his work that I overcompensated by saying, "Anytime you want to run a poem by me, whether we're looking at it in class or not, you can always email me. I'd be happy to send you my thoughts."

"Thank you, Professor," he said, over his shoulder, and disappeared into the hallway. I had an almost pathological desire to close the door, lie down on the floor, and read something, alone forever. Bishop. Prose. Her letters. I wanted to hide inside Elizabeth Bishop's letters, to stop my mind from thinking its own language and instead live in hers.

But another student, Julia, popped her cheerful head

in, and then Candor, and then Sasha, a parade so earnest and intense about their work that I thought maybe I'd been wrong—they didn't know about Leah after all. And then it was 4:30 and Leah herself was carried in on a wave of her own exuberant energy, inhaling, sparkling, pushing into the door (which she left open), and lounging on the green chair, opening a notebook, opening her legs. Was she sitting that way on purpose?

"I was hoping to ask you about something," she said airily, and incredulity rose up in me. Was she so proper that in order to ask me about a poem, she was still going to show up at my actual office hours? She crossed her legs now, the way Charles might, ankle over knee.

"Of course, what is it?"

"It's something I wrote," she said.

"You want me to have a look now?" I asked.

"Yeah."

I reached out, thinking about her body, her teeth hitting mine, the taste of her mouth, tight cords of her neck, all the inches of her, even the bottoms of her feet, which I'd felt against my calves. I saw her foot on the bathtub faucet, turning on more heat, pouring water over us—and then, mixed in, I saw my own death, Alexi, and Thomas Hardy. I was thinking of "In Wind and Rain," chilled as I'd always been by its last line: "Down their carved names the raindrop ploughs."

Leah put a piece of paper on my desk as Sean had, as so many students had over so many years. The papers were leaves and raindrops, piling up only to evaporate and crumble. I breathed in and looked at her poem. Except it wasn't a poem. It was a letter.

The first line read, "Dear Sam," and I glanced up to find her staring at me. I rushed my eyes back to the page.

There are some things I want to say to you that I don't know how to say. So, I thought I'd use what you've taught me. Here. I wish I could have made this a poem, and that it were good. Your writing has changed the way I read and think, and I want badly for my writing to matter, not just in the world, as you like to say in class, but to you. Because you're the only one who can—

I stopped reading and looked up.

Now Leah had closed her eyes. She was leaning back in the chair with her arms behind her head, looking luxurious while she waited for me to read her letter. I looked at her throat, her collarbone jutting out of the V-neck T-shirt she had on. I traced the shape of her jeans down to the boots she always wore, tied somehow today with velvet laces.

She opened her eyes.

"Let's go somewhere," she said, as she had the first time she invited me to her apartment.

"Yes," I said, obedient parrot, kept pet. "We can go have a cup of coffee and talk about this piece, okay?"

I followed her out of my office and had the distinct sense while walking that I was a man. That what Leah wanted was for me to care about and admire her work, but what I wanted was Leah herself, a situation I'd never imagined I might find myself in. And although I wanted to suggest we go to her apartment, instead we led each other to Coffee Queen, where I ordered a double espresso and she asked for a vanilla steamer with whipped cream.

I almost said *Humbert Humbert* when they asked what name to write on the cardboard sleeves.

We sat with our drinks. I took out the letter. "Do you want me to read the rest of this in front of you? Or tell you what I think about the opening, which was all I could manage to read in my office?"

"Either way," she said. She was sipping her drink, leaving light pink marks on the lip of her cup. I could taste all of it just by looking—the color, the gloss or Chapstick or whatever it was itself, the foam, her mouth.

"Your work is full of brilliance and promise," I told her, thinking it was mostly true. *Brilliance* was optimistic— hopeful, but not entirely false—and without it, *promise* would have felt like a death sentence. "It's lively, unpretentious, and engaging."

I almost added, "like you," but knew that this too would diminish the compliment. "I want to see you keep writing more poems like the one about the farm, want you to read Annie Proulx or someone like her, someone who writes landscape the way you do—I think she'll inspire you."

She kept waiting; the praise was too faint.

"I think you're a wonderful writer," I said.

"Maybe read the rest of the letter," she suggested.

I had failed a test, but was relieved in any case to be able to move my eyes away from her face, so full of a different hunger than the one I felt. The letter went on:

I have never wanted anything the way I want you, and I don't know what to do about the way that feels.

I stopped reading again, folded it up, and put it in my purse. So maybe the hunger wasn't that different.

I said, "I have to read this a little bit at a time," which was true but didn't mean what I knew she would think it meant—that it was so moving I couldn't take it all in at once without perishing from emotional overload. In fact, it was just so awkward and hard to deal with that I needed to cut it into tiny pieces and swallow them without chewing.

Was it possible that I had never read a female character as disgusting as I was turning out to be? And if so, what did that mean for me as a human being?

When we headed from Coffee Queen across the quad, the wind blew Leah's short hair into a strange halo and she turned to look at me, her eyes glinting with some combination of desire, anger, and maybe fear, a mix I tried not to wonder about. We started toward her apartment effortlessly, without having to suggest it out loud.

But then—I suddenly saw Alexi's best friend from childhood, Siobhan, and I turned like a crazy puppet to press my face into the window of the bookstore, almost licking the glass, wishing I could dive through.

"Sam?" Leah hadn't noticed me stop and so had doubled back. My heart was throwing itself against the rubber walls inside me.

"Just wanted to glance at—" I had nothing. But at least I could now see the back of the head that was maybe Siobhan's a block away from us. If I went extremely slowly and she didn't turn around, we wouldn't see each other. And if we did, so what? So I was walking with a student, having office hours, discussing poetry. I was that kind of teacher, generous to a fault, always giving extra time. I would just introduce them, and—

We were home, back at Leah's, safe from the town and Siobhan and discovery.

LEAH TURNED THE deadbolt on her light-blue door and we took each other's clothes off without speaking, without reading more about her work or desire, without much work or justification by either of us. Falling onto the futon against Leah, feeling the raw heat of her, letting her bite my lips and ears and shoulder—did I have a choice?—I got to be every version of myself I'd ever been: a teenage girl, a twenty-something-year-old hungry poet, a newly young old woman.

But nobody's mother or wife.

CHAPTER FIVE

WHEN CHARLES DID NOT COME home that night, I thought at first maybe he had died—been in a wreck, been lost, hurt, or damaged. But then I realized I deserved the not-knowing, that he was punishing me and I had no leverage, not even enough to text him and ask if he was okay. But I did that anyway at three in the morning, and he texted back simply, "Yes."

So he was angry. Of course he was angry. And maybe he knew I was fucking around. Of course he knew! What the hell had I been thinking? I had nothing to text back to his "Yes," so I held the phone, waiting for bubbles that might signify he was writing something else, something more, but they never came.

So I went and got a sleeping bag from the downstairs closet and carried it up to the third floor. The third-floor staircase was carpeted, because Alexi's room was at the top and she found plush rugs cozy.

At the top of the stairs, I climbed into the silky bag and slid down the stairs: bu-bu-bu-bu-bu-bu-bu-bu-bu-bump.

Then I did it again.

And again, banging my butt as I went, but still.

The sleeping bag was a cocoon, the ride down the stairs an amusement park-inspired transformation. Maybe I would emerge from the bag a lovely butterfly.

I went again. Bu-bu-bu-bu-bu-bu-bu-bu-bu-bump. It wasn't quite as fulfilling as I remembered it being when Hank and I used to stair-sled as kids, but of course we went headfirst. I tried sliding down on top of the sleeping bag once, but went bonking straight off and landed flat on the floor.

In the morning, Charles still wasn't back. I was listening to radio news about the dead girl who had exploded and getting dressed when Alexi called.

"It's only six," I said, "what are you doing up?"

"What are *you* doing up?"

"I'm always up early, you know that," I said.

"What is going on with Dad?"

"What do you mean?" Again, the hollow, metallic clatter of my lying voice. Did Alexi know more than I did? Had Charles called her last night? It seemed impossible, given his reserve, but since we'd called off all the rules, who knew? Maybe she'd just guessed, the way kids can, maybe she'd sensed impending trauma.

"Mom. Don't give me this bullshit. Tell me what's going on or I'm coming home."

"Since when is you coming home a threat? I would love for you to come home."

"Don't deflect."

"We're having some issues, that's all. We'll work it out, Alexi. You know there are some things that really aren't your business."

"Are you going to be those horrible people who wait until I'm in college to tell me your whole marriage was a lie and that you kept it together 'for my sake?' Because if so, you should know that this is still my sake. If you get divorced now, that's not better for me than if you had done it while I was still around and could see for myself that you were going to survive it, okay?"

"Slow down! No one said anything about getting divorced."

"Are you?"

"Am I what?"

"Getting divorced?"

"Honey. When you've been married for twenty years, you'll understand that there's ebb and flow, that people go through difficult moments, and this—"

"Are you getting divorced, Mom?"

"No," I said. "We're not. Why? What did your father say?"

"Since when do you call him 'your father?' And he didn't say anything. Why? What would he have said?"

I sighed. "Nothing, obviously. Listen, I have to run. I have to get ready for a doctor appointment," I lied, wishing to escape the need to lie more, by getting off the phone, "and—"

"I bought a ticket."

"A ticket to what?"

"Home."

"Alexi! We buy your tickets. You're still our kid. Don't do this, please—it's not making anything easier, either on me or on you. Anyway, I'll reimburse you. Are you coming in the Wednesday night before? Or did you have to make it Thursday morning?"

"I'm coming in tomorrow. I took my finals early."

"Three weeks early? What about missing a month of class? What finals?" She was lying. There was no way she'd taken her finals between my telling her the news and today—what, in three days?

"I told my professors you have cancer and that I'm going home to be with you. I can do my work from there, and the tests I needed to take I took. I'll take the rest whenever you're better and I'm back. Don't pick me up at the airport, I'm taking a cab. But I thought you should know I'll be in the house tomorrow, in case."

"In case what?" I dissembled. Had she guessed about Leah too? Did she mean in case my student was lounging naked in the house with me? But she had hung up.

My mind circled like a foaming dog—part frantic joy over any chance to see Alexi for any reason, and part—get this—*panic*, because how, if Alexi was going to be in town, could I see Leah? I could not, and I would tell her today that my daughter was coming home and we couldn't be in touch except during class and office hours. Of course, by the time Alexi returned to New York, I would have had the surgery and Leah and I would be broken up, since I didn't plan to tell her any of it. Today would be the last time I'd see her, at least in any real sense.

I dressed in running clothes, but also put on lipstick—part of the ongoing contest between my vanity, self-loathing, and fear, which inspires me to shellac myself in chemicals and then plunge into torment over whether the air stockings, lipstick, and mascara are seeping into my bloodstream and giving me cancer. Which, it turns out, they have been. And the trophy is getting to hate myself for the entire enterprise, including the self-loathing that makes me wear makeup in the first place. It's an incredible cycle, really.

I ran out our back door into the park. The dead leaves had tripled, and the sound they made as my sneakers crushed and pushed them was of matchsticks crackling, scratching, igniting. That dead girl's body was no longer underground, but I felt it everywhere, her ghost hovering over the murderers I sensed were waiting between trees, ready to creep out and steal female runners, kill and peel us.

I ran faster, my heart bracing against my chest, the back wall, the front wall, the cancer maybe bouncing inside wall-to-wall, this time like a superball, pinball, beach ball. Think, I reminded myself, of outside things. I began to count the trees I ran by: endless, though the rush of them helped calm me down. Trunk, trunk, trunk, branches, branches, leaves, Sam, breathe. I ran uphill to the edge of the park, then down a hill Alexi used to sled down, one the kids called Demon's Dive. I used to clip Alexi's mittens to a bright-pink parka Hank's wife Sarah bought her, then put her on my lap in the blue plastic sled. Charles sometimes came and gave us a push at the top of the dive.

I stopped running and made my way slowly along the grass, fewer trees now and several other runners. I said, "You're not scared" to myself, instead of, "I'm not scared." Neither was true. I was so scared all the time that I didn't recognize the newly electric scent of my own skin, fear rising like light off of me, a kind of shocking shine. I was the bipolar sky before a tornado, so bright the look of it rang like sound, smelled like metal, shimmered like Hopkins' shook foil.

I ran home fast and gasping, peeled my clothes away,

and climbed into a bath so hot it could lobster me. With my paperback Hopkins, I hid until the bath chilled, reading "The Windhover," imagining dapple-dawn-drawn falcons splashing, wishing for faith in religion but consoling myself that faith in a religious poet was next best.

When I climbed out, dried off, and looked, it was still only 8:34 a.m. A donut commercial leapt into my consciousness—what was it, Dawn Donuts? Was that even a real thing? Why did I have a song in my memory that went, "Before the sun comes up, we're busy making donuts, Dawn Donuts!" Somehow, even that jingle sounded dirty, and remembering it made me feel certain that I couldn't remember whatever was most important. All the space was taken up on the drive of my mind.

I dressed my body in a dark skirt, a light-blue blouse, and two silver necklaces stacked on top of each other, and sped to campus for my faculty meeting. Who knew what fresh hell was in store for me here?

By 9:26, I was an adult again, punctual, upright, walking into a conference room smiling and trying to look natural, coaching my own small coach to keep whispering into my ear: relax your neck, shoulders back, no one knows, and if they know they don't care and if they don't know they can't tell, they're all thinking about their own scandals and cancers, no one knows your private business, walk to the chair, take a scone, pour some coffee, have a seat, there. Parenting myself, in other words.

"Good morning, Frank," I said, my voice neutral and even. Good man, Frank, my favorite colleague, a harmless dog with more Ginsberg on his tongue than any human should have. Our students loved and mocked him in equal measure, finding it both eccentric and mildly worrisome that he seemed to live among the Beat poets even though they were all dead.

"Greetings, Samantha," he said. "What a reading, don't you agree?"

He meant last week's event—a performance by two poets we invited, so full of pathos (both theirs and our students') that I watched from the back of the room as if at a performance of Oedipus, magically the only audience member in on the dramatic irony. Maybe cancer allowed me a kind of Teresius-style insight; that would explain why I alone noticed the event was catastrophic and risible.

The man we'd invited gyrated and wept, so moved he was by reading his own poems. He swung his hips from side to side so violently he forced himself out from behind the podium, all while stopping for ten-second breaths at the end of each line, lest we forget this was poetry. Naturally, the self-loving interpretive dance made it impossible to hear any of his words.

The other poet read right after him, her eyebrows arched so high they looked as if God were yanking them from above. Probably she hoped to compensate for the male poet's horrendous performance and save face for poets everywhere, because she absolutely snapped with sarcasm, both while reading her own work and then during the "conversation" "moderated" by Frank. Feckless Frank, asking hopefully about lyricism, narrative, and discursive flights of fancy, only to have her hiss in response, "Those are your words, not mine. I write about nothing, because that's the real challenge—writing about something is easy, right? But try to make lyrical lines out of nothingness, that's what writing should be."

I admired both her anger and this notion that to steal drama from anything "real" or with inherent stakes was a cheat, but the thrusting co-poet was deeply offended. Some of his inaudible poems had apparently been about war, which was, as he said furiously, "the opposite of nothing." Frank, tasked with keeping the peace, gently intervened, proposing something limp about counterpoint and nuance. In other words, it was business as usual.

"Oh, yes," I said, "illuminating. Remind me who's next up?"

Frank didn't say who was coming next to gyrate at our podium, because the latest chairperson of our department, Melody Ames, cleared her throat to indicate it was time that we took seats and settled our paper napkins and scones. Melody had Republican senator-style hair, blonde and blown so it curled under, and always wore a scarf tied too tight around her neck that it seemed to hold her head on. My student and her pale, naked skin—so many points of contact (hips, toes, knees, fingers) replacing my terror with desire and pleasure—was surprisingly not on the long faculty meeting agenda now being distributed by our administrator, a hyper-detailed, deeply sad man named Daniel Rosen, whom Melody had once presented with a pink vase, at a department Christmas party.

When Daniel opened it, he looked stunned, and a graduate student standing behind me said, "What asshole picked that?" I think he thought that his question would be lost in the ambient noise of the party, but everyone heard it. Daniel had looked up and I thought he might cry.

I nodded thanks and glanced at the agenda Daniel had made us, then looked back up at him. Maybe this agenda was part of a long-term plan—slow-drip revenge for the vase or more, for the relentless, patronizing thanks he received from everyone in the department, always along the lines of, "We couldn't run without Daniel. What would we do if you left, Daniel?" smashed harassment-style between degrading remuneration and a litany of odious tasks, including showing all the old professors how to use their computers, fixing the new copy machine we broke every twenty-five seconds, and teaching the entire faculty at the beginning of each semester how to register our students again. Again and again.

His evil plan was working. The agenda made me want to kill myself, although there was no need, since we'd all die of natural causes after having lived through the forty-five thousand items on the list, each more devastatingly redundant and tedious than the next. How could anyone be thinking of modular learning, credit numbers, course sequences, or event calendars when Leah's earlobes and wing-bones were available for analysis? I felt loss and grief at the revelation that we would spend at least ninety irreplaceable, newly precious (to me) minutes of my now-clock-ticking life discussing our invitees for next semester and an annual romp of lists, votes, identity politics. And then the issuing of invitations to the same three celebrated poets we—and every other poetry department in America—invited on a rotation that reminded me of a rotisserie, the fat and joy dripping into a drain somewhere, the poems hardening into burnt bones.

But we would hear them again this year. Embedded into this conversation were all the usual social slights and delights—who knew which famous person well enough to "reach out with an invitation," i.e., be the faculty member who wrote the email naming the lecture, praising the work, hoping for the response, and modestly addressing the shameful question of the modest honorarium (always slightly too little not to require apologetic vocabulary surrounding it, but also big enough that most of the poets we invited showed up).

I decided to rock the faculty meeting boat. Even the feeling that I might do something outrageous—or honest—turned my blood to grape soda and gave me a delicious feeling of plot. Suspense. What might I do to redirect the emotional traffic toward something other than *I don't give a shit?* I sat through hundreds of bullet points as if they were Tic Tacs, dissolving in my mouth, tasty mint turning to grit. All the while, I planned what I could say or do to upset the meeting, tracing my fingers sexily along the edge of the mahogany table and rerouting my thinking to a long road of grudges until I arrived at a good one: the time we tried to hire a man that I'd confidentially told my colleagues in charge of the search committee had tried to stuff my hand into his Dockers at a summer writers' conference.

When I repeated this quietly, burning with shame over it again, I was on the junior faculty. I had agonized about whether I could possibly tolerate telling my male colleagues and decided I couldn't stay in my own skin if he came and worked here, plus it seemed criminal to provide him access to our students when I knew he was that guy—which, by the way, is not an event but a characteristic.

The committee not only invited and fêted him anyway, but also offered him a job.

I used to wonder what happened in the meetings after I told them my humiliating anecdote, remembering my surprise at his hand on mine, the furious loop of (with hindsight) preposterous justification—*maybe this is fatherly, he's holding my hand in a fatherly way, maybe this is nothing, maybe I'm flattering myself, if I take my hand away will he no longer think my poems have merit, maybe this is just old-fashioned, chivalrous,* all that vocabulary still playing in my mind when he moved my hand onto and then into the fly of his khaki pants, unzipping them deftly without undoing his belt so I felt his hard-on through the stretchy, unmistakable fabric of white briefs. Was I still on *maybe* and *fatherly* when I got the measure of his pulse in the palm of my hand? Had I accepted what it was by the time I found myself running, tripping over twigs and ditches in the forest where we'd gone to hike and "discuss Wordsworth?"

So, *what,* after I'd re-experienced that, did my colleagues say to each other during their committee meetings? How euphemistic did they even feel the need to be? Did they say, "Maybe that good old poet was having a bad day?" Did they propose to each other that it had, after all, been fifteen years ago—ask, can one such event really define a person forever? Or maybe they didn't believe me at all and wrote it off that way—they didn't have proof, of course, other than my word. Which was, of course, true. But likely they said the things men say, about the reasons they had to give him the benefit of the doubt. They couldn't smear his reputation just because of *one accusation* by a woman they'd known literally for a decade and who had never even intimated such a thing about anyone else.

I re-riled myself up, finding the rage a delicious side dish to my fear and recent insatiable desire. I arrived, as I had many times before, at the most obvious hypothesis: the men in my department had believed me, but hadn't given a single rat's emaciated ass. It was true, I hadn't been this man's student at the time; they probably told themselves he would have a more hands-off approach with our students when we hired him to work here. They loved his work. Please come, they begged, fuck our female faculty and students. We so admire your syntax, the violence you write so believably.

He declined our offer, which he used as leverage at the school where he taught already, so I don't know whether that final joke/insult was on me or the men who blew off what I considered to be an egregious sexual harassment anecdote. In any case, my pulse flooded my arms and legs, even my lips vibrated, and I thought of the cold feeling of the contrast dye being injected into me, freezing my feet and lips, lighting up that fucking spot of calcification that turned out to be cancer. This was the opposite of the contrast-dye cold—this new feeling, the panic of impending social conflict, turned my whole face feverish. What if I didn't do it, I thought, but it was too late, the fire had already lit inside me. I needed only a segue to my grievance—what, hiring?

Title IX. That's how I would get there, straight through that stupid training back to the forest of my Wordsworth hike and resentment.

I said, "Before we all leave, I wanted to address the Title IX training we all just had to do—"

Heads snapped up as if they'd been yanked from above by a tyrannical puppeteer. Me.

"Go ahe—" Melody started, but I didn't need her permission.

"—since three years ago, when I brought up the egregious and obscene sexual harassment perpetrated against me by your favorite male poet, we immediately invited him to speak and give a job talk and then offered him a job anyway. I was interested to read that any allegation of sexual harassment at all must be reported to the Title IX office by faculty. Even if the allegation is by a student."

"Well, *especially* if it's by a student," said my colleague Karen, who wore plaid vests and glasses so thick they made her eyes look like small beads pushed into the doughy model magic of her face. She was daft, and hadn't heard the actual not-even-subtext of what I was saying.

"Yes, thank you, Karen," I said.

"Well, Samantha, I'm so glad you bring that up," Melody said, and I chuckled, not because I was unable to suppress my laugh, but because I wanted to laugh. I wished I could snort and shout with laughter, but that would have seemed insincere and anyway the derision of a chuckle was apt and good enough.

She waited for me to stop laughing as if she were trying to outlast a child in a tantrum, which she was.

Then she said, "I think we can all agree that the outcome of that, of his—" here she cleared her throat instead of saying his now-embarrassing name "—not coming to teach here—was an effective resolution of the situation. Which, when it was brought to my attention, was of course a matter of great concern for me, as I know it was for many of us."

Ah! The spears of blame, pointing out from Melody Ames's double-speaking mouth. She was blaming Henry, who had gone ahead with the invitation before I went to her (not yet chair then) and told her, incredulously, that I had reported this story and it had been completely ignored. That she had ended up ignoring it as well was what it was, obvious and unstated. I accomplished nothing except stirring hostility and misery and biting back the tiniest bit, but it felt so good—so much like sex with Leah—that I wished I'd spent my life screaming rage from the rafters and rooftops, rather than being an A+ goody-two-shoes every second until cancer started eating me from the inside and allowing the smallest bit of rebellion to bubble up.

That's what this was, a pathetic outburst. Leah, a slightly bigger but still pitiful expression of something repressed inside me. But what was I going to do that wasn't pitiful, go postal? I didn't have that sort of impulse, could never hurt a body, was sick at the thought even of taking a splinter from the flesh of another human being. Plus, my privilege. I was—am—always checking it. In the context of other people's unhappiness, how big a deal am I really entitled to make of my own? Should I write a fucking book about it?

I kept talking. Talking and talking, so Melody could say nothing else. I added, "All of this meaningful reflection brings me to the Title IX training itself, about which I feel I must ask: are we joking?"

Everyone stared. I smiled—kindly, I thought. "Did everyone do that two-hour Internet training? The one where it asks things like, *If a student comes to you and says she or he is being harassed, do you a) tell her to prove it by dropping her pants and showing you where he touched her, or b) tell her it's just a fact of life and to buck up, or c) report it to the Title IX office?* Remember that illuminating multiple-choice experience?"

"Are you suggesting you'd prefer that we approach the training some other way?" Melody asked, and the confusion on her face looked genuine, almost like hurt.

"Ha ha!" I cackled. "I'm suggesting we all stop bullshitting each other constantly about every single fucking thing, that's all. And that by asking questions that apparently and egregiously asinine, the 'training' actually makes a mockery of the real problem of sexual harassment. It's trivializing and idiotic and if I'm asked to do any such training again, I'm going to quit. I'm saying unequivocally: fuck such hypocrisy!"

Needless to say, crickets.

Into that agonizing silence I almost whooped with joy, almost leapt up onto the table, kicking papers and donuts in a jazzy dance. But I didn't want to overstate my case, of course. Wrecking the faculty meeting had become like the end of a play, the bad sort where the actors devour the scenery and sob and scream and then it ends but the audience isn't certain it's over, and so doesn't clap, just sits in silence until one person (the playwright, probably, or his horrified wife) begins to clap. Clap, clap, clap. Clap, clap. Clap.

"Well," Karen finally gasped. "I must apologize, but I have to teach in four minutes, so I'm afraid I'll have to—" Everyone shuffled furiously and stood. And that was that.

I remained sitting there, after-glowing while my colleagues filed out, grabbing final damp donuts to scarf down alone in their offices. Melody and our newest hire, a man named James who appeared to my now well-trained eye to be just out of adolescence, were clearly setting up a gossipy debriefing session in heavy whispers, as were Susan and Henry, who if they hadn't had an affair yet were headed for one. I lingered at the table long enough that Frank, before closing the door and leaving me alone, asked, "Is everything all right, Samantha?"

"Oh, yes," I said. "Fine. I was just—"

I don't know what he thought I was going to say, but he cut me off, "Well, of course. It's a crazy time of year. All the final projects and Thanksgiving right around the corner."

I nodded. Academics talking about how busy they are always reminds me of young people without children talking about how busy they are, in other words, delusional. If you don't have children, you aren't busy. You definitely took a long shower and/or played a video game or read some non-essential article in the last week—which, if you had kids, you did not do. And if you work two semesters a year, i.e., twenty-eight weeks, teaching fourteen or maybe twenty-eight times and grading twelve papers at the end of each semester, you aren't busy.

Even if you have to "do your own work," as I do. I've done my own work, such as it is, and taught, and even managed to frolic naked with my student on her futon. All while finding time to try not to die of anxiety as I brace for amputations! And welcome my angry, suspicious daughter home (i.e., parent her?). And here I am, not too busy to teach, write an occasional line, and lie on the floor of my office for giant swaths of time.

Which is what I did after the faculty meeting. Oh, office floor beneath my back, how like a lover you are! While lying there and staring up at the edge of my desk, I called my mom and asked if she wanted to have dinner. She said, "Meet me at Trax," her favorite restaurant because the trains were visible just outside, rattling by every so often, making all the silver and glasses shake on the tables. My mother has always liked to watch trains—it makes her feel, she has said, like she could escape any minute, go anywhere. When we lived in the city, she mentioned this all the time, and then when she followed Charles and me here, she was delighted to find a restaurant near the tracks so she could continue to fantasize about going elsewhere.

By that time, I had stopped asking, "Escape what?"—a question to which she'd always responded with laughter.

"Not you, darling. I would never want to escape you. I just mean the feeling—the trains give me the feeling of being free." She never said free of *what*, not even after she moved to this tiny theatrical set of a university town, wanting, she said, to be close to her only grandchild. That sounded logical—she only had Alexi, and who wouldn't want to be close to Alexi? But was this the escape my mother had dreamed of?

Now I wondered. When we were kids growing up in the city, was it Hank she longed to escape? Was it me? The memory of her appalling marriage to Hank's drunk, veiny, bulbous-nosed father? I met him only a handful of times when he came to pick Hank up, and Hank stood trembling in the doorway, while his father shouted at our mother. Or maybe she longed to escape the lonely secret of being the only one who knew who my father was? If she even knew. She'd always said she herself wasn't sure which of the many men she'd enjoyed sired me, which was too disgusting a notion for me to pursue, obviously, even now in my forties. She would just laugh as she had in the past and say, "Well, it was the seventies, honey, you know how things were. Monogamy wasn't exactly the rage."

"It's going to be fine," she told me now, looking meaningfully into my eyes from across the table. She meant the surgery. I was thinking about how there were trains everywhere; unless you were trapped in your own body, you could almost always enjoy the feeling of being on the brink of possible escape. Leah was a train for me.

My mother was pressing one of her hands flat against her left breast, reconstructed all those years ago after her doctor found the "insignificant" cancer, still contained in her milk duct.

"It's a good thing I nursed you so generously," she said,

"or I'm sure my cancer would have been worse and I would have gotten it sooner."

What did this mean in terms of me? Did she not realize that my cancer *was* worse—it wasn't in situ, so it was bigger and not contained and maybe fatal and anyway—even if my mother *didn't* realize that, she did know that I was forty-two, and so *had* gotten it sooner? Was she relieved not to be me?

And I had nursed Alexi a full year longer than my mother nursed me. Had I failed anyway, eaten too little broccoli, used deodorant full of parabens, smoked cigarettes at clubs, been chemically careless? And would I be on the receiving end of people's unbearable, self-righteous Hallmark shit about cancer, now and forever? Including my own mother's?

She was sipping a gin and tonic—which she'd instructed the waitress should contain "only a tablespoon of gin"—and watching me lovingly from across the table. I floated up for a moment and considered what it would feel like if I were the mother in this equation, sitting across from Alexi, if there were something wrong inside Alexi's body, something that was going to require Drs. A and B to take and replace her tissue. It was the most unbearable thought I'd had yet, and I pushed it far away from me, all the while thinking, at least it's me. At least this was happening to me and not Alexi, a giant mercy.

My mother was talking about broccoli. "All that broccoli I made you, all your exercising, you know, the swimming you do," she was saying, "none of it is a waste. I know it sometimes feels like this is so unfair, like why me? I didn't smoke. I hardly drank—well—" she chortled and held up her drink. "—I drank a tablespoon of gin once in a while. But it's so unfair to get cancer when your behavior was blameless, right?"

"I don't think it's unfair, Mom. I don't think anyone deserves cancer, no matter in what behavior she's indulged—"

"Don't be pious, Sam," she said. "My point is—you're young. Even if you were going to get this, sixty would have been better. Or seventy or eighty. Or never, preferably never. But what I'm saying is that none of that good behavior was a waste. Because it makes you stronger and healthier than you would have been—it will be an easier recovery for you."

The waitress arrived then with our salads: spinach with candied walnuts and blue cheese for me, a Caesar salad for my mother. She set them down quickly, almost sliding them at us in her eagerness to escape our table, I thought. She didn't ask if we needed drink refills and I was glad, because I had finished my glass of wine and was planning on having another as soon as I could. Her fleeing would delay my inevitable drunkenness and headache. The doctors, one after the other, had asked if I drank more than seven drinks in a week. I had to think for a minute about the math—one a night? More than one a night? Not really. "I'm a Jew," I told one of them, a resident in the oncology office.

"I'm sorry?" she said, meaning, *what the hell are you talking about*, not, *I'm sorry you're a Jew*, although that would have made sense too, given that my genetic predicament seemed to me to be the result of thousands of years of my ancestors marrying each other.

"I just mean I don't drink. Jews have other ways of self-medicating."

"So not more than seven a week?"

I sighed. "Right." At least Charles wasn't in the room for that one. The thought of Charles sent me careening and plummeting. Charles! We had known each other for longer than I could even remember myself, and now what? Did we suddenly not know each other anymore? I missed him, wanted to call him, to go home, apologize, climb into bed. But then what? How could I get from our bed back to Leah's?

My mother was staring at me, probably trying to memorize my face for later, when I was gone. "Alexi is coming home tomorrow," I said.

My mother's face bloomed, then withered. "You told her to come home? But she has—"

"Of course I didn't tell her to come! Why are you provoking me? I told her not to come, but she bought a ticket."

"Don't you guys buy her tickets?"

"Mom."

"What, Sam? I'm trying to help. Tell Alexi to come and stay with me. I would love to have her. We can have a Nanover." That's what they called sleepovers when Alexi was little and my mother stuffed her with candy and let her watch hours of consecutive television and eat syrup for dinner. I used to have to unparent for a month for every hour Alexi spent at a Nanover.

I rolled my eyes and missed Charles again, even though I would've been irritated if he'd rolled his eyes with me. Or if he hadn't.

"I would love to have her too, but I don't want her dropping out of school to take care of me."

"Of course not. She's not dropping out of school. It's sweet she wants to be here for you. Let her come. Charles and I will take care of both of you."

I hadn't told my mother anything about anything. Now, I held my face still and tried to eat some salad without changing my expression, even as I chewed.

"Sam," my mother said, "what are you not telling me?"

"Nothing."

"It's about Charles, isn't it. Is it about Charles?"

Charles! Charles! Could he hear or sense me panicking over him, wishing I could go back and erase this major trespass, while also wishing I could continue to descend into it? "No, it's not about Charles, Mom, it's—"

"Oh my God, Sam. What's happening with you and Charles?"

I looked up at her, my mouth full of the same bite of salad, which was underdressed and terrible and which I felt I couldn't possibly swallow. I kept chewing and chewing and chewing, but the tangle of leaves between my teeth only increased.

"Is he leaving you?"

I swallowed the whole dry forest. "What? Of course not. Why do you always jump to the worst possible scenario? We're arguing, that's all." Even this wasn't true. We weren't arguing. I was fucking my student and unlatching myself from the tedious shackles of everything about me and my life, including Charles, even though this wasn't his fault. Which was pretty simple, actually.

"Arguing about what?"

"Nothing. It's a small thing."

A plate of scallops appeared in front of me; they looked like erasers on a bed of shredded notebook paper. Maybe cancer was like pregnancy and I would eat nothing I'd liked and love what I'd dreaded and hated. My mother was cutting into a lamb chop, her left eyebrow raised slightly. She knew I was lying about Charles.

"If you're leaving him," she said suddenly, "I want you to know that I understand. And I support you."

"Thanks."

"Is that sarcastic?"

"I don't know, Mom. Are 'I understand' and 'I support you'—when I haven't said I'm leaving Charles at all—passive-aggressive?"

"I can hear what you don't say almost as clearly as what you do, Sam."

"That's creepy. And irritating."

"Well, I'm sorry. But I want it on the record that I'll be on your side no matter what."

I sighed. She was trying. This time I said thank you in a tonally improved way, as if I'd meant it all along. Then I cut into one of the scallops, watched its rare insides gleam, and felt my own turn.

"Are you not feeling well, honey?"

"Just not hungry for some reason."

"You're under a considerable amount of stress."

"Indeed."

"Can I pick Alexi up at the airport tomorrow for you?"

"I'm under direct instructions not to pick her up."

She didn't respond to this, and I figured it was because she was going to betray me, text Alexi, find out her flight information, and pick her up herself. Which was fine. I wanted nothing except to escape the dinner without having to consume anything slimy or that had once lived—even as a plant—and go to Leah's ridiculous apartment to numb my mind with her body.

A branch scratched the restaurant window, alerting me to the fact that there were trees. I thought of Plath's blackberries, her hideous birds fat with blue-red juices, stunned by their feast, as I felt by mine. Even though it was one bite of sickening salad. Of course, in the poem, the birds believed in heaven, having stuffed themselves to a point of disorientation. And the only thing then to come was the sea. Not so for me.

I WENT STRAIGHT from dinner to Leah. I found her in a tank top and leggings, barefoot, holding a mop. Some music was playing, lyrics about a tap in someone's heart, about drunkenness.

Leah looked tired, lavender shadows puffing under her giant eyes. "I have to shower," she said. "I was cleaning the place up for you."

"No need to clean on my account," I lied.

She said, "Don't lie."

I asked, "How can I thank you for the letter?"

"I have an idea," Leah said, and my pulse pounded through me. But then she turned and went into the bathroom; I heard the shower run, its curtain rings clatter.

When she got out of the shower, she told me her idea: Bananagrams.

"Bananagrams?" I asked, wondering again how to make this matter less, feel less real.

"That's how you can thank me for the letter."

She looked so young then I felt like an animal consuming its own offspring. Her wet hair slicked back looked like a shadow. Her jaw was set in some kind of defiance, maybe against me. She didn't try to kiss or ravage me, didn't suggest the futon, although she put on nothing but a pair of boxers and a see-through white tank top. I thought that maybe she was furious. And I wanted her more than I could remember ever wanting anything.

That's why I played Bananagrams with her. Well, that explained the first two games. Addiction and furious competition accounted for the five matches that followed. We almost fought each other and rolled off the futon onto the floor, punching and kicking, but we managed to avoid that (narrowly) by joking around the margins of clicking tiles and words we couldn't help but gloat over: *precipitous, allegorical, ramparts*. I was both proud and ashamed to report that she only beat me once. I pretended to have let it happen, but in fact she won fairly.

Bananagrams reminded me of soap boppers, words I had wrong working themselves out, like the lyrics, "New York City," in some song my mom used to love, which I grew up thinking said, "Do your shay-shay." I was still doing my shay-shay when I was fifteen and saw that the lyrics read "New York City" on an album insert.

Leah and I were exhausted, our eyes spiraling letters, so I stripped to my underwear and borrowed one of her tank tops—and we climbed into her bed together. I felt like a happy fourteen-year-old at a sleepover with her best friend, except I rolled over and pressed myself against her, feeling her breasts flatten and her stomach, hard as a flat stack of books. I reached around to pull her in so close that the boundaries between us dissolved. I put my hands up the sides of her boxers, found nothing but her underneath them, and I was so consumed by my own desire that there was nothing else. She tasted minty and burning, like tea, and afterwards, I slept as if I were someone safe, someone else.

But I woke at three in the morning, my phone choking with texts from Charles, who apparently also still panicked when I didn't come home, as I had panicked when he didn't come home. How had I not at least written to say I'd be late? I texted to say I was okay, that I'd had dinner with my mom, and then sat shaking, remembering who I actually was: a mortal, middle-aged poet whose cells had turned on her, whose own body was trying to commit suicide. Whose furious daughter was arriving, walking into a banal landmine of my selfish making. It all called to my mind the wings as well as the white and pewter lights in Plath's blackberry poem—its final, intractable metal, all that beating, beating, beating. Like my stupid, hopeful heart, Leah's body against mine, the pages of a book I was smashing shut.

CHAPTER SIX

I WALKED INTO THE HOUSE AT 4 a.m. to find Charles sitting on the couch, asleep behind his glasses, a book open on his chest. I wanted to cover him with a blanket, to apologize, to make something better, but I couldn't and didn't and anyway he opened his eyes.

"I was really worried, Sam," he said.

"I'm sorry, honey, I had some things to do. I'm okay."

Would he tell me not to call him *honey* anymore? We looked at each other and I felt a desperate kind of empathy, as if I were Charles, the one wronged here, the one I was wronging.

"Will you come and do something with me?" I asked, and he stared at me, probably unable to believe that I was going to make whatever this nightmare was stranger or worse. I remembered how we used to surprise each other—first with cooking; we learned to cook and made different meals each night, showing off. Then with other things, books, ideas, sexy suggestions. We used to joke that keeping it surprising was the key. But it turned out there was a kind of surprise that was unwelcome—who knew?

"Do what with you?" he asked reasonably.

"Come. I'll show you."

He followed me gamely to the closet, where I collected

the sleeping bag, and then he watched me walk up the stairs, pass our bedroom, and climb the carpeted flight up to Alexi's nest on the third floor. Charles stayed standing on the second-floor landing.

"What is this, Sam? What's going on?"

"Hank and I used to do this when we were little," I said quietly. I set the sleeping bag on the top step and put my legs in it, keeping my upper body out so I could maintain eye contact with Charles—and my dignity. Then I slid down the stairs, bumping and rattling as I went, slower, I thought, than when Charles hadn't been watching me, aghast.

"This is what you want me to do? Watch you throw yourself down the stairs in a sleeping bag in the middle of the night after you came from . . . God can only guess where? Are you serious, Sam?"

I said, "Please?"

And Charles said, "Please what, Sam?"

"Just try it."

"Just try it. Just get in the sleeping bag and fall down a staircase and then what, you'll be happy? You'll stop whatever insanity you're indulging in and we can treat you and get past this moment?"

Everything he said was so reasonable. I nodded. "I hope so, yes."

He climbed the stairs. I followed him and handed the sleeping bag over. "We used to go head-first," I said.

"Yeah, well, that's not happening, Sam."

He put his legs in and sat at the top of the stairs, and I had a pure surge of hope and longing that—what, Charles would love my game? That he'd feel the risk and the rush and understand something in me that was incomprehensible, even to me? Maybe just that we could go back in time, be young again together. Or play a game that required shedding our judgmental adult selves, stripping away the mortal fear and ruin of our shared life's vows, and sledding. In our house.

He bumped down the stairs even slower than I had, sitting so straight he looked like he'd stuffed a chair into the bag with himself. He looked very charming with his Muppet hair bouncing around on top of his head, though, and I thought it was sweet that he was willing to try the sleeping bag game. I had an urge to call Hank to tell him what was happening, to see if he'd come visit.

Charles was at the bottom of the stairs, taking the sleeping bag off his legs. He turned to look at me, a strange half-smile on his face. "Okay, then," he said.

I asked, "Was it fun?"

The smile dissolved. "Come on, Sam," he said, sighing. "I'm trying to be a decent person because I know you're freaked out, and if sliding down the stairs in a sleeping bag—or watching me do that—is what makes you feel better, I guess I can take one for the team. But if you're leaving me, or cheating on me, or having a nervous breakdown, I can't really see how this game makes that okay. So no, not fun."

Fair enough. I said, "I'm so sorry," and then, "Can we watch something on TV?"

He shook his head, so exhausted he looked like a puppet or a scarecrow. When he finished shaking his head he looked me over sternly. "It's 4:30 in the morning. I waited for you for almost six hours, Sam, and now I'm going to sleep. You should call your mom in the morning. I called her when you didn't show up and didn't pick up or text me, so she's probably awake too. Good night."

I had the audacity to wonder if he might sleep in our bed—to wish for it, even—but he disappeared into the warm light of his office, and after I watched the line of light at the edge of the door for a while, it went out. I stayed awake for the rest of the night, watching TV as if it were an abstract collage, moving from thing to thing, face to face, color to other color, all shapes, no story. I sent my mom a text, lying about having gone to the library after dinner, hoping she would wake to it and let any lingering questions go.

I finally took my phone to bed like a lover and lost myself in that lit rectangle, following meaningless links deeper and deeper until I was Alice, in a hallucinatory rabbit hole.

When the sun came up like a hot, bright fist, I flew out of bed, delighted—until I remembered my appointment with the nurses at nine.

Sure enough, my blood pressure was so high that they sent me to the drugstore to buy my own home cuff.

"Take it when you're not anxious," they said. I laughed.

"In case this is white coat syndrome," they explained.

WHEN I PULLED up at home, both Charles's and my mother's cars were in the driveway. So, she *had* picked Alexi up at the airport! I was happy to be coming from a blameless doctor's appointment, and I planned to do a fantastic job of seeming totally fine. I left the drugstore bag with my blood pressure cuff in the trunk.

Alexi came running to hug me, like a puppy or a toddler or a chimpanzee seeing Jane Goodall again in the jungle after years away. I pulled Alexi as close to me as I could, sniffing and schnarfing and snuggling and kissing her, then held her back so I could look at her. Her face was different, both familiar and strange, slimming into its adult self, bones more prominent than ever. Was she too thin? Just growing up? Reverting in my memory to a baby whenever she was absent, forcing me to measure the distance each time she reappeared? When was the last time she'd had cheeks? She was so tall, taller than I was—which she had been since she was thirteen, but it still surprised me.

"You're too thin!" I told her, pulling her back in, holding her so tight I could feel her trying to escape me. "Where are your chubby cheeks?"

"You're one to talk, Mom. Jesus," she said.

"Well," I said.

"Well, what? You haven't started chemo yet, right? You should be gaining weight now, not losing it." She was Charles's girl, no doubt, always critical, practical, right.

Of course, she only knew the barest outlines of what was happening, or she would have been significantly more judgmental. She only knew I was sick, that I needed surgery and treatment, not that I was out romping all over town, ruining my marriage to her father, and probably her sense of self and core confidence forever. My mother, who knew more than Alexi but less than she wanted to, was sitting at the counter watching us as if she were at the US Open.

"Hi, honey," I said to Charles. The word tasted like fake

grape candy, but an image bumped down the staircase of my mind: Charles's agreeable head last night, poking out of the sleeping bag. I walked over and stood on my tiptoes so I'd be tall enough to kiss him, kissed him, felt him flinch away. So much for appearances.

But Alexi had her head in the fridge. She was pulling out individual tubes of yogurt and I wondered gratefully who had bought them. Charles? Of course, he'd known she was coming home. What had they said about it, about me—that I needed to be protected, was a little off lately, was buckling under the stress? Had Charles come up with buying kid yogurts for the first time in Alexi's life even though she was nineteen because he was practicing for being her only remaining parent? She'd always liked those—squeezers, she called them.

Now she tore the edge off one, a green tube full of pink that she drank. I felt nausea drape me, even though watching Alexi eat usually filled me with joy and relief—some primal sense that the human race would continue, my baby wouldn't starve, my purpose on earth had been served.

We all sat together for a minute at the table, and I thought resentfully about how every time Charles took Alexi anywhere as a baby, he lost one of her shoes. Or her coat. Or her backpack. Now he was making coffee, though, and my mother and I each drank a mug, Polish pottery she'd bought us years ago at an art fair. Charles had been very sweet to her about it, talking endlessly about the potter and the pattern. Maybe I could let the baby-shoe grudge go?

Alexi made so many trips to the fridge I began to think

she knew everything and was having some sort of quiet, WASPy anxiety attack. At least Charles's blood coursing through her diluted the toxic genes she might have inherited from me. Please God, I thought, even though it had occurred to me that it was precisely because I only contacted God in selfish crises that she/he had forsaken me lately.

Please don't let Alexi have this odious gene. And please, don't make me ruin her adolescence further by having to tell her it's a possibility. Then what? She'd have to begin considering prophylactic mastectomies at nineteen? It was too medieval even to consider, and Alexi's practicality terrified me. She would look at the numbers, decide any possibility of death wasn't worth it, and mutilate herself. But was it up to me to keep the information from her at nineteen? Soon she'd be twenty-one, a real adult. I knew I wouldn't want to tell her then any more than I wanted to tell her now. But I would. I'd have to. If I wasn't alive, should I leave a note?

Dear Alexi,
I'm sorry I orphaned you while you were still in college, darling. Now that you're twenty-one, I thought you should know that there's a fifty-percent chance you have the gene that killed me.

Maybe I'd just leave that—and everything else left in the project of parenting our baby—to Charles. He'd do a fine job. In a way, it was a miracle I married someone so sane and loving. He'd been glorious with Alexi, and since he wasn't an irrational lunatic prone to fits of fear that melted everyone within a two-hundred-mile radius, he was probably a better candidate than I was for this conversation anyway.

"Tell me about school," I said to Alexi, trying for a natural cadence and missing the mark. "How's Amy? Andy?" I was like a crazy, shrieking bird. Amy was Alexi's roommate and Andy her boyfriend or sometimes-boyfriend, I couldn't always tell. Their triple-A names made me feel like her life in college took place on the set of a 1980s sitcom.

"School is fine," she said, sucking the last of the yogurt out and rolling the tube into a ribbon. "Are Pops and Ez coming for Thanksgiving?"

It was November 7th. My surgery was in fourteen days, Thanksgiving in sixteen. Would Pops and Ez come? It was unimaginable. Pops was Charles's father; Ez his terrifying mother, the nickname Alexi's babyish bastardization of Elizabeth. I didn't know what he'd told his parents, if anything. I used to ask him everything all the time, and then when this all started happening a month ago, I stopped. Because I was tired. And because I didn't want him asking anything back, so I'd dropped off using question marks, except in my mind. Why did I doubt he missed my questions?

Neither Charles nor I spoke for a moment, and my mother raised her eyebrows and twitched her lips. "Well?" she asked. My mother couldn't stand Charles's parents, but loved to be politer to them than they were to her and get credit.

"Charles?" I asked.

"What?"

We stared at each other. Of course, it was inconceivable

that he would have made a plan with his parents himself, that I wouldn't have been the one to issue the invitation to them for Thanksgiving, or to respond if they invited us. To buy the monstrous, rubbery animal and pull its innards out of its ass, even though I don't eat meat and neither does Alexi. To jam the thermometer into its pimply body in the oven and pour its juices—mixed with whatever marinade I'd spent a day making—over its roasting flesh. Fuck Thanksgiving!

Every year we brought to life the split screen in *Annie Hall*: Charles's family of self-medicating ice-people and my outrageous, interrupting lunatic clan all stuck at a table together, so panicked it was as if we were about to be told that we must kill and eat each other to survive.

Then we enacted the same script with only the tiniest of variations. In the face of my brother Hank's sorrowful speeches about the decay of human civilization, Charles's father James would become increasingly agitated, until he finally leapt from the table and ran into the study to watch football—always an unstrategic move, since Hank would invariably follow him. My mother, aware that James sat in judgment of Hank, clucked and simmered with judgments of James and Elizabeth, who sat sipping gin and not speaking, so intense were the judgments of my mother and me coursing through her.

I wished Charles's mother would break free of herself and say whatever the hell she was thinking, rather than letting it rise up in tiny, passive-aggressive bubbles, breaking like carbonation at the surface of a vodka tonic. At each meal we shared, she vanished more and more into her own pinched self, like a giant ball of resentment magically contained in a glass bottle, the neck of which was as thin as a thread.

Alexi alone loved our holiday meals—all her grandparents, even Pops and Ez, whom she considered "judgy but elegant," in one place. I consoled myself by remembering she preferred (as we all did) my mother, doting Nana Sophia, not to mention Aunt Sarah, still cool, even by Alexi's stringent measures—which was miraculous, considering she was awesome when I was Alexi's age. Even though Charles and I were no Aunt Sarah, Alexi usually mostly liked us, even liked to have us around, presiding nearby, not just at Thanksgiving or Hanukkah or Christmas, but even when she had sleepovers. The kids were always at our house, in the basement or up on the deck. I made sure there was endless food of the sort children (Pirate's Booty, Goldfish, cheese wrapped in red wax) and then teenagers (pizzas, burritos, vegetarian chicken patties) liked. I let them have privacy, talked to them like real people, cared what they thought—what all kids really want. I was always grateful that Alexi preferred to be at home than anywhere else, to have the mountain brought to her. So maybe I'd gone insane not just because I had this poison growing in me—not just because my body was trying to devour itself—but because my girl had left our house.

Sometimes, even before the diagnosis, I woke in the night and thought I could hear a sucking sound, something inside my rib cage howling: where was she? Then I remembered: New York, in college, in a dorm, a metal twin bed, her roommate Amy sleeping beside her, and

I felt both better and so panicked I actually thought I might have a heart attack. So I would get up and go and sit on the deck, the cold night settling on my skin, stars relentless above me. I was already old. Now I was older, even older, hiking the rungs up a ladder that vanished before we saw its zenith—or maybe descending the ladder's rungs, now that I thought of it, since in my corrosive belief system I would end up moldering in the ground, rather than ascending into some alcoholic afterlife with Charles's ancestors.

Now, in our kitchen in front of my mother, Alexi said, "Mom? Dad? What the fuck is going on?" She was still holding an empty ribbon of yogurt packaging.

I walked over and buried my face in her hair, which smelled more hippied-out than the shampoos I liked; she washed her body with mint and her hair with lavender, and ended up smelling like a patchouli incense stand. In middle school, her best friend Siobhan had told her that if you used "drugstore products," they would fill your body with chemicals and your "chemical load" would be so huge that you would absolutely have cancer by high school. I guess I don't get the last laugh about that anymore either.

Maybe I'll never been right about anything. Is a side effect of a cancer diagnosis that you forfeit the right to gloat ever again? If so, I hope Charles and his father never get cancer.

To Alexi, I said simply, "Nothing, honey. We're fine. I'm behind is all, haven't talked to Pops and Ez yet."

"About being sick you mean? You haven't told them? Why? That's insane, Mom."

A spear of panic eviscerated me. Was I insane? It seemed likely. I let go of Alexi and held onto the back of a kitchen chair, which must have made me appear faint or compromised, because my mother shouted, "Sam!" while sitting one foot away.

"I'm fine," I snapped, and I saw Charles roll his eyes at both of us, our dynamic, the whole irritating business of having married me—and by way of me, married my mother as well. I felt for him. We were incredibly annoying. Even I longed to escape us. But why couldn't he be generous? Why not pat my mother on the shoulder and comfort her, after years of her adorning him with shirts from Brooks Brothers and miscalibrated gifts of fixtures for the house? Why did he have to be so judgmental all the time, when his parents were so judgmental it was impossible to breathe with them in the room, noisily inhaling all its oxygen? He came by it this way, of course, so maybe I should have been more generous in my thinking about him.

I took a big Lamaze breath, counting a full ten-second exhale. "I haven't told Pops and Ez yet because I don't want to worry them," I said gently and calmly to Alexi. See, Charles? I can be nicer than you, even more blameless! Look how he'd been so mean in his glance at my mother and me, and now here I was being careful of his parents in the same breath.

"Fuck that," Alexi said. "I'm going to tell them," she added, not gently, to me.

"Well, everyone! I'm heading to the credit union and the Farmer's Market," my mother shouted. "Alexi, darling, will you tag along?"

Alexi looked at me and I nodded, gracious. Let her go, I thought, remembering watching her rock climb once when she was ten-ish; she scaled a wall of rainbow nuggets, and I had to whisper to myself, *don't look, don't look, okay look, let her fall, if she falls it's okay, falling is part of it, she's belayed. She's belayed.* If I died, Alexi wouldn't be belayed anymore.

"Have a good time, you two. Bring some flowers, will you? Lilies, maybe," I said cheerfully. "And caramel apples. No nuts."

"Of course," Alexi said. She slid off a chair I hadn't seen her sit down on and glided like a gazelle across the kitchen. Please God, let me die before she does, but not yet, not on the table, not of this, not while she still might need or want me. Not while I still needed or wanted myself. I wanted to see what Alexi made in the world, who she would become, how she loved whoever was lucky enough to be hers.

As soon as my mother pulled out of the driveway, I followed Charles into the living room and collapsed onto the couch, where he was already sitting. We weren't touching.

I said, "If I die on the table, please give her the files on my laptop in the folder marked *Alexi*, okay? And put Sarah in charge of birthdays. I'm going to buy some gifts to have in stock, just in case. And teach Alexi to throw herself down the stairs in a sleeping bag. Have fun—please."

I could see him tighten his first, trying to get control of his irrational wife and her stupid, sleeping-bag bullshit and fear and illicit desires. I wondered if he would count his exhale as I had when he rolled his eyes at my mom and me. He took Lamaze with me before Alexi was born, so he knew the breathing moves.

But he had no need of such measures, and went for words, of course. "It's a controlled environment." Maybe he meant this as a reassurance, but it doubled as a dismissal and I was pissed. Then he punctuated it with, "You're not going to die on the table, Samantha. You're probably the safest you'll ever be while you're under general."

I disliked the abbreviation, as if he and my comatose state were intimate, even before I was unconscious. General? Ugh. He was looking forward to it. Who wouldn't have wanted to knock me the fuck out. I knew this because using all the syllables of my name meant he hated me. He'd called my procedure by its nickname, but referred to me as Samantha. We were strangers.

In any case, I didn't want to be talked out of my neurosis. I wanted to saddle up my own fear and ride it to its furthest possible reaches, to imagine the worst possible cases and prepare myself for them. Charles's consolations, as always, felt belittling.

"Sam, there's no way you're dying of this. I know you're scared. And I'm so sorry this is happening to us. But the numbers are promising—no one dies on the table during mastectomies. No one. And this cancer—they caught it early. We found it on an MRI; if you hadn't been so vigilant about finding out about the BRCA, about getting screened so often, it might have taken years for this to show up. You've done a good job of doing everything you can to fight this already. You're in good hands and good shape. Try to be rational about the fear."

I tried to ignore the reliance on cliché, the boring syntax of it, and focus on how kind of him, how good of Charles it was to have said "us," that this was happening to "us." I think that was really how he thought of it too. Why, in the blaring light of my most hideous behavior, had Charles turned out to be a mensch to his core? Or was he not that great and just looked especially generous relative to me?

I said meekly, "The whole thing about fear is that it trumps rational thinking." What I was thinking was that Charles had never been afraid of anything. Or guilty about anything. Or crazy. And that I hated him for those facts, even though they were maybe admirable—or enviable, anyway.

Charles sighed. I could see him wanting to sit next to me, to put his arm around me, comfort me. He shifted his weight from one big, handsome leg to the other. "I know it feels that way, Sam, but it doesn't have to."

"It does for me."

Then he did put his arm around me. "Okay," he said. "You're allowed to be scared, of course." I didn't argue with this, didn't point out that I no longer needed his permission—hadn't ever, and what, to be scared? He found my fear annoying, I knew, and not only because it was irrational—and therefore pointless—but because there was nothing he could do about it. It wasn't something he could fix or litigate. This was both generous and unbelievably entitled, arrogant, self-loving.

He continued, "And I know you're struggling." Here, his voice changed, and he took his arm off of my shoulder, remembered something—maybe how monstrous I now was, maybe that I wasn't the wife he'd thought I was, wasn't his for real. Can anyone be anyone else's for real?

Charles's voice broke over the surface of the next few words he said, and I felt fished from our life and gutted. "Sam, I'm trying to give you whatever you need. If it's space, you can have that. If it's something else, well..." He trailed off, and I felt an urge to fill in the awful silence but resisted, because what the hell would I have said? Plus, he was crying.

I reached up and touched his face, tried to wipe the crying away, but he stood and turned. "We'll talk about it after your surgery, when you're in better shape," he said, "but I have to ask you this—are you in love with someone else? Is that what's happening here? Is this about our marriage? Or just about your—our—well, the cancer?"

He was crying openly now, and I could feel him being drawn, as if by magnets, toward his office, toward the comfort of his immaculate desk, toward work at which he was adept, away from the chaos I made and was and caused.

My voice was a whisper. "Of course I'm not in love with anyone else."

"But this is about sex, yes? Is this about sex?"

"It's about my body, I guess."

"Your body," Charles said.

"I'm sorry," I told him.

"Sorry about what, though, Sam, what's going on?"

"I don't know yet, that's the thing. I don't know what's going on."

He said, "Sometimes, I think acting—" he wanted to say *crazy*, but we'd had enough fights over the years during

which he'd called me crazy that he knew better, so he settled on, "—out, acting out—you know, being wild or out
of control or whatever this is—is a way to avoid the fear
that you feel when you're most—" Here, he wanted *sane*
or *rational* and he was right. I was acting insane because
it let me off the hook, the horrible hook of what sanity
required, which was a performance of bravery and calm
in the face of my mortal fear. Sometimes I forgot that
Charles had a brilliant analytical mind, because I found
his analysis so irritating.

"I know what you mean," I said. "I'm acting crazy
because letting myself be insane is easier than facing
this—a kind of self-inflicted insanity to save myself from
the horror of sanity."

An edge crept in to his voice. "I didn't say crazy, Sam. I
didn't say insanity."

"I know. Thank you. But it's more than crazy. Or less.
I guess I'm sick of making everyone happy, sick of being
kind, generous, pleasing in any way to anyone at all,
including myself."

He responded, predictably and justifiably, "What
about Alexi?"

Of course I couldn't answer him, other than to say,
"She'll be okay. There are things about my private life she
doesn't need to know."

"Maybe, but I have to know. Are you having an affair
with someone? Is that what you're telling me? And is that
what Alexi doesn't need to know? Because I think she and
I both know that we need to get you help, we need—"

"I need to do what I want. For ten minutes of my forty-
two-year life."

"That's rich," he snapped, turning white. Now he was angry. I was glad he was enraged; it was so much better than having made him cry. "You've been doing what for the last forty-two years, what *I* want? What someone other than you wants? This is some self-actualization moment for you?"

I could see the regret creep up inside him. He had shouted at me, even though I was sick. He tried to recover.

"Let's get your health back together and then try to cope with whatever depression or mania this is. Please. Just try to keep it together. For yourself, for your own sake."

We were quiet for so long that I thought maybe we'd both died and this was what hell looked like, my own living room coated with misery, impending loss, fear, and impossible silence. Charles cleared his throat as if he were going to say something final, and I rode a huge wave of my own relief that the pause would end, we'd be saved, even if he said something awful. The furniture was heavy, the lid of our shared life closing, all light shut out.

Charles didn't speak, didn't save us, just sighed. Tears moved down his cheeks again, this time so many they made neat lines, rows of tears, an absolutely drenching parade straight down his face. When he turned away from me I felt seared with guilt and gladness that I didn't have to see his wet face. Now I could avert my eyes.

So I did. I sat there, stunned numb, staring at walls that now seemed padded, brushed with color that wanted to but couldn't prevent decay. Why do we enclose ourselves in silky mahogany boxes when we're dead for real, just to taunt and make the worms work harder? And are our houses advance, rehearsal-style versions of our coffins, even though we move about inside them?

Maybe my once-strong, balanced Charles got inside his office and laid down on the floor, staring at the bellies of his bookshelves. For how long did he keep crying, and who would comfort him, since I was the one causing his suffering? Sometimes I thought I'd made Charles into someone more like me—someone worse, crazier, cancerous, fragile. I was contagious.

Lying on the couch, I made a list of bodies, a record of each body I'd ever touched. This felt like my hobby of alphabetizing condiments, gorgeous order in the form of a map of my own desire: Andy K, I thought—in fifth grade we kissed at recess under a concrete awning where girls usually played jacks. We were "getting married," two eleven-year-olds saying vows and chastely bipping our lips onto each other's cheeks each day. Three days after Andy's and my wedding, he kissed a different girl, one named Kara Lipsky, without even the guise of it being a game or ceremony; he just wanted to put his lips on her freckled cheek. I'd always suspected she was the cutest among us. Halfway through the day, which I spent in a haze of humiliation I mistook for love, Andy K. made sure I was clear by passing me a piece of paper torn from a spiral notebook. On the smudged and crumpled page, he'd written, "Were divorced," and I shouted, "It's 'we're' with an apostrophe, stupid!" And everyone stared.

Already, punctuation and grammatical superiority were my best defenses! Don't want me? Too bad for you, because that comma you used should have been a semi-colon! Ha, ha! How will you edit your break-up notes without this green-eyed, rageful girl, Mr. Death?

A long list of other boys followed, so many names they felt like sweat, eyelashes, tube socks, and video games on my tongue—and later, maybe joints, glasses, college bedsheets, paperbacks. Boy nouns, in other words, and the boys themselves, ones I kissed in circles with objects spinning at their centers, the few girls I kissed or felt up on dance floors in high school, usually for the pleasure of the boys watching us, occasionally for our own enjoyment in each other's basements. Those encounters were rare and embarrassing enough that we called them "experiments" or "practice sessions," euphemizing ourselves out of the hot cauldron of our own vulnerability—and possible real desire for each other. I somehow never dated women for real, never even had full sex with a woman until Leah. Why? Why not? Maybe my entire heteronormative life had just been one giant failure of imagination.

College was my legs up the wall of a boy named Steven who lived across the hallway, his angular body my favorite hobby. I was so starving for him I couldn't eat or read and every time we had sex it proposed an epic set of questions, at the core of which resided: how could I stay in this moment, keep this feeling, never be anywhere else, never feel another way than this? He was the best present tense I'd ever had. And then he told me he was gay, that he really had felt something for me; I was the only girl he'd ever felt this thing for, but it was done—both the thing he'd felt and the things we were doing, and I ate my own heart until the past and the future collapsed into a new present tense.

Additional boys, thin-hipped, quick-witted, so straight they were the notebook-paper lines onto which Andy K. had penciled his divorce note. I kept pace and track of all the boys who followed Steven like a queen. I said I wanted nothing but their bodies, quiet, unless it was books they wished to discuss—then I could correct them, I thought, trump them, not be hurt. I picked boys I believed were least likely to like each other: Derek, Matt, Jackson, Ben, and Charles.

Charles! The end of the path of boys, the finish line I thought I'd crossed, only to realize in my forties that it was chalk.

Once, when Charles and I were seniors in college, I had an affair made up mostly of email, but so intense it merited inclusion high on the list of mouths on my mouth, bodies in my bed, and heart pulp in my wake. In fact, that one was a terminal degree in what I thought of the world, a mirror in which I fell in love with myself by way of a boy named Nate. I met Nate three times in person and slept with him only twice. We met at a party. He had come by train to New York from Boston, said he was at school in Boston the way people who are either modest or pretending to be modest say it when you ask where they go to college and it's Harvard. I couldn't hear his words anyway, because his mouth was so glorious when he spoke them, each word that came out reshaping his lips, I almost fell forward leaning toward him. We stayed up all night in the stairwell of my dorm because I was too afraid to sit with him in my room, knowing I would tear him up and devour him. While he talked about whatever he talked about, I repeated on a wildgirl-loop all the reasons I couldn't kiss or touch him: because Charles, because I had a serious boyfriend, because, because, because. A rushing sound originated in my ears and crowded out even the words I was saying to myself. I could feel each breath that entered and left him, feel the words coming from his mouth as if they were three-dimensional and caramelized, wanting to eat them, to suck whatever he spoke straight into myself, to pull him onto me, push him under me, to be crushed by him and to crush him. I felt the heat coming off his arms, felt my fingers pull toward what I knew was the hot groove between his neck and shoulder.

I sat utterly still, as desperate to be blameless as I was to consume him, until he said innocently, "I need a shower before I head back to Boston; will you take one with me?"

"Um, I think that breaks the code," I whispered, so close I could smell his skin, the whiskey we were drinking from a shared glass slightly antiseptic on him, reminding me of the dentist's office, rubbing alcohol pads, mint, medicine.

He said, his mouth creeping up into a smile, "I won't touch you. I promise."

And so it went; we climbed up the staircase to the dorm bathroom, locked the door, and got into the shower together. We kept the lights off, and I felt him bobbing against me, hard but true to his word; he never touched me. I almost died of desire.

And from that platform we plummeted into the lava of an insatiable correspondence, writing, writing, I still had a boyfriend, still felt we couldn't meet up, still knew we would never be together, still wanted him like some part of myself I'd lost. And that me was still in this one; I knew because I saved our emails, printed-out and crispy like antiques I took out to check: who did I use to be? Had I ever loved anyone?

The emails were so young they made me want to unzip my skin and run; they were narcissistic in all the predictable ways. But I don't know why teenage love gets such a scornful rap from adults, because the funny revelation of those letters is that we were in love—legitimate, devastating love. It counted at least as much as mundane, late-life or even long-term love. Why not, if the measure of something is how pathologically it's felt, rather than how epically it endures?

Nate and I fell in love with ourselves by way of each other, but that didn't, for some reason I couldn't articulate even now, discount the purity of the excruciating love or desire in those letters. The writing was sophomoric and reading it for the first time in twenty years, on the eve of losing the body that boy I never really knew brushed against in my dormitory shower, I thought, well, good, I've loved a few people. And one of them, at least once, was me.

CHAPTER SEVEN

ALEXI. ALEXI. HERE WAS THE thing, or one of the things. When I thought of Alexi, I also thought of Charles. I kept remembering what he looked like when I first told him I was pregnant, how his face opened up like some wild book I was dying to read and re-read, how he cheered about the baby project because he was a good and fully rendered person, even when we were so young we might as well have been toddling about ourselves. Back then, I thought his kindness and joy over the idea of a baby were the result of his being older. Twenty-eight! Ha!

He wanted to have kids someday anyway, wanted to get married. I was slightly more equivocal, but my mother had just had her cancer, which, although "insignificant," had terrified me, and I'd decided it might be up to me to make sure the human race continued. It seemed reasonable to do so before she was gone, so she could meet the baby and buy grandma presents and be someone our baby knew—so I wasn't equivocal enough not to have the baby we'd just made. If I let the radical, self-justifying version of me (who now romps around town with my young, sexy student) take over my mind and rewrite my history, I could persuade myself that what was really eating away at me (other than cancer) was the feeling of having been ensnared. I felt trapped, and wondered—had I been trapped forever? And if so, by whom? Myself? Charles? Was Charles happy we got knocked up because it meant he got to keep me?

It was difficult, even for me, even now that I was the worst version of myself I'd ever been, to justify the idea that I was an object of Charles's and always had been, but it had a little, twinkling, wind-chime melody of truth in it somewhere. Charles had been *relieved*—a gentler way of thinking of it—that a baby would bind us together, would mean our future had more security than he'd previously hoped for (well, until now). Charles was a secure person, liked stability. I wonder what horrendous crime he committed in a past life to deserve loving someone like me. Well, not just someone like me, but me in particular. It must feel to him like a curse.

Of course at the time, getting married was actually the opposite of stable. It wasn't what anyone thought we'd do or wanted us to do, other than Charles. There was something almost subversive about getting married and having a baby before everyone else in our cultural bubble. Charles's friends behaved like absolute bro movie, infantile frat boys, crying and whining that he was leaving their "tribe" and joining mine, that he was pussy-whipped, no longer a bro's bro, etc. They weren't as funny as Judd Apatow—didn't quite get the measure of the Hollywood humor they thought they were enacting. And of course, they didn't realize (as most man-children don't) that it was, in fact, *Charles* who drove the proposal, who wanted to get married long before I'd stopped to consider it, who was abducting me from my own promiscuous youth and delivering me into early-onset middle age. Stability. Safety. Of course, little did he know that even stable safety is subject to the whims of a brain that's aging. In other words, time.

The side effects of marriage were trappings his friends, apparently having watched too much television, assumed all women wanted. This misapprehension must have also been partly the result of their never having asked a single question of a woman, or listened to anything an actual human woman said. Their perspectives were myopic, and the outcome was a surprisingly long-lasting inability to be either adults themselves or friends with the adult version of Charles. That version, not incidentally, was the only one I'd ever known; he'd always been more grown-up than I was, so it seemed strange—even early on—that what his friends wanted most was to coax him into fake sports teams and long, drunken nights of homoerotic banter. I always recommended just sleeping together, having whatever actual sex or intimacy with each other it was that they wanted, admitting what it was, and keeping us—women—out of it.

Sometimes when Charles traveled on business, he would make plans with one or the other of them, but they never reclaimed their boyhood ownership of his time or undivided attention, and thus never recovered from his marriage—which was, in fact, a romantic slight to them.

I was interested, walking by his study and slowing slightly, to hear him on the phone with one of them, the recently divorced, almost-done-with-my-sci-fi-novel novelist among them, the one who at forty-eight is now spending a stint living with his parents in Missouri, even though he tried to make a Bohemian novelist's life for himself (and I guess his estranged wife) in Madison. He was supremely well-read and had flashes of brilliant, surprising self-perspective (even on his own narcissism and inertia), but no amount of analytical clarity was adequate to the task of changing behavior that had led to the divorce and would likely soon lead to him pushing a cart of philosophy books from his undergrad days through his middle age. I could see him doing this back on the streets of Wisconsin, none of Madison's students able to imagine that he had once been one of them—all promise, nothing hardened into failure yet.

"It's unclear," Charles was saying, and I heard him drop his voice into a quieter register, maybe having heard me walk by outside the door.

I noisily straightened a bowl of keys on the altar table in the foyer, signaling that I didn't want to surprise him. I had an interesting surge, thinking maybe I was wrong that he was on the phone with Kevin, thinking what if it were a woman—what if Charles had been cheating too? And now that I was cheating, did it even count as cheating if he did it? Or were our vows so broken that he could now do whatever he wanted?

I wondered how deeply I might care if the person on the other end of the phone were a woman. Maybe it was one of his colleagues—he'd had his eye on someone all this time, and now, liberated by my bad behavior, he could fly free with another lawyer from his practice, maybe Katherine Harris-Walters. She'd be a good pick for Charles, with her tight suits and perfectly calibrated heels, her arsenal of frank and essential vocabulary about rights.

Or if he wanted to climb out on a more dangerous limb, maybe Alana Ingersol, brash Alana of the holiday parties, the toasts, the one-of-the-boys way she took on her male colleagues. If I weren't a pedophile, maybe she'd be fun for me. But here, in this fantasy, it was Charles stripping her trousers. Or maybe there was someone else—maybe he was on the phone with a fresh-bodied intern, some youngster who picked up the phones for him and filed court briefings. Anyone it was could be a useful dress rehearsal for my death.

But then I heard him discussing basketball, who owned what players on their team and how many points their players had scored. The names of the teams? Hand Bananas and Free Ballers. Ugh! So it *was* Kevin. Was it disappointment I felt? Maybe. Maybe I loved the chase, the game, the newness of Leah, or maybe just newness itself. Maybe Charles and I would still get to grow old, and we'd be those weird people who opened our marriage up like a sharp-edged can, slicing ourselves up on the sides of our lives, bringing other people into our bed, hopping from apartment to apartment but "not falling in love with anyone else," as if such rules could be followed. Occasionally we would tell each other the dirty details, even share people who were willing.

It sounded like an absolute Hieronymus Bosch painting to me, a hellscape so fresh and 3-D I almost fell in and dissolved just thinking about it. My own googly demon eyes stared out at me from my mind. How did other people cope? What did I deserve? If I'd lived hundreds of years ago, I'd have been burned at the stake for this shit. Maybe three hundred years from now, women like me will be considered heroines for our liberated springing. Or maybe not.

The door. Squeaky sneakers. Alexi came in with her arms full of lilies, an orchid, and a bag stuffed with apples, cider, and donuts. She set everything down on the foyer floor and then went back out to the porch to retrieve a pumpkin.

My mother wasn't with her, and I didn't ask where she'd gone, just hugged Alexi and took the pumpkin.

"Let's carve it," she suggested.

"Okay?" I asked. It seemed depressing to carve a pumpkin after Halloween was over, but the idea of her as a child again, gagging at the melon's guts while I roasted seeds, was irresistible. I went and got a marker from the drawer under our coffee maker, still full of the neat stacks of mini origami and a rainbow of Sharpies I'd kept in there for writing notes to put in Alexi's lunches her entire life, until the instant she left for college. I was still writing love notes her senior year, still making her lunches, gently lowering crustless sandwiches into steel lunch containers, filling compartments with peeled carrots, pickles, olives, sometimes cheese puffs of the less-evil varieties. How many notes did I write over the course of her whole school life, I wondered? All those notes are gone now; I saved nothing because I didn't think then that I would die. How many, how many? I could do the math—she went to school for thirteen years, five days a week except summer and winter breaks; that's a lot of tiny notes. Some of them rhymed.

When I managed to make her lunch the night before school (especially on nights when I staggered up from her toddler bed after she'd fallen asleep, rather than sleeping there with her myself), I sometimes sat at the kitchen table with a glass of wine and made her a pop-up note, taping folded-paper components into live springs, under which she could find poetry about her. I recycled the words *love*, *dove*, *above*, *glee*, *she*, and *free* until they lost meaning, became a chant or refrain.

Later, when she was older, vowel rhymes were sufficient, and when Alexi went to dance day camp for a week in the summer after seventh grade, I rhymed *leap*, *eat*, *please*, and *breeze*. I didn't know whether she ever noticed the notes; I'd always assumed she'd realize what went into the enterprise when she had a baby of her own—and that I would get to see her have that revelation, and enjoy both her joy and my own told-you-so moment. Now I wonder.

"Mom? Help me draw the face," she said, so we made triangular eyes, bumping the ink messily over the pumpkin's ridges. I drew a small eyelash coming up at the corner of each eye and Alexi made a nose and mouth with two teeth—one rising from the bottom and the other descending from the top. I felt vaguely faint and reminded myself that comparing my own body to the pumpkin my child was carving was not only crazy, but also unproductive. In terms of not sticking my head in the oven.

She cut a neat circle around the stem, then through the strange orange innards to lift the top straight off. She sawed away at the yuck, then set the lid down flat on the table. "Can you get two spoons, Mom? We can scoop this out."

I couldn't control my thoughts, felt my brain send the message to my legs: walk, Sam, across the kitchen, use your hand that's still attached to your arm and your arm, still coming from your shoulder, to open the drawer.

In this way, I collected spoons, a gut bowl, and a colander for seeds. My mother came in then, her arms full of a giant assortment of white flowers: lilies, hydrangeas.

"Who died?" I joked, but no one laughed.

"Seriously, Mom?"

"I dropped Alexi off before the credit union because that's boring," my mother said. She set the flowers down and tousled Alexi's hair. "You only have to come on Nana's fun errands and get a pumpkin, darling. That's why I'm late, though, because of the credit union."

I was thinking how no one cares about anyone else's logistics, and how sad and lonely that was because logistics take up ninety-six percent of any adult's life. My mother cared that she had generously dropped off Alexi before going to the credit union, but there was literally no one else in the world—including Alexi and me—who could possibly have given a shit one way or the other.

"Thanks, Nana," Alexi said, "I appreciated that! Look— we've already started carving."

So she was nicer than I am. No surprise.

ALEXI WAS SCOOPING the pumpkin clean, running its stringy insides through her fingers to comb for seeds. I dug in too, felt the side of the spoon scrape the hollow pumpkin, and came up with a cluster of guts and seeds, which I squished separate. When the colander was full of hairy seeds, I rinsed them in the sink, picked tiny bits of white or orange off each, and spread them on paper towels to dry. The meticulousness of the work felt satisfying, but I thought better of comparing myself, even in my own mind, to a surgeon. Alexi and my mother were discussing a humanities paper Alexi had just turned in on Thucydides.

"Are you going to write anything about this?" my mother asked, and it took me a minute to realize she was talking to me, that "this" meant cancer.

"Oh. No, I don't think so," I said. "I'm not planning to tell anyone, really. I'd like to get through it and then be on the other side and consider what story it is."

"That's really weird, Mom," Alexi said.

"Maybe. But what are the possibilities? I don't want to shout this from the rooftops and suddenly become either a victim or survivor. That's weird too. Plus, this is my private medical business."

"Can I tell Siobhan?"

"Of course."

"Good, because I already told her."

"You're allowed to tell your friends anything you like, Alexi. You're the protagonist of your own story."

"Yes, I know, Mom, thank you."

Usually I told Alexi this when she was feeling insecure, broiling under the watchful, critical eyes of everyone else in the world, and I was trying to convey to her the absolute fact that most people were thinking about themselves, not her. Or me.

"You could write a book like that one when—what's her name, the elegant old writer? With the—when she lost her husband, and then Vanessa Redgrave played her in the movie?"

My mother was fluffing the white flowers and the kitchen smelled funereal. "Joan Didion," I said. "It was a play."

"Right, I know, Dingbat—we saw it together!"

Dingbat? I tried not to roll my eyes, because I sensed Alexi watching me and wanted to model kindness to one's mother, even when.

Joan Didion's diamond-y prose about (her own) suffering was one of the innumerable reasons why I didn't want to write or say anything about this experience, or any experience. Because could a book be myopic and narcissistic and still be good?

Because if not, oh, shit. If I were one of my own students, I'd write a poem about the pumpkin, into whose eyes Alexi was stabbing the dagger. She wrecked the eyelashes I'd made; I tried to look away, but found myself riveted. The pumpkin ended up with only one tooth, the bottom one having been sawed off accidentally. It looked as if it had two noses, one growing up from its mouth and the other down from its eyes.

Maybe I should never write anything again. Even if I don't die.

"Tell me about studio," I said, sprinkling olive oil and salt on the seeds, knowing they weren't fully dry yet. I couldn't stay still.

"I'm working on a painting of this woman who hangs out at the corner of 112th," Alexi said. "She's okay with it, and she's always there, so I drew her first, sitting across from her."

"What is she doing there?"

"What is anyone doing anywhere?"

"I know, but I mean—is she homeless? Or selling things? Or—"

Alexi raised her eyebrows at me, and I felt sheer delight at the fact that she was still an unsophisticated teenager, that she still thought she knew more than I did. Of course Alexi thought I was a dinosaur for asking whether the women she was painting on the streets of New York was a homeless person. I loved this kind of interaction.

"She's making her way, okay? And she said I could make a picture of her."

I knew better than to ask if Alexi was paying the woman, even though I was curious.

"Did she ask for money?" my mother asked from the sink, where she was washing our mugs by hand even though she knew I preferred they be put in the dishwasher. I hid my smile.

Alexi was more patient with my mother than she was with me, because my mother got the handicap points of genuine old age. Alexi expected no more from her than such questions.

"Of course not," Alexi said, and then she paused, turning the pumpkin and setting its lid back on. "But I offered, because I'm using her image and her time. Nans, I want to show you something."

She pulled up "Humans of New York" on her phone. They sat, my mother's silver head touching Alexi's blonde one and I watched the tops of their heads, smelled the pumpkin, the cooking seeds, autumn coming in from the window, thought *please don't let me die yet*. The smell of

146

bone, ground, dirt, and the dead girl rose from the news and straight up the other side of my consciousness, and I coughed until I was able to slam something down in my mind, some sense, hold my breath, then gasp for clear air again. When I turned back to my mother and daughter, they were both staring at me.

"Jesus, Mom, are you okay?"

"I'm fine, yes, sorry—I—I inhaled something."

"Well," my mother said, pouring me a glass of water, "you need to drink more water. I think you're dehydrated."

"Thank you, Mom."

She eyed the oven window, her eyebrows rising. "Those pumpkin seeds weren't dry enough."

"They'll be okay," I said.

My mother turned to Alexi. "Is Andy okay? I noticed he hasn't come up." Again with the questions I would never dare ask.

"Yeah, he's okay. I mean, he's fine. We're taking some time off."

"Oh, I see."

"We can talk about it more when Mom's doing better."

"I'm doing just fine, Alexi," I said, irritated, in either case, to be used as an excuse for her not to tell her grandmother about her dating life, or, if she was serious, to be spared. I was happy to be irritated; it felt better than being terrified, distracted me from the smell of death I'd what—imagined, experienced, understood?—a moment before.

Being terrified all the time was an incredible predicament, the opposite of an out-of-body feeling—something constant, acute, physical. Maybe I could ask Drs. A and B to take the horror out with my tissue and cancer, to biopsy the biology of all the fear I carried. My eyes were vibrating. I suddenly went to the fridge and poured myself a glass of cold white wine, not giving a shit that it was daytime.

Once I'd had a few sips, I told Alexi, "You don't have to protect or patronize me. Tell us whatever it is now—have you and Andy broken up?"

She eyed me, trying to determine whether I was competent to stand trial. I remembered the director of the first daycare she ever attended, Sally, giving Alexi twin compliment and criticism when Alexi was two. Sally told Charles and me that in forty-three years of running a daycare, she had never met a toddler with as vivid an interior life as Alexi's. I waited, aware of a chilly shift that suggested the impending "but." Sure enough, she added, "She's also the only two-and-a-half-year-old I've ever met who can show genuine contempt for adults."

I blamed Charles. He was judgmental and contemptuous; I was more of a pleaser. But I felt a surge of pride, too, and hope that our girl would be more like him than she was like me. She wouldn't wilt in the devastating climate of caring what everyone thought. She would speak whatever her truths were, no matter how appalling, and not worry about whether people liked her. I'd never been able to shed that care myself. Now I'm trying.

"Well," Alexi said, standing up, eyeing the wine in my hand, and slipping her phone into her back pocket. "I'm just not sure who I want to be with right now—what kind of person, or whether I want to be with anyone at all."

I got my bearings and finished the wine, which felt sparkly and cool, the glass sweating in a way I found delicious. It gave me a giddy rush, which I knew would transform momentarily into a headache. But in the meantime, I cleared the pumpkin refuse, scraping it into the garbage.

"What do you mean by what kind of person?"

"You know, gender, or whatever. Maybe I'm just off boys for a bit."

"Oh, wow, okay," I said.

"Wow? Okay?" Alexi asked. "What does that mean?"

I backed up, spinning the pedals of every second of conversation so far. "Just that I'm happy for you, honey, I want you to experiment and explore and do whatever is most fun and fulfilling—" Why did everything I say sound desperately sexual?

Alexi said, "Ew, Mom."

"I know, gross, right? But I just mean—take your time, or—"

"I'm sorry I brought it up. I'm going to go call Siobhan and check out her dorm. Bye, Nans." She kissed my mother on the cheek. "See you in a little bit, Mom." She kissed me, her cool papery face right up near mine.

"Have fun, honey," I said, glad Siobhan was in town, so this—Alexi coming home mid-semester, missing her actual new life in New York—might feel slightly normal.

I went back to the fridge and poured more wine, thought about Leah's fierce eye contact and how she'd offered me booze, said she didn't drink. How sad it was not to drink.

I wondered why she'd decided—maybe her own

addictions, but more likely one of her parents was a raging alcoholic. Her dad? Her mom? If her mom, then was that what she'd meant when she said that my poem about motherhood made her think it would be okay to become like her mom? That there were also forgivable aspects to her mom, so she could focus on and relax into those likenesses? Or maybe it was her mom who was the alcoholic and being with me even for a few minutes had made her think it was okay to be a drunk predator too. Add that to my CV!

As soon as Alexi was out of the kitchen, my mother sprung over to me like a wild cat and grabbed my arm with her claws.

She was grinning ludicrously. "Does this mean our little Alexi is a lesbian?"

"Ew, Mom, come on," I said.

CHAPTER EIGHT

I WOKE SHELLACKED IN MY OWN freeze. Pure black. Nothing from outside, so night, still night. The sound of wind oozing, slow and cold, branches against the skylight. I took more stock, groped around in my mind: Charles?

I scrambled to remember where he was, why not in bed. Yes, because Leah, because my whatever-this-was leading up to my surgery. Surgery! I sat up. Cancer! What! Something—terror, maybe—was puppeteering me.

It drove me from bed and out onto our deck. It was nighttime, those hours so long that fear made me prowl them, looking for something that wouldn't be visible even if it were lit. Unable to bear the blank dark, I opened my phone and fell again into links, following one meaningless dot to the next until I felt full and sick, as if I'd devoured straight fast food, fat, and flour into my brain.

I wanted to try to be more like men, or some men— my colleagues maybe, or Charles or his father. In other words, to care less who thought what of me. Here, you hate me? Fuck off. You think it's shameful that I'm sleeping with one of my students, that I ran the clock out on patience and affection and appreciation for my husband? That once I thought I might be dying any minute, dutiful love seemed suddenly not enough, not exclusively anyway, not forever? You think I'm shallow, merciless, ruined, vain, a shadow of some other, better version of myself? I've thought so first. There is nothing anyone can think or say about me that will be crueler than what I've thought, whispered, even repeated like mantras. Try to criticize me more harshly than I criticize myself—I dare you. You can't possibly succeed.

I used to believe in the fundamental empathy of all people and to think that empathy was the most important ingredient, not only for a decent life, but also for any reasonable writing. But what if I've been wrong, and brutality works too, in both life and writing? Maybe all the mansplaining I've endured over a career of being dutiful has paid off; I've learned to be more entitled and selfish. I am working on unapologetic.

A fingernail of moon was scratching at the sky. I said the word *stop* over and over until it filled my mind and drowned out both my thinking and the night noise.

Once my mind was quiet, I decided to climb over the wrought-iron railing of the balcony to see what it felt like—a trapeze, maybe. I lifted my legs up carefully and sat, then swung my legs, after which I turned onto my stomach, feeling the wet bar across my hips and imagining I was an aerial artist, high above a ring with people applauding below. I let my legs dangle, now behind me, over the two stories of our house.

If I fell, I'd probably break some bones, but not die. Our bedroom was only on the second floor, although we had high ceilings, so I might have been twenty feet above the ground. If I slipped and broke my legs or arms or even spine, people would likely think I'd meant to kill myself—by *people*, I meant Charles and Alexi. Hanging from the second-floor bedroom deck was such a pitiful and domestic way to commit suicide, what my fourth-grade teacher would have called a "fizzle ending." Boring. I hoped I wouldn't fall, but I didn't want to climb back to safety yet. I lowered myself further, felt the muscles in my arms ripple—all that swimming? This was apparently why I'd kept fit for so many years, so I could swing like a delusional monkey from Charles's and my deck.

The whole cold night was behind me. I no longer felt like I was under the impossible sky; now I was part of it, side to side with it, hanging. I was like a blinking star a million miles from myself, outside of my dangerous, vulnerable, stupid body. My hands were so cold, and the railing was wet. The feeling of my feet tugging me toward the ground woke me up somehow, alerted me to the very real possibility of slipping.

And it was this, a feeling more than a thought—a primal bone-knowing that I was slipping, that I would break my legs and maybe my back—that sped my blood back up to straight panic and made me yank myself up until I was on my stomach again.

In other words, my body saved my mind. Even though I'd thought these days were all about my mind trying to save my body.

I stayed there on the wet deck, knees to my chest, exhausted, pajamas soaked, hair stuck to my face, until the sun began to pour dirty yellow light along the horizon and the leaves flared. I stood slowly, sore and pretzeled by both the hanging and the lying twisted in a single position.

Inside, I peeled my soaked pajamas off, feeling that

the water was dew that had settled on my limbs because it thought they were branches, dead things, dirt. Even morning dew now seemed personified, thinking critical thoughts of me.

I stood under a scalding shower and washed my hair. The shampoo was called "Theory," and I thought suddenly that I could have had another life entirely, been someone else, someone who named products, or who mixed and sniffed cosmetics. I longed to be that person, a stranger to myself and my own mind. I'd been teaching about *subject* and *object*, thinking about how we're always both when writing. What if I could divide into even more versions of myself than just the narrator and the character? I wanted to be a crowd of strangers, so I could be someone different every day, never have to recline into the rut of a single, diminishing identity.

I put on clean leggings and a hoodie and then peeked in on Alexi, a grown-up sleeping in her twin bed, cheeks flushed, hair a tangle. She looked like a baby, as she had the night I came back from a poetry reading in Wisconsin when she was actually a baby, maybe sixteen months old. She must have heard the keys in the door or my heels on the floor, or maybe Charles said, "Mama's home," because when I came running into the room, she was standing in Charles's and my bed in a blue romper with a tiny pig icon on the chest, an orange zipper, and the words, "Oink baby" on its side. She was holding her arms out and crying, stretching up, trying to get to the edge of the bed as fast as she could to reach me, and I was no more mature than she was, had run so fast up the stairs to our room in my stockings that I'd shredded them on the floor, slid across the wood, and flung myself onto the bed, crying too. All this because my flight had been delayed, because I wasn't supposed to—wasn't willing to—be away from her for the night, just for one day.

In our bed that night, I couldn't stop exhaling, because I felt I had narrowly escaped dying of heartbreak—a six-hour delay! Alexi, for her part, fell asleep whispering, "Mama, Mama," like a love-struck Shakespearean character, like she'd won something, reclaimed her own heart. The way I felt about her. I knew I'd never love another human being as much as I loved her.

"Hi, baby," I'd said into her hair. I said it now too, "Hi, baby," and she stirred, turned in her sleep, stuck her foot out of the covers.

She'd grown up, even though I didn't take her for granted, even though I tried my best to absorb every minute of her when she was in our house. She'd left for college, as she should have. I heard the sucking sound again, felt the arrhythmia of my collapsing heart—thought, shut up, Sam, be a fucking adult, she's *home*. Why can't you absorb *this*, appreciate this—and how about keeping your marriage to her father together and trying not to wreck everything she needs and cares about?

That silky teenage foot sticking out of the covers agitated me, her toenails half-painted, her toes as familiar as my own. Even though I slept that way as well to cool myself down, I couldn't bear the idea that her foot might get cold, so I covered it back up. She kicked it back out, turned, and opened her eyes, squinted up at me. I'd woken her. What kind of a person was I?

"Hey, Mom," she said, yawning. "What time is it?"

"Six, maybe," I said.

"Ugh!" She rolled back over.

"Do you want to get manicures and pedicures today?"

"Uh, okay. But I don't think those places open at six."

"You'd be surprised," I said. "They're mostly staffed by slaves."

"Nice, Mom, let's support that industry then."

"I'm going downstairs to make pancakes."

I patted her, then bent down and kissed her hair. She snuggled back under the covers. "I'll be down in a minute," she said, "by which I mean three or four hours from now."

Charles was at the kitchen table, reading the paper on his laptop. He looked up at me, his eyes as clear as child's, and took his glasses off.

"How are you feeling?" he asked, and the kindness of it, the nothing sharp in his voice, the real fear I could hear, made me feel savage inside. What if all these years, my kindness was fake, and his lack of outward kindness—or lack of performative kindness, anyway—was actually a real sort of generosity and care? Maybe every nice thing about me had been bullshit and this was who I was.

Once, my friend Isabelle, married to an abusive drunk, sent me an article about how cruel drunks are just cruel people who become their real selves as soon as they're freed to do so by alcohol. In other words, you weren't someone nice made mean by drink—you were just a dick, and when you drank we all saw you. Maybe fear was that for me, a cocktail freeing me up to be my real—what, philandering, unhappy, desperate, crazy self?

Or, after the surgery, if I survived whatever this test

was, would I go back to wanting to host brunches with Charles, showing up for everything with my blameless game face on?

"I'm okay," I said. I walked over and put my hands on his shoulders. He didn't move or throw them off, but he didn't reach up, either. He was wearing athletic clothes, a shiny shirt and track pants. "Are you going running?"

"I'm playing squash," he said. "What's your day like?"

"I'm going to take Alexi to get our nails done. And grade student poems and papers. And read Bishop and Li Bo and Hart Crane. And swim, if there's time."

He pushed back and stood. We both heard the foot of one of the chair legs scrape the floor, a noise it shouldn't have made. Charles flipped the chair and took a look, checking whether the soft pad was lost, I knew. His face was very still. I felt we were in a play, suddenly, about domestic life—one that starts banal and then ends the way such plays tend to, with people screaming and throwing things, torturing the audience as much as each other. Or maybe a movie, in which case the torture would become literal; it would end with a murder-suicide. Flesh blowing off bones underground, a peeled body. His, mine, whose?

Or maybe nothing would happen. What if life were real life, no narrative form imposed on it; what if I had cancer, had surgery, had an affair, and fucking nothing came of any of it? Then I'd have been a human being, just like everyone else, I guess.

I loved Charles's inexpressive face, found his refusal to be publicly or visibly riled extremely sexy. In general, I preferred people whose faces made it impossible to imagine what they looked like having sex. The mystery made me want to see it, to watch someone normally reserved lose control. This contributed to my appetite for conservative men in my youth; I never liked the rockers, who always looked like they were having sex anyway, even when they were just talking or eating French toast. What was left to discover, in that case? I liked to shock the shy ones, watch them slip off the edge, free of whatever usually held them back.

Leah liked to shock me, it seemed. I found her brash and brave, maybe how Charles had once found me. I tried to push her away to the furthest horizon of thinking, whispered *stop* to myself.

"Sam?"

"I'm just trying to remember my French toast recipe is all," I said.

Charles looked away and left the kitchen, went into his day, away from me. I felt relief and desperate sorrow in equal measures, added teaspoons of salt and cinnamon, whisked milk and eggs. Challah. I used to make challah every week with Alexi, rolling the dough into perfectly even snakes after rising it in the warm kitchen all day on Saturdays, right when—if I'd actually been observant—I would have been prevented from working at all. This amused me in those days. She helped me braid the snakes, twisting the challah into a raw, doughy chain, and then we rose it another half hour before giving the twisted bread snake an egg bath.

"Isn't it funny, mama," she asked me once, "that if those were real snakes, they'd eat the egg instead of getting bathed in it?"

"It is funny," I agreed.

This challah came from Whole Foods. I didn't bake anymore once Alexi left—where was the joy in baking for adults?

I sliced the store-bought bread slowly, watching the serrated teeth of the knife bite into its shiny crust and soft insides. Again, I thought of writing a maudlin poem, something about all the cutting that happened in a daily life, all the boards onto which we rest inanimate things and dismember them. Each mattress on which we rehearsed our deaths. Please God, forgive me for not believing in you and prevent me from writing any such poetry.

Alexi came schlumping into the kitchen, wearing plaid pajama bottoms and a Girls on the Run T-shirt from fifth grade, one we'd bought so big it still hung down past her hips.

I hugged her, full-body-tackle style, and sang, "I'm going to teach you to eat a peach at the beach and schnarf your beak for a week. I'm going to tickle your belly like a big bowl of jelly and schnarf your beak for a week. I'm going to sniff your head and throw you in bed and schnarf your beak for a week—"

"—you done, Mom?" she asked.

I wasn't, but I nodded.

"Can I have some coffee, please?"

"Of course." I jammed the portafilter into the machine and we stood staring at each other under the storm of grinding beans. Then I tamped with my entire body weight before hooking the portafilter back into the machine and pushing the espresso button.

"Why is everything with you a full-contact sport?" Alexi asked, yawning again.

I hugged her again. "Because I'm happy you're home."

I foamed some milk and tried to draw a picture with it on top of her coffee, but it looked like an enormous butt. She laughed when I handed it to her. "Did you make it look like that on purpose?" she asked.

"It was supposed to be a heart, goddammit," I said.

Charles came back up then, carrying the chair. "Hey, Dad."

"Hi, baby." He flipped the chair over and pushed it back under the table; this time, of course, it made no sound. Charles didn't use to be handy. When we first got married, we called some other person whenever anything broke, but then eventually, he took to watching the workers, and feeling, as he did about most things, that he could do a better job. Then he bought various tools and studied manuals and figured out what part of which machine was broken, and then how to replace and reassemble. I liked this; it reminded me of the scene in *Mad Men* when Don Draper goes over to Pete Campbell's house and emasculates Pete by fixing his wife's kitchen sink. Of course, Don Draper does it in a skintight wife beater, so that's part of the charm.

"Thank you for fixing that," I said to Charles, the formal strangeness rattling around in my voice. Alexi, always a hawk for awkwardness, looked askance at me.

"Who wants French toast?" I asked.

Now I was in a TV ad for Lysol or something; next I'd be dancing through the kitchen, scrubbing, twitching my sexy body while cleaning, the way pleasing women like me did. Except I wasn't pleasing anymore, was just human, cheating, maybe about to be gone from the planet.

The soft feeling of Leah's body and the cricket noise from the back of her throat came at me and I turned away from Alexi and Charles, lest they see her on me, in me, around me. I took out a frying pan, threw butter in it, began to dip the slices of challah into batter. The smell of cinnamon reminded me of Leah's short red hair, the color of the bread her beige apartment, the butter her wretched cheese sandwich, my daughter, her vocabulary.

Had I imagined the entire thing, and if so, starting from where? The diagnosis? The futon sex? Maybe I would never recover from having done whatever I had done, or maybe it wasn't a big deal at all, and we'd have forgotten it by next fall, a blip, some bad judgment during a time of stress. If I had torched my entire life with just a few nights of sex with my student, just a doctor's appointment gone wrong, did it mean our lives were more fragile than I'd thought? Or not? How high were the stakes of the mistakes I was making? Had anything happened at all?

Breakfast elapsed faster once Charles went to play squash—with his colleague Cotty, I learned, because Alexi asked him in the friendliest way, wanting to know more about his day the way you want to know the details of the life of someone you love unconditionally. She hugged him the way I'd hugged her, so fully she might have been tackling him on a football field, and he laughed with abandon she'd always inspired in him. Watching him love her reminded me how much I used to love him. Did I still? Could I later? Maybe I'd just paused my heart for the duration of this episode, put it under general, cut the circuits—although it was awake for Alexi, somehow.

CHAPTER NINE

at the nail salon, and an ad came on. Alexi and I both watched, riveted, as a bearded hipster got tickled by a Twizzler.

"Are you too serious? Have some fun!" the ad told us. I was inspired.

"Let's get some Twizzlers when we're done here," I told Alexi. "We can go to Kilwins."

"Wow, that ad worked fast on you," Alexi said. "I thought you hated beards."

"I do. They remind me of feet. But I like licorice."

"Whatever you want, Mom."

"Or Deli Kat. Are you hungry?"

The massage chair Alexi was sitting in was rattling her and she looked silly inside a vibrating outline of herself.

"Ow," she said. "What's with this thing?"

She fiddled with the remote. I reached over from my chair. "You can turn it to *knead only*," I said.

Now the TV was playing a sexy cooking show, *Chew* or *The Chew* or *A Chew*, a bunch of hosts talking about turkey, about relatives, about how drunk to get to make it through Thanksgiving dinner. A guy with tufts of golden hair was mixing a red cocktail with a giant ball of ice at its center. He was laughing, but I couldn't hear what he was saying, didn't want to. The ice was turning red and it looked to me like a breast, whole but disassociated, tissue about to melt.

Alexi was on her phone, texting, smiling, blowing hair out of her face. I looked at her like she might pull me from a well in which I was drowning. "Hey, so, do you want to tell me about what happened with Andy?" I asked. "And your recent change of heart?"

"It's not a change of heart, Mom. It's nothing so—I don't know, formal, or whatever. I just don't want to shack up at nineteen. He's too serious."

We looked at each other, both waiting to see if I would do the clinical narcissist thing and make this about me and/or Charles. "That sounds right," I said. "Is there anyone else you're interested in?"

I could hear us both thinking *good job*, knowing I had weighed other possible responses and ruled them out.

"There is someone, actually," she said, my reward for not having rerouted the conversation toward myself. "Her name's Bekah."

"What's she like?" I asked, scoring 100 percent on this test so far. A+! The woman doing my pedicure, named Julie, was scrubbing my legs with salt so sharp I thought it might draw blood.

"She's great, really smart and fun, and funny," Alexi said, and then maybe realizing that there was absolutely nothing in this to hold onto, she added, "She's the head of an intersectional feminist group on campus."

"Tell me about intersectional feminism," I said. Now Alexi eyed me, searching for sarcasm. I held my face as straight as Charles's.

"It's the radical notion that not only straight white women should benefit from society's progress—if you think there is progress, I mean. It means we should pay attention to how the overlapping identities of women—and sometimes the diverging ones—I mean, gender, race, class, and so on—matter to each woman's experience of injustice."

Maybe Alexi mistook my excited silence for stupidity, because she added, "You know, Mom, the idea that we should, like, listen to people who aren't the same as us. That we should stand up for people who don't have interests identical to our own."

"That sounds right," I said mildly, wanting her to keep talking, not wanting to get this wrong, or be a fossil, or even a contemporary hypocrite. Alexi believed she could make the world better, and if that required her thinking that I had failed her, then she'd be no different from any other human being ever to have grown up.

Maybe she heard me thinking these old-lady thoughts, because she looked over gently. "It's not like your generation didn't do anything for ours," she consoled me. "It's just . . . we want something different in terms of modern civil rights and fair representation. Not just in the law but also in art. We want all kinds of women to be represented."

"What's not to love about that?" I asked, and she rolled her eyes even though I'd meant it. Oh, her delicious, crusading self, yes! The small girl I'd snapped in and out of rompers, carried like a leaping marsupial until she was so big I fell over. Now she would burn the patriarchy down! Of course, I couldn't help looking at the line of women in the chairs, and the line of women washing and painting our feet. I said nothing, felt the guilt wrack and wither me, but some mirth must have risen in my hypocritical eyes because Alexi narrowed hers.

"This was your idea, Mom," she reminded me. "I never would have—"

"I know, I know. I feel terrible," I said. "But I hear you. I think people can change, even once we've become chunks of our own essences."

"Ugh, Mom, really? Why do you have to put everything so grossly?"

"I'm a poet! That's what they pay me the big bucks for." I laughed at my own joke while Alexi waited patiently for me to get over myself. "I'm just saying, I hear you. And I'm going to work on my intersectional feminism. In the meantime, why don't you invite Bekah here? I'd love to meet her."

"You're way ahead of me, Mom. We're not even— whatever—yet."

Did *whatever* mean they weren't having sex? Or that they were, but not solely with each other? I began to pray that Alexi would never, ever find out about Leah. I planned to end it immediately, to tell Leah I could never see her again, that I shouldn't have involved myself (obviously) but that I was in a small crisis. I would say how sorry I was to have hurt her, to have raised her hopes or expectations, either of me or of the world, how talented and fabulous she was, what a wonderful life I expected her to lead. As a writer.

I would do anything to get out of this.

ALEXI AND I sat at the dryers, our toes glowing under lights that probably gave us cancer and fans I imagined spreading it. Her nails were light blue; mine were silver, looked like metal or jewelry on my body, less human, less frail. Less like me.

I watched Alexi's beautiful hands hold a Reuben sandwich at Deli Kat, and she looked up at me, guiltily, I thought. I felt fear, but then she asked, "Is it okay if I go meet Siobhan?"

Maybe it will come as no surprise that I didn't hesitate for even one second, and not because I was such a generous mom that I didn't mind Alexi running off to spend one of my last days on earth with her friend. In fact, I had to work to suppress a rush of excitement that almost toppled me. I had been so thrilled to spend the morning and early afternoon with her, but now the rest of my day was opening up like the door to Leah's apartment.

OH, LOOK! There I was, at the door. I was going to end it, to let her know gently that my daughter was in town and it would be impossible for me to see her again outside of class. Or in office hours. I would say it all right away, so there could be no misunderstanding.

But she appeared in nothing but a tank top and striped boxers. It would be disingenuous to pretend I gave what happened next a thought at all. I skipped the part about telling her it was over. Instead, I lunged and kissed her so hard I bit her lip. She bit mine back, on purpose, harder than I had bitten hers, so hard I pulled away and my skin tore.

"Ow!" I said, unsexy.

But she didn't seem to mind, because she ripped my shirt while pulling it off and I fell out of the fun again, wondering how bad the tear, how I'd explain it at home, whether I'd have to borrow something of hers, what lumberjack dungarees and her rhino tank-top? At least I didn't say *ow* again, just let her tackle me onto the futon, reaching everywhere at once with her hands, mouth, fingers. We were naked in less than a minute, and afterwards, it seemed the wrong time to make my speech about how I'd realized the importance of my family trumped all other considerations.

I had a hand on her hard stomach, tracing patterns downward, when she turned over. I ran my fingers over her back, the smooth dip of its arch.

She said, "I wrote something," mixing business and pleasure, but what could I do, really?

"Do you want to show me?"

"Yeah." She stood from the couch, naked, flushed, and luscious. I wanted to go back twenty minutes in time and do it over. And over and over. I knew I could never break it off with her, no matter what it cost. Charles was right; I was crazy.

She came back holding a notebook with a skull on the cover.

"Can I read it to you or do you want to read it yourself?" She asked, and I thought, please God, neither, please neither—but I touched her naked shoulder, squeezed the muscle right underneath her skin, put the skull out of my mind, and said, "Either way."

"I'll read it, then," she said. She cleared her throat, her white neck contracting a bit. I tried to listen. "Okay, so it's called 'Snow, for Samantha Baxter.'" She took a breath, and so did I.

I'm sleeping in a dream where someone says you best decide what
to do with the corners of your mouth. Who uses best like that?
I consider shapes: a lipstick tube, a snowflake, origami
Or a hollow ball with words inside: luxurious, alphabetically, and why?
I fold my guesses forward, meaninglessly awake in incoherence.
You are here at my house, you make
coffee for me, make the bed I want to lay in, show me you and how I
might someday write poems, might someday be. Now
it's snowing but I am no longer dreaming. You are naked, I am
naked, too, we watch out the window as I say and write your name, Sam,
I'm hungry for this moment not to end, for you, for snow, open the door,
let's go out to the street just like this, no clothes on, for
breakfast, flakes will melt all over us and in our mouths, no two
the same, each one original as this as me as you.

I arranged my face into a shape.

"It's amazing," I squeaked. "Lively and technically wonderful."

Her expression collapsed. "It's a love poem," she said.

I shifted myself onto her, lying flat against her body, feeling her whole front flatten, her stomach, thighs, and knees underneath mine. I lined us up, entwined our feet. "I noticed, yes," I said. I considered sliding a hand between us, but guessed it would seem gauche to cop a feel, that it might reveal how vast was my hope to avoid conversations of actual content or even the slightest depth. How did men manage? I rolled off of Leah's body. "Let me see the poem—can I read it on the page?"

Her eyes brightened, and pitiful though her need was, I knew I could love her for it more easily than I could for any of her more-worthy qualities. It wasn't as if she'd gotten drunk and unloaded some horrid confession onto me. She wasn't stalking my house or texting me uncontrollably. She'd written a mediocre poem, and wanted—with more intensity than she wanted me—my approval of her writing. This trumping desire in her, to have created something meaningful in a poem, flipped a small lever inside me, one that made me feel Leah was more admirable and serious than I'd originally believed. I thought, well, maybe, maybe she'll manage it, she'll be what she wants to be, by sheer determination. And maybe years of work will make her writing better.

So, I skipped ahead to that optimistic possibility and said, "You're the real deal," knowing even as the chattering words clacked out that if any student ever wrote "the real deal" in a poem, story, or paper, I'd write in the margin immediately, "Avoid cliché."

Now I read Leah's poem again, to show I meant this, took her and her work seriously. I read it lying there on my side, trying to make my eyes and mouth into shapes that suggested deep contemplation and appreciation, because Leah was looking straight into my face. Some of the poem, I told myself, was genuine; it showed talent. I could handle this. It would be like appreciating the unlovable partner of someone you love, a practice I'd perfected over the years by finding the two good things about that person (everyone has at least one or two—well, not everyone, but most people), and focusing entirely on those qualities. In other words, averting my eyes, as usual.

"The rhymes are very fine," I told Leah. "Subtle, and yet they give it shape and form. I'm not sure about *laying*, think it should be *lying*, and maybe the snowflake metaphor—for originality—is something you want to rethink? And what if you lost *all over* and *in our*, so that the snow melts the poet and her, uh—her friend, and you know, so the line ends: *melt us and our mouths*, instead of—"

Mayday! Mayday!

She got up from the futon fast. Obviously, I'd crashed catastrophically, wasn't supposed to have said anything critical, wasn't supposed to have workshopped her poem naked. But what the hell? I felt defensive and trapped; how was I to learn suddenly some other way to talk about student work? I felt I had already done an Olympic job of euphemizing and pretending Leah's work was better than it was. What more did she want from me? I couldn't respond to the content, obviously, because what possible response was there to the fact of the drivel being a love poem? To say *what*, that I loved her too? That we were, in fact, as original as snowflakes? Impossible.

"I have to go, Sam," she said then, slipping into underpants and jeans, buttoning a blazer over her black tank top. No bra, I noticed. Dr. B had said I would not have to wear a bra anymore after the implants were in, should I choose not to. And I could not—or, would not *want* to, anyway—wear anything with a wire. What did it feel like not to wear a bra? When Dr. B told me this, I thought that maybe it would be scandalous, showing up at faculty meetings and dinner parties knowing I had no bra on. But now it was difficult to imagine that my wearing or not wearing a bra would register on the new seismograph of my life's turbulence.

"I'm sorry, Leah—I didn't mean to hurt your feelings. It's a wonderful poem, and I'm, uh, moved—by it."

"It's not that. It's fine," she said. "Thank you for reading it, and for your response. It's just that I have class now."

"Oh," I said, relieved, fake cheerful. "How nice. What class?"

She eyed me, checking whether I might be challenging her. I widened my eyes and tried to look innocent and loving, a difficult combination given the context. "Professor Harding's Ginsberg to O'Hara seminar—Beats to NYC Poets?"

Of course, Frank's class. At the mention of him, or any seminar, I felt frantic with nudity. "Right, right," I said, and I sounded like Frank.

I leapt up and pulled my skirt back on, debated whether to return the plastic bags Julie had wrapped around my freshly painted toes so they wouldn't be ruined by my socks and boots, decided against it. It would seem vain and frivolous to be rewrapping my pedicure at a moment like this, especially in front of Leah, who seemed so, I don't know, *above* pedicures. Or boyish, or critical. I remembered dating, suddenly—all the distress of sex with people I didn't know well enough to want to guess at the aftermath conversation. Charles had been easy this way from the start; he didn't demand to know irritating things like *what you are you thinking*, didn't fish, didn't require post-game analysis. For him, sex itself was adequate intimacy. For me, too. Now I resented Leah's sensitivity, and longed for the clear, self-explanatory sex of my marriage.

I decided to put the plastic bags on after all—why ruin my toenails right after getting them painted? I wondered what Alexi was doing at Siobhan's. She lived on the quad. Were they close by? Would I run into them with Leah? If so, say what—office hours? I didn't think Alexi would suspect if she were to see Leah. It was too preposterous.

But I said goodbye to Leah in her lobby and went to Coffee Queen, where I graded student poems until I was sure she was in class and I was in no danger of running into her and then Alexi and Siobhan. Which, because the possibility had occurred to me, seemed fifty percent likely to happen, even though the odds must have been infinitesimal.

As soon as I knew there was no chance of seeing all three of them at once, I braved campus, walked to my car, drove home, and made a pesto lasagna because Alexi and Siobhan both loved it. I made chocolate chip cookies too, dissolving the baking soda into hot water and adding them to the wet ingredients so the cookies would rise evenly and beautifully, because Alexi didn't like her cookies flat.

When Alexi and Siobhan came in, they were laughing. I lifted my face, felt warmer, better, alive. Siobhan ran straight to me and threw her long arms around my neck. "Mrs. B, oh my God," she said. "You're going to be fine, right? Lex told me. I love you!"

"I love you too," I said, guiltily untangling myself from

173

her wildly sweet hug, thinking about how I could possibly be gallivanting with Leah when I had pushed Siobhan, only a few years younger, on the swings with bars to hold a toddler in. "And yes, I'm going to be just fine, thank you, honey." My voice pitched up artificially and Alexi raised an eyebrow, so I said, "I made chocolate chip cookies."

Alexi already had one in her mouth. "So I heard," she said, swallowing the entire thing and reaching for another.

Siobhan took one cookie politely, delicately, the rings on her fingers and bangles on her arm catching the final four o'clock light from the window. "Thank you, Mrs. B."

"Of course," I said as their childhoods reeled by me— first sleepovers, Siobhan's elegant parents bringing pastries and coffee over when the girls were small, always staying the entire time in case she was a burden to us (impossible). Then later, taking Alexi to dance concerts and even Martha's Vineyard one summer. Siobhan's mother taught in the law school and her father was a businessman.

We used to have dinners and brunches with them. Now they would hear that I had fucked my student, lost my job, ruined my family, and had cancer.

As if on distract-me cue, Leah popped into my mind like a pornographic puppet, dancing naked, lively, scandalous, the opposite of Charles, the opposite of me.

"How are your folks, Siobhan?"

"They're good," she said. "My mom's in the Netherlands teaching at some human rights thing, and my dad's here, babysitting my brothers."

"It's not babysitting if they're his kids," Alexi reminded her.

"It can be," Siobhan said, reaching for another cookie.

"I'd love to see your parents. Tell them I'm going to call them and invite them over," I lied.

"I will, Mrs. B."

Alexi pushed her chair back, stood, and then sat on Siobhan's lap. "Oh my god, Fatty," Siobhan said. "You're crushing me!"

"Freshman fifty!" Alexi said, and they laughed and sprayed cookie crumbs all over each other and the table.

I shoved the breast cancer and Leah and my impending surgery and wrecked marriage into my body for later and laughed with them, lived for one oblivious, glorious moment in the present tense. This was what all the spiritual assholes had been talking about all along. Maybe they were onto something.

I fell out of the moment fast, though, thinking—who had I been listening to all my life? Myself? And had that been stupid? Maybe I should have run off and followed an Eastern religion. What core beliefs and values would have equipped me better for getting through what really should have been a small mess? Compared to other people's suffering, this was nothing, so why was I unhinged?

We ate lasagna and the girls talked about their high school friends so fast and referentially that I couldn't follow and didn't try. I just sat there, tomato sauce and basil in my kitchen, two tousle-headed teenagers at my table, and let myself feel normal joy for the whole meal. Maybe Siobhan noticed I had unplugged from the conversation, because she looked over at me and asked a few questions about my teaching and writing (insanely sweet, when children try to encourage adults out of our shells, no?). I turned the questions around and asked her about her classes. She told Alexi and me about the professors she found "inspiring," as well as those she found patronizing or boring. I wished I'd been Salinger, a perverted recluse locked in a cave where I belonged. Siobhan was a biology fiend headed for pre-med, so at least I didn't know that faculty and they didn't know me, which was obviously just as well. She laughed with Alexi about swimming requirements and pretentious people pulling con-stant all-nighters and various political insights. I tuned most of the words out, got to relax and watch the metal prongs of their forks, delivering energy to their lovely bodies.

Then my phone rang, flashing "unknown caller" across the screen, and I picked it up, heard her voice call-ing, "Hello? Sam? Professor Baxter?"

"Hello? Hello?" I shouted, as if I were on a distant planet and deaf. My heart had pole vaulted up into my mouth and I thought I might cough or spit it up onto the table, where Alexi and Siobhan now sat, staring at me like I was mad.

"I can't hear you—try to call me back," I said, working on a more normal cadence, swallowing.

When she called back under six seconds later, I sent it to voicemail. "Who was that?" Alexi asked.

"I couldn't tell," I said. Then we looked at each other, and I thought she knew—but knew what? Had she heard a girl's voice on the other end, and if so, wouldn't that make her less suspicious that I was doing anything wrong or out of the ordinary?

"Hey," Siobhan said, snapping Alexi and me out of what I thought had become a kind of staring contest. "Mrs. B. Let Alexi and I do the dishes—you go rest, okay?"

I thought, Alexi and me, Alexi and me, let *me* do the dishes, not I, but of course I said nothing—I wasn't that much of an asshole. Yet.

I stood there, immobilized.

"Mom!" Alexi's face was a half-half mask of horror and bafflement. "Are you okay?"

"Yes, of course, thank you for offering to clean up." I wandered out of the kitchen and into our tasteful, clean, modest foyer, and looked at the stairs I was about to climb up to my howling bedroom. To do what, read? I couldn't imagine taking in words, or even seeing them and leaving them seen but unread on the pages.

I slid my hand across the slim, wooden in/out table, pushing mail, keys, a green celadon vase, and a glass bowl to the floor. The vase and bowl broke, and both the shattering noise and the sight of the pieces splintering out into piles—that I'd now get to sweep up and throw away—filled me with purpose and peace.

Alexi and Siobhan came out into the hallway. I grinned at them ludicrously. "Oops," I said, and went to get the broom, vacuum, and a bucket. While they did the dishes (and probably had meaningful eye contact over my insanity), I would clean this up and mop for extra measure. See? I could be productive.

I picked up the individual pieces of glass with my

hands, gently, being careful not to slice open my skin. Then I swept up the smaller pieces, green chips of celadon, dust. I mopped the floor with lemon-scented wood soap and dried it with rags.

When I finished, my good feeling of having a goal was replaced by an adolescent sense of doom I remembered clearly from my first adolescence, the one that took place when I was actually fourteen and not just acting like a fourteen-year-old. It was a kind of being trapped in the tunnel, seeing no end, not being able to imagine what would come next—and so, assuming in an almost primal, unthinking way, that *nothing* would come next. This would be it forever, whatever *this* was, usually something terrible—heartbreak, say, or illness. I couldn't see what was coming or who I'd be, and so I felt like I'd be this me for the rest of my life, which, whether short or long, was an utterly sickening sentence. My phone was ringing and ringing and ringing. I turned the power off, planned to cross the Leah-as-stalker bridge when I couldn't possibly avoid it.

I despised myself. And wanted to survive. As always, both ways, both ways. What I couldn't have and most wanted.

CHAPTER TEN

CHARLES CAME HOME LONG after dinner, by which time Alexi and Siobhan were downstairs, eating more chocolate chip cookies in front of *A Clockwork Orange*.

I was perched upstairs, brittle, thinking I could hear the part where they cut the nipples out of the girl's shirt, but I couldn't have been right, since that part only happened once in the film and I thought I heard it eighty-nine times. My own nipples were now a suspenseful plot mystery to me; the universe knew whether they'd be spared, but I didn't. Did this mean they were both spared and not spared?

Chances were strange and I was no scientist, so whenever there was a chance of something—my nipples being lost in the surgical shuffle, for example—it felt to me like a fifty-percent chance, like maybe running into all the girls on campus the other day, or dying on the table, or having the cancer everywhere inside me, a surprise party of cells ravaging my bones. Fifty-fifty. This irrational, anti-mathematical method was my favorite for considering my odds, even though (or maybe because) Dr. A has said repeatedly that it is "most likely" that they'll be able to "spare" them. And that if the cancer isn't in the sentinel node they carve out, it is "statistically unlikely" to be elsewhere or to reappear, especially if I do a five-year regimen of Tamoxifen or some other estrogen-crushing drug.

It's all going to go one way or another, and my not knowing which way doesn't change the odds. Cat in the box, dead and alive—both, right? I have no agency. And nipples I've had my whole life—parts of me—are gone and not gone. The outcome is of course already determined; I just don't know yet what it will be.

Thinking about it, wishing, figuring, and guessing also had no impact. I found it difficult to accept these terms. It was too bad I wasn't religious, but I found it impossible to accept those terms too.

I heard Charles come in, and in case the girls were listening, called out, "Hi, honey, there's lasagna in the fridge. Want me to heat some up for you?"

He didn't respond, but I heard him go into the kitchen and open the fridge, so maybe he ate something? I was, by then, hiding in the bedroom, not reading—partly because I was punishing myself and partly because I couldn't focus. I was lying in the dark. Solitary confinement, staring at the ceiling when I couldn't even see it because there was so little light. I stayed like that until I fell asleep for what felt like thirty-six seconds, only to dream I was coughing up flesh that looked like it had come from a chicken, tangled innards, lines of something bloody and solid.

In the dream, I had a message from my regular doctor, who in real life always said in voice messages and live on the phone, "It's nothing to worry about Sam, but give me a call," or, "Don't panic, I'm just calling with some test results and they're fine." But here, in the horrible logic of my nighttime mind, both clear and imagined, she said, "Samantha, give me a call at your earliest convenience, I'm sorry to have to say." Just like that. I called right then, 6:19 p.m. on the dream phone I looked at, and she said I had a rare and incurable disease called "internal dysmorphia," which was eating my insides away, so everything inside me was falling and therefore could be coughed up. The dream skipped time and found Charles and me standing at the counter in the kitchen, where I was hacking whole pieces of meat from my lungs and mouth into the sink and trying to hide them from him. I felt a cough come that I knew was my last, and I leaned forward to kiss him, knowing I was dying—this was the final moment and I had to say something about it but couldn't speak. I coughed as I fell toward him, my mouth an open O, dying, jerking awake, kicking the sheets away, and already standing by the time I knew I was up.

I went to the kitchen and turned every switch on. It was 3:13 a.m., and the dark outside closed in like black walls containing the blinding burst of light. I opened the freezer. There was a turkey in it. Charles had bought a frozen turkey.

So, he'd do fine without me. Alexi would have squeeze yogurts and health insurance; they'd have Thanksgivings with his parents.

The turkey looked like a human baby, vacuum-sealed into its rubber package, legs tucked up at its sides. He had never bought a turkey before; I had been, for all the thousands of years of our marriage, in charge of the holiday food and like most women, the cheer. Oh, spine-cracking work of putting on meals (without complaining) for dozens of family members, most of them savagely critical and disappointed. Oh, smiles glued to our spackled faces, menorah lights twinkling, dreidels spinning, Christmas decorations ringing like wind chimes from trees we'd practically sawed down and dragged into the house like huntresses with carcasses. I closed the freezer and opened the fridge.

We had a lot of condiments, and I felt a compulsive, almost delighted desire to organize them. Alphabetically, of course: applesauce, blueberry preserves, blue cheese dressing. Then I came to Bedekar chutney, and wondered if I should go back and alphabetize by brand, rather than content. What about Heinz ketchup? H, or K? What about the strange catsup Charles had brought home? Did that go under C, while the Heinz Ketchup went under K? I peeled the C label from Charles's catsup and put both in K. This decision—to stick to the content—pained me. It meant the two bottles of Ghirardelli sauce, one caramel and one chocolate, had capers between them, a short, stupid jar I almost threw out. But I wasn't that crazy. And tabasco was tabasco, so I had no choice but to put it under T. P, for pepper sauce, or H, for hot sauce, seemed wrong. The H category was full of horseradish from Passovers past. I missed my mother, wished I could call her at three-thirty in the morning without panicking her. I wished I still felt married to Charles, so I could wake him and be with someone else instead of alphabetizing the fridge alone.

But I didn't deserve him or anyone. So, I got a sponge and washed all the glass shelves in the fridge, even the ones that hooked into the doors, before putting the lined-up bottles back in. By the time I finished the freezer, all those veggie burgers and rectangular boxes of filo, the sun was up and I went outside for a run before showering, putting on lipstick and mascara, and making pancake batter so Alexi would wake in a cheerful house, to a mother who appeared sane.

We had no buttermilk, so I poured milk into a glass measuring cup and added a tablespoon of white vinegar from the Mason jar in the cupboard. Years ago, when Charles and I were young, we visited friends who had a cabinet of perfect dry goods, all evenly spaced, each containing visible contents. I flew home and threw out all of our half-eaten chip bags, misshapen boxes of crackers, and bags of rice and pasta. I put everything into neatly labeled glass Mason jars, and felt pure, relaxed joy each time I looked at our pantry. Maybe simple pleasure, or maybe a complex feeling of finally having conquered some small corner of chaos. Either way, even now—in the most catastrophic moment of my marriage and physical life—I smiled when I opened the door to our food supply, upon finding it neat, lined up, contained in glass, labeled.

Watching the milk curdle, on the other hand, made my insides twist, and I leaned on the counter for a moment before retrieving the baking soda and chocolate chips. A teaspoon of baking soda dissolved in two teaspoons of hot water. The slight sizzle brought me back to Alexi's pre-school volcanoes, which gave me the poet Anne Carson's volcano. Baking soda in the kitchen, love on obsidian, ballast, basalt, the words like lava in my mind, bubbling and boiling up until they reached my eyes, blew blood vessels up, poured out.

Crying, I skipped the next ingredients and went to my computer, wrote a note:

Dear Alexi,

I can still see you standing on the small wooden step with your name in rainbow puzzle letters, cherry apron around your tummy-waist (as you called it), your eyebrows furrowed. You were stirring. "Why it's not exploding?" you asked, and the universe answered you, the vinegar finding its opposite and blowing the top straight off the tiny plastic mountain we'd bought you, white lava pouring all over the counter and down onto the floor. You looked up at me then, the way toddlers do, asking if we were afraid or not, and I laughed and you laughed too. I felt like your best mom in that moment, letting you laugh about our wild volcano mess, giving you permission not to be afraid. "Exploding!" you told me, and I said yes.

Naturally, this was too much about me, too little about Alexi—what child wanted an elaborate and self-loving account of her own mom's best parenting moments? Ugh. I deleted it and opened my email. A note from the dean's office about Title IX made my heart shrill and twitter:

Sexual harassment or discrimination violates Title VII of the Civil Rights Act of 1964, a federal law prohibiting discrimination or retaliation in cases of complaints or charges of discrimination. It is also not in keeping with our commitment to a safe and inclusive campus community. Sexual harassment includes unwelcome sexual advances, requests for sexual favors, inappropriate verbal or physical conduct, domestic or dating violence, and stalking. No such behaviors will be tolerated in our community, and the University will take action to prevent all forms of sexual misconduct, and

is committed to investigating any and all complaints, to the fullest
extent of our power, so that we may take disciplinary measures
where appropriate.

Was this a form letter? Or something sent only to me? It didn't have my name or a salutation; it had gone to the entire faculty listserv. But why at this exact moment? Coincidence?

I snapped the laptop shut and returned to my denial-pancakes, even pulling out cookie cutters so I could shape them into cute animals with chocolate chips for their eyes. Alexi would be little; I'd be young. Things would be okay again, because I'd make time reverse. Tired light from outside came through the window and formed soft blocks of color on the floor, contradicting my hope of going backwards, shifting forward like video-game pieces. I turned the oven light on and off in some pattern I thought might resemble the sunlight on the counters and floor. On, off, square shifting in line into rainbow, into *gone.*

My back began to hurt so much that I bent over the counter, and the pain moved down into my right leg, sharp and bright like the light now collecting morning force and intensity as it speared through the window. Maybe this was cancer in my bones. I stretched out on the kitchen floor until I thought I'd seen the girls' feet on the stairs—was it hours later already? Maybe. I stood and propped my devastated puppet body against the counter, reminded myself to stay present, make espressos, try to feed Alexi and Siobhan bunny- and bear-shaped, chocolate-chip-eyed pancakes. But they didn't appear. I hadn't heard them. I got back down on the floor.

When Charles and I were first married, I toppled over one day from back pain so agonizing I thought someone had shot me. As soon as I realized I was alone and there were no bullets anywhere, I sat up and tried to focus on the pain, tried to locate or understand it. A searing pain zoomed from my lower back down my right leg, so intense I hopped up instantaneously, leg aflame, but standing set my lower back on such blue fire that I sat again, only to resume feeling the torment in my leg. I spent the next few hours in a frantic dance, writhing on the floor, trying to find a lying, sitting, or standing position that didn't ravage me with pain.

Nothing worked.

I assumed, even then at twenty-two, that there was a fatal, underlying, structural cause for the pain, that I had been injured and would never recover. My doctor sent me to a physical therapist, who used a hot wand and hot pads and an inflatable cushion with inflatable spikes and made me do thousands of excruciating and tedious exercises every day.

"Until when?" I asked her.

"Until the pain is better," she said.

I stretched my legs and back and rolled on a giant rubber ball endlessly, epically, tortuously, like a damned soul dragging my own twitching spine up a hill. I complained the entire time, even wrote poems about lying on my back on the floor, and tormented Charles about how women were destined to have to spend years on our backs no matter how hard we fought for rights—a joke I found more amusing than he did.

A chiropractor cracked my neck on an awful table over and over, and I saw myself as a character in a graphic novel, the same panel forever: me on the table, the sound of ice, the sound of glass, the sound of bones cracking. I tried on onomatopoetic words for what that noise was: *crrrrk*, *krick*, *clik*, something with an X, *xrick*—devastating, breaking sounds that never made me feel any better but kept me thinking I was doing what I could, what I should, what the doctors had told me to do. Sort of how I felt now, about to have my breasts (and maybe my nipples) removed.

What other choice did I have? Do the wrong thing, or nothing, and then die of that choice? Leave Alexi to believe I didn't try to save myself? That I didn't love her enough?

Two and a half years into my rigorous physical therapy and chiropractic regime, I happened to catch a post by a guy I went to college with, streaming by inconsequentially on one feed or another; it was a rapturous, almost clinical rave about a book on back pain. Flanked by twin forces of skepticism and overpowering hope, I ordered the book, even as I thought sarcastic thoughts about anyone gullible enough to be the member of such a cult.

When the paperback arrived twenty-seven hours later, I threw salt into the bath because my back was in agonizing pain, added a few drops of eucalyptus oil and some bubbles, and poured a glass of wine. I cleaned my reading glasses. It was like getting ready for a hot date, just with a paperback on pain. I slid into the hot, salty bath, pine-needle steam rising around me, and started reading. Within one chapter, I was laughing. This doctor had written his book to me! About me! *For* me. We were in love. Every case study described exactly my misery, the pain across my horizontal butt muscle—the name for which, the physical therapist had told me, was *piriformis*. Had there ever been a more hideous word, with peering and putrid and deformed and *mis* all jammed in? Leave it to humans to take a string of horrible, painful, butt-cheek muscle and call it *piriformis*. I had tried to reform mine, cure it, stretch it by lying on my back with my knee to the side, pulling my leg toward me by wrapping my arm behind my knee, desperate, writhing.

And then this doctor, writing out from his mind straight to me, told me that there was nothing structurally wrong with me, that fear of back pain and its potentially terrible underlying causes was itself a main cause.

My back pain—caused by repressed fury, fear, and anxiety! Of course.

I went years after that without back pain, never even finished the book. Once, we were at a dinner with a client of Charles's, an epic mansplainer, who—in addition to being a businessman on a trip of great importance to all—was also a writer. He told me when he found out I was a writer. When I asked about his wife and what she did, he said, "Well, nothing, because she's just had back surgery."

"Oh, that's too bad," I said, glancing at Charles and raising an eyebrow. Charles lifted a glass to his lips.

"She's had a herniated disk," the man said, and then took ten minutes describing how the disk rubbed the nerve and had to be shaved down in the surgery.

"Did it work? Has it helped?" I asked, pretending to be sympathetic but actually callously and delightedly catching him in a trap, while Charles—who knew now that back pain was caused by repressed fury and anxiety, and who would have been predisposed to doubt such hippie bullshit had he not seen me cured instantaneously after years of misery—nodded unwillingly at me behind his client's back.

"It hasn't fully worked," the man said, "because apparently it can take a long time for the nerve to heal. Sometimes you have to do a repeat surgery for the really chronic back problems."

"Maybe she just hates you because you never ask her a single fucking question or listen when she tells you what she's thinking or doing," I didn't say. That's what I would say now if I had that dinner back. If I hadn't been so conflict-averse, I would have shoved the good doctor's book into Charles's client's hands, would've told him it had saved me, would've said, *listen*. For once, listen. You might hear something important.

Alexi and Siobhan slept so late they never came down. I left the pancakes in the pan, still in their cookie cutters, and put a lid on top and a note on the table: *Breakfast for you, lovelies. Sorry I missed you. Off to teach.*

Then I read my own note, as if I'd written it to myself: *Breakfast for you, lovelies.*

Sorry I missed you. Off to teach. Off to teach?

I headed, incredulous, into my day. To teach. Off.

CHAPTER ELEVEN

I WAS DRIVING TO MY OFFICE, the date splattering on the windshield with fat globs of rain. November 9th, twelve remaining days with my body, with this self. I slid the car along Maple, onto Oak, from there to University. I could feel its wheels gripping the road as I turned. How the fuck was I going to teach? I had been awake my entire life, couldn't remember ever having slept except the time I dreamt I was coughing myself out.

The rain was happening in such small drops on the windshield that at first, I thought it was maybe just wiper fluid, something internal to the car leaking up and across. Or dew. I thought maybe I was elsewhere, the disoriented floating feeling more and more familiar after my diagnosis; maybe since I couldn't be sure what was happening inside my body, I also no longer felt much confidence about the things going on outside me.

But it was rain. I turned the wipers on, smushing the drops into a sheet of wet, and considered the short walk from the lot to my classroom. Would I arrive soaked, looking like an angry cat? No more vulnerability seemed possible. Where was my umbrella? I was turning off of University onto Main when I remembered there was an umbrella in the trunk. The sky had turned apocalyptic but I felt an oversized thrill, having thwarted nature by accidentally leaving my plastic umbrella in the car.

I parked in the Humanities lot and sat for a minute. And another minute. Rain was percussive on the roof and when it slid gray down the windows, the tears of it hit and provoked each other into streams, lines, a flat, wet map or some system I couldn't understand. I felt strange, illiterate, trying to read a pattern where there maybe was none. I climbed inside the parked car to reach over the backseat into the trunk for the umbrella and grabbed it, but even once I had it, I still didn't want to open the door or get out.

Instead, I slid open the cloth part of the moonroof and watched drops flatten and pool on top of the car. A sense of utterly stunning inertia came into me, rainwater turned concrete. I knew I could not get out of the car, ever. I would sit in the backseat forever, and be discovered—by whom? Leah? Charles? Alexi? My mother? Siobhan? Siobhan's extraordinary, talented, competent, lawyer mother? No. Whoever found me would be someone who didn't know me, obviously. Only in soap boppers did such meetings happen coincidentally between people who'd already been introduced. A way to keep the casts manageable, I guessed, or the stories intertwined and coherent, if implausible. Do most of our daily interactions take place between strangers? Or, given the amount of time we spend with our families, between people who know each other well?

If they found me fossilized in the car in the parking lot, what would those who'd known me say? That they were "so surprised?" That I'd always seemed "so normal?" Maybe not. Maybe that I was a "creative type," so this sort of insanity was within the boundaries of what could be accepted, even if it hadn't been anticipated.

Perhaps in the vaults of their deepest thinking about me, accessed only in the event of my tragic death, they'd all be unsurprised. I'd been insane, they'd known, of *course* it had come to something like this. At least I hadn't gone wild and shot up a faculty potluck, meatballs from the crockpot splattering the walls like brains.

I slid down until I was lying flat in the backseat, holding the umbrella. Hopefully, I was invisible to anyone walking by or also parking in the lot. Summers, we used to drive across the Midwest, my mother and Hank and I. I could read if I was lying on my stomach, but if I was sitting or lying on my back, it made me sick. So, I spent those long trips face-down in the backseat, buried in books about girls with worse lives than mine. Out the window above me now, I saw a tree moving, gallons of rain pouring over it. Its branches ran the water off, but appeared to me to be absorbing light and further darkening the sky. What if I really did stay here forever in the backseat, and no one found me? I might sleep this off—the cancer, the insanity, the whole enterprise—to emerge eventually as someone else, Rip Van Winkle, but to what effect? And to what world?

Would everyone be dead and I'd find myself walking through the sort of dusty, tedious, post-apocalyptic context everyone else loved to read about and watch on TV? It would be, in a sense, the perfect penance for my having been me.

Or maybe my own hell was this waiting. It was such awful waiting, infused with the slowest dread, slowing the pace of our lives so that time felt thick and stretchy, misshapen like sickening taffy. The moon sank miserably at the end of nights so long I was out of my body already, out of my brain, waiting for the sun to struggle up over the horizon, turn the sky infection-pink. Maybe my wounds would be septic and festering? I was waiting to find out whether I would bubble over with bacteria, cancer, psychosis.

I was too afraid to get out of my car in the parking lot I parked in three days a week. No one cared, I told myself, or knew that I was sitting in the backseat, that I had been listening to the rain for an hour, had missed all of my pre-class office hours because I was trying to get my brave on enough to walk to my office, walk to my classroom, talk about Elizabeth Bishop, and keep my wits close.

I burrowed deeper into the backseat like a little kid, totally incapable of getting on top of my own fear. I was a fearful kid, because I knew the realities of the world were being hidden from me: if you swallowed a mothball, you would die. If your coat touched the berries outside our porch, and then you touched your coat and then you put your hand in your mouth, you would die. If a stranger spoke to you on the way to school, then you would be like the girls my brother and I overheard about on the news: stolen, raped, murdered. Some of the girls they never found. And the one this year, the peeled girl whose flesh blew off her bones underground? I felt like I knew about her decades before she was even murdered, before I heard that horror on the news. I always knew that the worst possible violence could be visited upon girls, *still* could.

When I was young, I understood death in a way I never had since, not until now, when my fear had begun to consume me again; I used to call it *understanding forever in the dark*. I assumed when Alexi was little that she must also be this sort of person because she was mine, and because it was familiar to me—the state of perpetual neurosis that kept me chattering under the covers at night. But she wasn't like me. She was tough and hardy, and my attempts at comforting her from her—my—fears only introduced the possibilities of such fears to her. The thought of Alexi's fearlessness motivated me to sit up. Get the fuck up, because what if she could see this? That got me out of the backseat.

Rain bounced off the pavement, and small shadows crawled up the sides of my maroon shoes, the ruined leather provoking in me a feeling of mild satisfaction. Some objects would not outlast me. Today, we'd talk in class about "The Fish," "The Armadillo," and a Li Bai poem about crows. In the crow poem, a girl weaves emerald green yarn while the crows caw and roost, and when she weeps, it's rain. Walking across the parking lot storm, I thought of the rabbit, fluffy and vulnerable, who makes an appearance in Bishop's "The Armadillo," its eyes fixed and also ignited. Animals. "The Fish," a poem shot through with sea lice and smells, flesh and barnacles. The streets smelled like worms, and I imagined them flushed from the dirt, drowning and pickling in the rain and then drying out, beached mid-sidewalk. I saw them entwined with each other and the roots, an underground network of flesh, some of it above-ground suddenly, our vision halved by the dirt and what we couldn't see beneath it.

I thought I might throw up. I bent at the waist for a moment before approaching the English building.

"Professor Baxter?" Timario Jeffreys was next to me, almost under the umbrella with me. "Are you all right?"

"Yes, I'm fine, thank you, I—" Why was I out of breath? Maybe the cancer was crowding my lungs, growing wildly like a vine up the side of an old, ugly house. The inside of my body, cluttered with weeds.

Not to mention—while I was suffocating, would people see Timario and me walking into the building together under my umbrella, like young lovers? And if so, what difference? Would Leah see us and think I was futon-hopping? I had the sense I'd had with the back-pain book—not of instant cure, but of the opposite, the dam broken, all my confidence about my behavior and position in the social universe evaporated with one wall down, water rushing everywhere, like rain, like the tears of the weaving girl who knows carrion birds are waiting to beak her bones.

"Professor B., let me take that."

Timario had reached across me and taken the book bag I was carrying, which I hadn't realized was heavy until he slung it over his own shoulder—broad, young—effortlessly. His hand was smooth. A spasm of pain rippled through my neck and shoulder and I gritted my teeth, tried not to shout. I remembered Sophia Loren once, having been asked how she stayed so glamorous and responding with the advice not to make "old-lady noises" when standing or sitting or picking something up. Here I was, just walking along, and I was about to be incapacitated, shouting with old-lady noise and pain in front of my young, handsome graduate student. Had I never noticed before how handsome Timario was? How unblemished and innocent?

"Thank you," I wheezed, ninety-six years old suddenly. My hand, bony and delicate, was the hand of a corpse. I was dying from the inside-out, my veins protesting, pushing up against the surface of my thin skin.

We climbed the stairs together, Timario and I, and I turned the full force of my thinking toward him, away from myself and my own woes. He had grown up, I knew from his poems, with a single mother ferocious about keeping him safe, and had gone on to thank her by becoming a poet! He had chronicled, in a series of poems ranging from terrible to terrific, his childhood in the South, his mother's disappointment at his decision to be an artist, and his monkish struggle to write against the grain of his family and community. Then he received our first-year prize, full-ride, and a teaching fellowship, and his mother came to the award ceremony with two of Timario's brothers and three grandchildren, and when I said how brilliant he was and how proud she must be, she whispered to me, "I guess he's going to be a real writer after all!" The grandchildren were beaming, and his brothers looked as proud and thrilled as any siblings can be expected to be.

I remembered one of Timario's lines now, *My swing your porch sidewalk meets the street.*

"How's your work?" I asked, feeling better already, the

worms diminished, the rain rolling off us, the foyer of the building opening up.

"It's going well, Professor B.," he said, and I heard some musical touch in the nickname Professor B., my formal title brushing up against that abbreviated B. What sort of musical touch, a snuggly one? Or something more than snuggly? Or nothing at all? I was losing track of the difference between something and nothing, a difference which I realized was everything.

"What are you writing?"

Now he looked confused and I realized my mistake: I was reading the work he was writing now, every week.

"Well, my thesis, of course," he said.

"Of course." I wasn't fully able to recover.

"See you in class in a minute, Professor B.," he said, and handed me my bag at the door to my office. I watched him walk away, then slipped into my safe, silent office, and sat, stunned at my desk.

When I was young, my preference was for men—shy ones, as I've said, the mysteries of their various repressions supplying the suspense I craved. No angry or aggressive or emotive men for me. Was there something feminine in the reserve I preferred? Or had I actually just liked to watch civility fade live, to tune into the eyes of those who could only turn animal once their superegos receded? Had it mattered whether they were men? Had I just assumed I liked men for no reason other than some default setting expected of me by everyone, including myself? Did it have something or nothing to do with my non-father?

I slipped student poems into my folder, thinking of

Dr. A's black folder, the un-poetry of my many medical charts and records. I stacked the Bishop and Li Bo poems neatly on top, held my thermos of ice water in my right hand and hung my straight flat purse on my shoulder. See? I liked order—but only in the small, banal quarters. The large-scale parts of my life I wanted to turn to absolute chaotic rubble. I wonder if the opposite held, whether people who appeared chaotic in the spaces or schedules or logistics they kept were actually sane in grander-scheme ways.

I turned the key neatly in the lock, cleared my throat, put my keys into my purse, and checked my lipstick in the mirror in the bathroom across from my office before walking up the eleven carpeted stairs to the second floor and from there to my classroom on the third floor. Eleven stairs. Why? Should've been twelve. Or some other even number.

I SAT AT the head of my seminar table, thinking, don't think, just don't think about anything and you'll be fine. But teaching required thinking, even for me at this late stage of my teaching career (and life), so I had to think.

I read the Bishop out loud and thought only of her lines, the fish, the beauty meeting the hideousness. My students were young and blinking, and I felt grateful for my glasses, a small shield between what I saw and what I let them see of me. I reached up and touched my earrings too, metal, invulnerable. Like my silver nails.

Oh, animal poetry in my classroom, fish with your aged wisdom, your beard of hooks and wires, lifetime of being caught and escaping. You gave way to the rabbit

Bishop calls a handful of ash, who gave way to the crows waiting for the ends of all of us, the ends of every poem, of this class and the next and the next and the next. I felt my own self and body staggering through stanzas, caught and released. I was trapped now, stranded like a worm washed from the soil onto the sidewalk, only to be freed a few days from now, when I woke up. *If* I woke up. *When.* This was a new way to imagine the surgery and I felt pleased. Maybe waiting was the worst trap—crossing the square of cement, hoping to burrow back into the dirt, safe and dry-ish, but not so dry I was a worm turned to fruit-leather.

My students made remarks that ranged from earnest to clever about the poems, noting the pitfalls of any writing that features animals: the rhyme, the work, the resonance between the different poems. Our analysis went so well I felt smug, although the smugness was followed by a dizzy feeling vast enough that I had to lie down on my office floor again during our ten-minute class break. Why was I always lying on the floor? What did it do? What did it suggest? It was like giving up in the middle of something. Or maybe it was the opposite, a power play to make time stop. When I was little, I believed that if I hid under my parents' dining room table, time would stop moving and I'd be safe; my and Hank's fathers wouldn't be ghosts. Mine wouldn't have disappeared before I was even sentient, and Hank's wouldn't have left us all in a rage. Maybe our mother wouldn't cry anymore if I stayed hidden and still. Instead, everything would be suspended, waiting for me to return to my right place at the center of the world's attentive action. I was an even more preposterous narcissist than most kids by the time I was five or six.

While lying on my office floor, I had the fully articulated—if disembodied—thought that I knew better now than to believe I could stop time by hiding from my students or refusing to sit or stand up. (If my father's non-existence hadn't taught me this in spite of my powerful wishing to know who or where he was, I would have learned it at some point anyway). I knew that if anyone saw me lying there, even if I saw myself lying there, staring up at the underbellies of my bookshelves, thinking about incisions under or over shelves of flesh, they would think something was wrong. But maybe time would just slow a little bit for me, if I stayed still.

I took a picture of the room, the naked underneaths of my bookshelves, the legs and feet of my desk and chairs. Then I stood up, wobbling like a Weeble, and pivoted out the door and up the stairs to my classroom. Dip and pivot, I thought, Hart Crane, *O harp and altar, of the fury fused.*

Back at the front of the seminar table, I felt dangerously crazy. I looked around at my young students and focused on trying, as I always did, not to notice those who had returned from our fifteen-minute break with full-scale meals: steaming, terrible bowls of chili, sandwiches reeking of violent weeds—onion, scallion, chive, garlic mayonnaise spilling out their fat sides while my poets tried to eat quietly, politely. Sometimes an unruly glob of meat or condiment even dropped onto the workshop table, or worse, the page. I kindly looked away. I told them at the beginning of every semester that I had a distaste for bureaucracy and any rules that existed for the sake of themselves. Hence, they could largely do and say what they wanted in class, as long as the conversation stayed constructive and interesting. As for food, I said that as long as the meal didn't draw unnecessary attention to itself—like vulgarity in a poem, for example—they could consume it. While we seemed to have different standards on this matter, I was unwilling to shame them, either about writing or about food. So, it went that semester after semester, people ate hideous things during my class while saying beautiful things about poems. In fact, now that I thought of it, maybe I liked the dissonance.

Leah was quiet today, dressed in a white tank top, work boots, and black cargo pants. My androgynous mistress! I tried not to notice anything about her, and she made it easy by saying nothing during our conversation about Bishop and Li Bo. We workshopped a poem by the slightly steampunk Candor—this name, I assumed, must have been assigned to her by someone other than her parents, or chosen herself. Her poem was called "Alone," and it had in it the appalling lines: "*Fucking my own demon triangle / instead of letting you in.*"

I lost access to my own vocabulary when she read this, and began to pray: please, please let someone else say how terrible it is, and why it's so terrible. But no one spoke. I contemplated just standing up, pushing my chair back, and running out of the workshop room. Instead, I tried clearing my throat. "So," I began, "what's at the center of Candor's poem? What questions does it ask, where is it doing its best work, and where can she invest her energy as she revises it?" I felt an urge to laugh creep up inside me like a tickle, and squirmed on my chair to suppress it.

Sean was staring at the table. Jin Yi was staring at me. Finally, Keisha, bless her heart, said, "I think its most successful element is its unflinchingness." Then she laughed. "Is that a word, *unflinchingness*?"

I said, "We know what you mean."

Then came Leah's voice. "Remember the thing that poet who visited—sorry, I can't remember her name—said? About writing about nothing? And how that's hard to do?" Oh, Leah, naked love of my mid-life crisis, why must you speak in workshop?

Apparently unable to hear my thinking, she continued, "I guess I think the—well, the—you know, 'fucking' part of the poem—it's the opposite of that, somehow? It's, like, taking up a lot of space because it's so . . . what Keisha calls 'unflinching,' but I think is kind of, like, borrowing value from its own profanity?"

Someone coughed, and I felt certain I heard something in the cough—something mocking, something—are you fucking kidding, how rich is this, Leah fucking our professor on her hallway floor and then coming to class to talk about how profanity in a poem is cheating? But maybe I was the one who coughed. Maybe I was the one who had that thought.

"So, I'd like to say something kind of on the back of that," Candor said, even though it was her poem. "I thought about doing the sex part in a more elliptical, or . . . I don't know, *lyrical* way, but it felt too smarmy that way." She looked, I was sure, straight into my eyes. "I wanted to address it directly, call it what it is—which is, in fact, fucking. I'm sorry if that offends anyone, but it's kind of like the elephant in the room."

This lit a wick at my core. "Indeed, sex in a poem, I mean—or anything that has inherent shock value in it—or, even if we're not talking about shock, dramatic value—can be well-done directly . . . can feel like a clearing of the air, an exposing of the elephant in the room of any poem, or—" Oh, how desperately I wished to make that elephant general, to pan out and have this conversation be about craft and not the inside silk of Leah's thighs, her mouth open, head tipped back, breath speeding up until—

"I guess what I mean to say is that of course it's always worth asking, as I think Leah just asked, what work the built-in shock value of that is doing, and whether it's worth the borrow—I mean, the way in which a poem borrows drama from its, well, most explicit elements."

Sean said, "I didn't really find the sex part that explicit, you guys. I think the word 'fucking' in a poem is okay. I wondered about 'demon triangle'—can we talk about that for a minute?"

"I took it to be a stand in for 'hellhole,'" Keisha said. And again, a bubbling, vicious laugh rose up in me, and I thought of all the words I'd never used in workshop, all the truths I'd never said, all the euphemistic renderings I'd made of other people's questions and my own responses, and I felt the laugh erupting out of my throat.

I gave in to the feeling of it, orgiastic, and I let my head lean back, opened my mouth and laughed and laughed until I felt so excited and exposed and horrified that I thought I might combust.

"Professor B., is everything all right?"

Timario. He looked around the room with wild eyes at his classmates, all frozen in positions of tormented silence, only their eyes moving, as they looked at each other. Only Leah was looking down.

I considered apologizing for laughing—for scaring them with my being an actual person rather than a heroine who lived behind the whiteboard and crawled out only to teach workshops. I didn't want to apologize.

"I think 'demon triangle' is quite funny," I told Candor, "So, if that's what you intended—" (Of course, the deep disingenuousness of this false clause was obvious to me and fell somewhere on the spectrum of the sort of euphemizing I was trying not to indulge in anymore). "—then I commend you. But if you meant to be serious or provocative, then I think you need to rework the line."

She was nodding, her face red, neck and chest lighting with hives.

"Let's do an in-class writing exercise," I suggested. I hoped the demon triangle of Candor's poem would leave all of our minds forever—which, even as I hoped for it, I knew would never happen. Did its hideous staying power make it part or a signal of something good? If you remembered something forever because it was disastrous, did that make it more meaningful than something—Leah's love poem, say—fine in its very forgetability?

"Make a list—" I proposed, all the alphabetized condiments in our fridge flashing by me. "—of lines that begin with, 'I used to X,' and end, 'but now I Y.' Or it doesn't have to be first-person or confessional, but there has to be a change recorded in each line. Something used to 'X,' but now it 'Y's.' Go."

They went to writing, whiplashed maybe by the change in lesson plans, yet so trusting, so willing to make the shift from that conversation to this one, to their own blank pages and their own minds, that I felt I could love them—in the good, old way of love, not the perverted new one.

Although—I had to confess that even as I took in the sideways part in Leah's hair, my eyes twitched over to Timario with a new kind of curiosity. As if slapping myself, I whipped my eyes onto the blank page in front of myself, tried to pay attention. The page and this exercise both made me feel young suddenly, and some kind of possibility opened up in front of me.

This classroom used to be mine but now I've defiled it.

I used to be me, but now I might vanish forever and never be known again, to myself or anyone else.

I used to wonder who my father was and think I might someday get to know him, but now I understand I'll never find him.

I used to think I could make up at some point for whatever and whomever I had loved insufficiently, but now my time is dire and I can only use it to make things worse. To love less by loving more. Or to redistribute.

I used to know something, but now I know something else.

I used to know something, but now I know only all I can't know.

I used to be above ground, but now I'm digging in.

I used to feel safe, but now my own death blocks me walking across the parking lot.

I used to sleep sometimes, but now my death pops up like a whack-a-mole in each of my thoughts and my dreams too.

Sleeping and waking used to be distinct but now they blur.

I used to be a body with breasts, but now I'll be a body with balloons.

I used to assume I'd always have nipples, but now I think I'll lose them.

I used to have the luxury of not wondering what it's like to have no nipples.

I used to sit in my office, but now I lie down.

I used to swim, but now I just save myself from drowning over and over, lap by lap.

I used to be an adult, but now I'm moving backwards.

I used to want a complex set of loves and things. Now all I want is Leah.

I used to protect what I loved, but now I destroy it.

I used to "teach" poetry, but now I just don't give a fuck. (Did I used to give a fuck? Or was I pretending and fell for it, too?)

I used to be unaware of the words "demon triangle," but now I'll remember them forever.

I used to be married to my husband Charles, but now—

I used to fuck that;

now fuck this.

I looked up, bored of my own mind and agitated. Leah's head was bent down over her paper. Her spiky hair looked tidy; I could feel the teeth of the comb combing it up this morning, feel her running her fingers through it with whatever product she put in. I could feel her bare neck, her mouth, whisper, flutter, swallow, gasp. Her lips, parted slightly.

Her eyes flickered up suddenly, and I thought of the eyes of the Bishop fish, flat and glinting, isinglass. But Leah's eyes met mine, lavender shadows underneath them. She looked exhausted, but her small mouth turned up into a half-smile, quick. My heart shook my ribs and I smiled at her, held her gaze, waited for my other students to look up, to notice, to know, told myself I didn't care. Leah, daring to her core, stared me down.

Other students began to look up; we stayed locked in eye contact.

"You can post or email these if you like, but you don't have to," I said, even as I kept my eyes on Leah's face. I could feel the flickering of everyone else's gazes on us, and my excitement was visceral, adrenaline pumping so fast through me and up into my brain that I felt high. No one spoke, so I kept looking at Leah, whatever I felt for her visible on the surface, I knew, of my face. I said, hardly moving my mouth, "We're going to reschedule next week's class for after the Thanksgiving break, so you have a little more time to work on your projects, and I'll see you all after the break."

If anyone was shocked by this slight change in plans, no one acknowledged it. What was one class rescheduled? I needed a moment to pause, to percolate, didn't want to try this again next week, wanted to bring on the surgery, the turkey, the other shore I still hoped to reach.

Leah stood. I kept sitting, watching her. Oh, after the break! By then, I would be somewhere other than mired in this moment, having paddled through unconsciousness and amputation.

Amputation. Charles criticized me when I used words like that, asking why I must describe everything as hideously as possible. But for me, arriving at what felt like the real words made me feel better, safer, secure, as if I'd found a way to write the thing I'd been meaning to write—or taken ownership of the worst possibilities, rather than letting them take control of me, or surprise me.

I RIPPED THE page of "I used to 'X' but now I 'Y'" out of my notebook and left it on the classroom table for whoever taught next.

AS I CLICKED across the lot to my car, done until after the surgery, a turkey galloped across my mind, red waddle flapping like an insult, layers of Thanksgiving's absurdity clarifying like rendered animal fat, my own complacency in honoring the holiday at all coming at me like an animal itself. Alexi used to make animal rights signs to hold up during our family photo sessions, Charles's father James humorless as he set up his camera on a tripod and stalked toward us, cursing when the camera went off before he was positioned. In at least one entire set of photos from a Thanksgiving we all spent together, all that was visible was James's back and the corner of Alexi's sign, a personified turkey holding up its own sign: *Why Not Tofurkey This Year, Murderers?*

I found this as adorable as James found it annoying. Charles was indifferent. I made a tofurkey that his father spent the entire night comparing to an NFL football while Alexi rolled her eyes accommodatingly and tried to persuade him to try it. His mother drank three vodka tonics and four glasses of white wine. I was counting. Counting felt like a hobby.

Why not the truth this year, liar?

NOW THE RAIN had stopped and the day was silver. I climbed into my car, feeling competent to drive, and to drive straight to Leah's apartment. This logistical competency was inspired by its counterpoint, the fact that whatever had just transpired in my workshop had unglued me completely.

I shut the car door and turned the engine on, thinking of Bishop, thinking, *And I let the fish go*. I let the fish go.

There were rainbows, rainbows I drove over in the steamy, shining parking lot and all I could think was *let the fish go*.

CHAPTER TWELVE

LEAH WASN'T EXPECTING ME because I had decided, naturally, that nothing about our liaison should ever happen or be recorded in writing, and I hadn't felt like calling, in my giddy moment of letting the fish go. Leah wrote her poems—apparently sometimes using my name, that I couldn't control—but there would be no data exchange, no texting or emailing. This was, of course, because I didn't want to leave evidence of our affair, but I pretended that it was for the sake of some sort of pure romance, just for the fun of it. A present-tense thing.

As I rang the bell, I imagined myself unconscious on the table, Charles and Dr. B and Alexi and my mother gripping my phone, reading texts to and from Leah. I wasn't stupid. Well, I was stupid, but not about that part.

Leah was cooking. It smelled like a farm, and I didn't even ask what she was making. Her apartment was a mess, half-unpacked groceries in the hallway, multiple outfits on the bed, shoes all over the floor. She was wearing a bathrobe with sweatpants underneath, and a face mask transformed her into Jason from the movie where he wears a hockey mask (I couldn't remember what it was called because I think I never watched it, but the image of the mask seeped into my consciousness anyway, of course). The mask she was wearing was white with tiny holes poked in it. She looked absolutely terrible.

"My God, Leah, are you okay?"

"Sam, I didn't know you were—" she said at the door. I could hear something bubbling in the kitchen. "About what happened in class, I, um—I—?"

"My fault entirely," I said, not moving. I felt like I couldn't move.

"Well, it's just—I'm having some people over in a minute."

"Oh," I said, embarrassed. "I'll go. I just wanted to pop in and say hi. I couldn't say so just now because, well, of course, but I wanted to tell you that my daughter's home for a visit, which is why I've been MIA."

I still didn't move. But now she came closer to me, and I could see that the mask with the holes in it was slipping, peeling away from her forehead. I felt electrocuted to the floor. My arms were buzzing, too heavy to lift.

"What happened in workshop—I'm sorry if I—"

"No, no—it's—don't apologize. That wasn't your fault. It was—"

I had a rule in my class that the girls, unless they'd hurt someone egregiously, were not allowed to apologize. Otherwise, they'd say sorry for breathing. And reading their work. And having written. And existing. But I didn't know what to say.

Leah's eyes filled up, and I had the strange sense that I was swimming in them in my elastic cap and goggles. I wanted to come up, un-fog what I saw, release the water from inside my sight and also around me. I blinked several times.

She said, "Okay. I'm okay," but I thought she was tell-ing herself that, not telling me.

"What are you cooking?" I asked, desperate.

"Lasagna," she said. "But the tomato sauce burned, so."

"Do you want some help?"

She stared at me, her wet eyes wide, relief so stark I felt embarrassed by it for both of us. Was the relief just because I'd offered something kind? Because I was here, turning out to be a human being?

"No, that's okay. I don't need help with the cooking, I just—" she started. "It's just—you didn't take any of my calls the other day, so I thought—"

This I felt I couldn't help with.

"I thought maybe you didn't want to see me anymore. Outside of workshop, I mean." One half of the mask flapped open. "Did you think that conversation today was—"

She paused, probably hoping I would rescue her, but I couldn't. Part of it was cowardice, of course: I didn't want to have difficult conversations with Leah. And part of it was that I felt incapacitated by the same revelation I thought she might be having about me: she was a fully rendered person, with her own ideas and stories, and this thing—this thing with me—was happening *to* her.

I reached out and touched her face, felt the wet mask slip further.

I didn't know how she understood this gesture, but she turned and went into the bathroom. I heard the water spraying from the faucet. When she emerged, she had peeled the white mask off entirely, but maybe not washed or dried her face of whatever it had offered—aloe? Collagen? Her skin looked wet and I thought of a sea lion, poking its head from the water, hoping for fish.

She stood very close to me then, wet-faced and waiting, and I kissed her lips, clean teeth, sea salt taste. She didn't object. I kept kissing with increasing insistence, partly because I wanted to drive my own thoughts away and partly because the vision of the sea lion drew me to Leah as much as it repulsed me. There was nothing consistent about me, or any of us. If anyone thinks her tenancy in the land of the sane and healthy was reliable, she should probably think again, because our bodies and minds have a million shards and parts, so many in contradiction with each other that we cannot count on ourselves not to revolt against ourselves.

In Leah's hallway, looking at her, feeling her, I realized I couldn't see myself anymore, couldn't tell who I was, had to feel more and more in order to feel anything. And because I was made of my own most sickening contradictions, what I most wanted was to feel nothing.

Leah, maybe because she wasn't middle-aged or mortal yet, seemed to me not to have reached this point yet. She was my perfect counterpoint: one sane, coherent person, tough, young, full of hope and promise. I felt jealous, proud, devastated. I felt that maybe I loved her, even without knowing enough about her to justify infatuation, let alone love. I thought I was crazy, thought I could stay forever in her hallway, never do or think about anything else again.

Leah leaned against her wall and pulled me toward her, sliding the robe off her shoulders. It fell to the floor, and she looked, as always to my unsophisticated eye, almost boyish, topless with her sweatpants riding low on her hips. I touched her neck, her collarbone, her breasts and her stomach, then pulled at the drawstring and the sweatpants fell too, into a pool at her ankles.

She kicked her feet free of them and she was naked, still standing, and I knelt until she collapsed onto the floor and we became a pile of parts on the floor, with only our own scraps of clothing underneath us. No doubt her burnt sauce was not improved during the twenty minutes we spent devouring each other on her hallway floor, but I collected myself and my skirt and shirt before her buzzer rang once, likely bringing with its alarm my other students. I felt oddly powerful. I said, "Tomorrow I want to cruise you."

"What?"

I clarified, "Tomorrow morning, meet me at Coffee Queen when they open, okay? In the first bathroom on the right. It's a code, so just punch in the numbers. I'll already be in there, waiting for you."

I slipped into the fire escape and took the metal steps down, wondering, had I just missed my students? Were they on the main stairs? In the elevator? Standing in the hallway where I'd ravaged Leah twenty seconds before? And did I want them to be? I could smell Leah's skin on mine, and I decided not to wash it off, not to care, not even to indulge in the erasing apology of a shower. I wanted to fuck her in a public bathroom, pretend I was free to cruise, to have the sort of sex shot-through with literal and also lyrical risk: get this, I wanted to be a man, preferably a politician, the sort who has an affair in his office or with the documentarian following him precisely because the possibility of getting caught is a hard-on. The feeling of almost ruining my life, counter-intuitive though this was, was a giddy counterpoint to my actual fear. At least this danger I was choosing. My heart pounded with excitement, with the way Leah had felt on her hallway floor, with the way my body still felt, with the way she would feel tomorrow.

I was freezing as I rushed home, as I wished that the world had waited to knock me flat with my body's betrayal and send me reeling into this insanity until *after* Charles's parents had passed away. It was hardly humane of me to prefer they were dead so I could torch my life—and with it, their son's—without having to consider their feelings or response, but there it was. I wondered, freezing, what he had told them, whether anything at all. Clattering as Alexi and I stayed up late, watching a movie so intense—*About Elly*—that at one point she and I turned to each other and both started laughing, the way you might at the funeral of someone you loved, out of pure shock. In the film, three beautiful, middle-class couples take a weekend vacation on the beach, and when their children run into the waves, you think they've drowned but then you realize the woman who followed them in—an outsider on the vacation and someone who shouldn't have been there in the first place—has vanished. Elly, in other words, the unsung heroine. I realized an hour into the movie that I wasn't breathing.

"What the hell?" I asked Alexi. "Who told you to watch this terrifying, life-wrecking movie?"

"My Iranian lit professor," she said. "We watched this

guy's other film for class, *A Separation*." Did she eye me sideways when she said that title?

I stared right back at her, unflinchingly. Like Leah, with tons of eye contact, no flicker of guilt. I wondered, though, why Alexi was watching extra films this professor had suggested. In other words, I turned my guilt on her.

"Did he suggest this to the whole class?"

"Uh, yeah. He loves the director, Asghar Farhadi," she told me.

I stopped freezing then, heated up, focused in. "Remind me who the professor is again?" "Professor Ibrim," she said, and her voice changed. I looked up, in spite of feeling that I should not blink, not acknowledge it.

"What," Alexi said. Was she daring me?

"What what?" I asked, even though we both knew.

"Why are you looking at me like that?"

"Like what, Alexi? I think it's great you're branching out and watching international films."

She un-paused the film and we went back into the search party, waiting for Elly's bloated body to be discovered, and somehow, Alexi and I both began laughing again and dropped it, whatever it was, about Professor Ibrim. I worked on my breathing, casting back to Lamaze and Bradley classes (I took both)—what a hilarious clusterfuck that whole enterprise was! A thousand hours of breathing and counting and also imagining I was on a river or whatever, and then Alexi jumped rope with her umbilical cord and tied it around her neck and I had a C-section. At least the breathing was useful now, as I watched to see whether Elly had, in fact, perished, or whether she had just decided to escape the vacation house without telling anyone where she was going.

When Elly's fiancé showed up in the movie, enraged to learn that she had been on this vacation—and to understand that there was one single man among the crowd of beach-goers—I realized it was about social shackles on women. *How much was I entitled to—information or opinion-wise—about my own daughter?* I wondered then. Did I get to have a view on whatever was between Alexi and one of her professors, if that's what the slight twitch in her voice had, in fact, indicated? Or was I just projecting, now that I wore whatever was the predator's version of rose-colored glasses? Was I a retrograde feminist, imagining that Alexi could be the victim of a romance, rather than the initiator? Leah had asked me to her apartment, after all—I hadn't started it. She had driven everything in the beginning, hadn't she? Everything until today, maybe, when she'd stood naked in her hallway and I'd been dressed. But even that had been her choice—she'd slid the robe down her shoulders, not I.

Of course, the staring in class was my fault. And I was the adult in the equation. I had always, my entire life, been the seducer. Why did I feel seduced by her? She had been running whatever show was taking place between us.

I missed the climax of the movie, tuned so completely out and obsessing, that I had to fake my way through post-film analysis with Alexi. I pretended to just be patiently listening to her, but actually I had no idea what had happened in the final half hour of the film, even though it was literally the most suspenseful movie I'd ever seen.

I came only to this conclusion: it wasn't my goodness or even an aversion to hypocrisy that stopped me from asking Alexi further questions. It was exhaustion—the pure, selfish sense that I couldn't take on another drama, even of tiny scale, even about the only person I thought I loved unselfishly. I didn't want to know.

As if on cue, Charles came in. "I went ahead and invited my parents for Thanksgiving," he said.

"Oh, good!" Alexi said.

I nodded. "Oh, good!" I said, trying to sound natural, to be nice, but shrieking accidentally, while Alexi and Charles stared at me. I grinned and nodded, idiotic.

Then I went to bed, hoping the hours between me and my Coffee Queen-cruising Leah might elapse faster, but I kicked all night like a trapped beast, twisting my night-shirt until it almost hanged me.

I WAS THERE before Coffee Queen opened, at 5:59, waiting for the doors like some crazy consumer on Black Friday, the first in line to order my cappuccino, which I carried to a table near the bathroom. We were a skinny morning crew of baristas, lawyers, and lovers. Who else wanted coffee out of the house that early? I typed in the bath-room code I'd demurely requested: 3694. I reminded myself not to care if anyone else had to wait. There were three bathrooms, I reasoned; they could use the others, maybe I was sick. I *was* sick.

In the mirror, I saw my face as if I were on an acid trip, the skin theater-white, my eyes green glass, lips a dark gash. I came close enough to blur and erase my face, and stayed that way, erased, the cold sink digging into my hips, stayed at the mirror with my eyes open but seeing nothing until I heard the beeping of the key pad.

It didn't work; it turned out they'd solved the problem of someone walking in on someone else by creating a digital system that didn't allow two people to use the bathroom at the same time. So, I opened the door and let Leah in. She smelled bright like orange juice and shampoo. I never wanted to see or think or eat or touch anything again that wasn't her.

She seemed uncharacteristically shy. "What are we doing?" she asked.

"Just meeting for coffee," I told her.

"What if someone comes in?"

I said, "Don't worry," and put my mouth over hers, to take whatever other, worrisome words might come out of it and swallow them, but she pulled away.

"I don't want to take my clothes off in here," she said.

This gave me pause; had I reached the point where I was going to compel a young woman to have sex she didn't want in a bathroom where she didn't want to be?

"How about my clothes, then?" I suggested. So yes, I was now *that guy*, unwilling—even though she didn't like it—to give up the fantasy I was planning on enacting with her.

She seemed to consider this. "Can we just do it with our clothes on?" she asked, meaning *quickly*, meaning she wanted it over with, didn't want to disappoint me but didn't want this. Because I'd said such things in my own life—because we were both women—I understood this subtext precisely.

She had no belt on today. I reached into the waistband

of her jeans, pulling them away from her stomach and pushing my hand down, wanting to take them off completely, wondering how much taking-off would count as my having defied her wishes. I kept my own clothes on because *she* was what I wanted, and I didn't care about my own state of dress. She stood still, getting younger and younger somehow. Or maybe I was just realizing she'd never been in charge. And what a true villain I was.

Once I was pressed against her, moving her into the wall, and she was breathing the way she did right before the cricket sound, we heard a knock. She jumped and stiffened, but I shivered with desire. Maybe we'd get caught. Was that what I wanted?

"Hello?" A voice called, a man's voice. Good, I thought, because as soon as he heard my voice, which said to him, "I'll be out in a minute," he would back off. And I was right, because women don't do the sorts of things in bathrooms that he was worried someone was doing in the bathroom. Ha!

Leah, for all her hesitation, came, bucking against me as I put my other hand over her mouth, lest anyone waiting—the barista, other customers, the police—hear the cricket sound I wanted to preserve only for myself. I didn't care if they knew we were fucking, even if they arrested us. But I didn't really want to share that sound with anyone else, wanting to believe for the moment that something about someone else could be mine alone. Even though I knew better.

Leah bit my palm, actually breaking the skin. Then she zipped her jeans up and walked out on the heels of her usual boots.

I let her go first, of course, because I knew she'd be embarrassed if someone tried to come in and she were already in there. I didn't care at all, so I sauntered out into the line of two people waiting for the bathroom. Maybe because they were there, Leah appeared to have left Coffee Queen entirely—not that I looked very hard or long for her. Her absence was probably a message, one that should have sparked in me some concern, or at least—in the absence of genuine caring—a performance of worry. But I felt buoyant, tremendous relief. I headed to the rec center, where I shed my clothes like guilt or rules and rushed straight into the pool. Steamy room of chlorine and arms wind-milling slowly out of the ripples.

Where the water met the wall were waving stems of sunlight, in my lane an elderly Chinese man I'd seen before and knew underwater, his head half-vanished into a silicone cap, his feet slim and powerful as flippers. I felt, although of course we didn't speak, that we were swimming in sync, agreeing on the rules of the lane, maybe even in love.

Twenty-six minutes of overlap in the pool, and when he climbed out, water pouring in even lines down his bright-blue swimsuit, I stood up in the shallow part of the lane and waved goodbye. He smiled and nodded before wrapping a towel around his waist, sliding into flip-flops and walking into the men's locker room. I remained standing in the water and watched him the whole way because I wanted to. How luxurious to do the things one wanted to, rather than packing those things into one's back muscles—rather than doing whatever was subtle, or polite, or even expected.

Once he was swallowed by the wet mouth of the men's room, I flattened my body right below the surface of the water again, made my hands into knives, and sliced only the thinnest layer of blue from the top of the pool on each stroke. I swam forever, until the water no longer felt cool, until it was soup, until my arms wouldn't windmill, until my legs cramped and refused to kick. Maybe individual parts of my body would begin to revolt, also at unpredictable moments—would mutiny and just stop working. My eyes might suddenly refuse to see, my ears to hear, my legs to carry me on the dubious errands I was assigning myself. They'd be smart to make such choices.

In the locker room, I spent eleven minutes in the sauna, trying to sweat some of my own cells out of my pores. My understanding of science, fueled and trumped by my hope, allowed for that possibility. Another woman came in when I had been in the sauna for six of the eleven minutes. I had been lying down on the top shelf when she arrived, my legs bent at the knees because the top shelf was short. As soon as she came in, I began fretting about her experience in the sauna—was she made to feel awkward by the fact that I was lying down? Was my towel gaping open in a pornographic way? Was she thinking how obscene it was that I had used three towels—one for my head, another for my body, and the third making sure even my toes didn't come into direct contact with the wooden slats?

I reminded myself I was now working on being someone who didn't care when another person entered the sauna or the pool, the sort who didn't move instantly to the shitty part of the pool right next to the wall when someone else decided to share my lane—who didn't sit up straight in the sauna now, or wrap myself tighter in the towels in an effort to be more polite or blameless. I was no longer going to apologize. This was a small matter, but it took every modicum of restraint I had not to leap up, cover myself completely, and leave the sauna, letting this woman who had innocently come in—and who didn't seem to mind that I was there—have the place to herself. I had only wanted to stay ten minutes, but I forced myself to remain there, in the exact position in which she'd found me, for an extra sixty seconds. And I didn't apologize when I opened the door and cold air rushed in. She didn't seem to notice me at all. No one did, right? So why had I been so apologetic and polite my whole life? I went to my locker, got my notebook, stood naked, and wrote:

1) *I used to want everyone to like me, but now I only want Leah to like me.*
2) *And I don't even want her to like me that much.*

ALEXI WAS AWAKE when I got home. I sat on the couch, where she was lying with her feet up, reading. She looked at me. "Were you swimming?"

Was this the real question? Did she mean to ask where I'd been? Or was it just kindness, as when she'd asked Charles which friend he was planning to play racquetball with?

"Um, yeah."

"How was it?"

"It was fine," I said. "Cold."

We were quiet for a minute. She kept looking at me,

though, didn't go back to her book. What did she see? Fear poured into my limbs, made me heavy, reminded me again of nursing, of being young. I wanted to be young with Alexi so much it felt like wanting oxygen I couldn't have.

"Are you going to tell me what's going on with your professor?" I asked, pinning blame, gaslighting.

Alexi tilted her face, pinned me with her grayish eyes. She blinked. "What professor?"

I knew her well enough to get which faces were faked; this expression was of genuine confusion and curiosity.

"The literature one who recommended the movie," I fumbled, hoping to get away from my original point without having to acknowledge it. I suddenly felt that I might cry out of pure self-loathing. What the hell was my problem? "Oh, um—I was just wondering what else he's recommended. Has he suggested any other movies? Something else we could watch now or later tonight?"

"Uh, yeah. We could watch *A Separation*, I guess," Alexi said, tucking her hands behind her head. "But that's not by the professor, just the same director as *About Elly*. And I've seen it, like I said. Why? Do you want to watch TV now? During the day? Why are you being so weird?"

"Was that weird?" It was *so* weird. Since when did I waste four hundred syllables to ask a meaningless question that could have been made out of six? I added, "I just want to hang out with you."

Alexi blew her bangs out of her eyes and narrowed her eyes at me. She used to keep one eye open and one eye shut when she was nursing, like a suspicious dolphin.

(Didn't dolphins sleep with an eye open in case they got attacked by sharks? Or was I misremembering that?)

"Do you think I'm, like, sleeping with my ninety-two-year-old Iranian literature professor? Is that your implication, Mom? Because he recommended a movie to me? What the hell is going on?"

"Of course not, honey, I—of course not."

I turned on the TV, just like I had assigned a writing prompt in my classroom—anything to flee the actual conversation I had started. Maybe this was what it felt like to be right-wing, politically dishonest, unable to finish a sentence, to have to peel up the ends of all your clauses, because locking down lies with punctuation was embarrassing and made them more difficult to escape. To deny having said anything at all.

The only thing on was a rerun of *Honey Boo-Boo*. I hadn't seen the show before, but I immediately loved it. Surprise! Is that even a surprise? Maybe it's perfectly in keeping with my being the worst person ever encountered that I loved *Honey Boo-Boo* pathologically, as if I'd been hungry and the show was the only food I could find, the perfect food. I didn't even feel nostalgic for my own youth or Alexi's babyhood anymore, because now all I needed was to devour endless episodes of *Honey Boo-Boo*.

While Alexi looked on in horror, I watched gluttonously, jealous of the woman at whose expense the show seemed to me to have been made: the morbidly obese June, who spent the episode resisting pressure to "slap some paint on the barn"—i.e., apply makeup to her broiling face—and joking with her daughters about farting and rolling in the mud and eating animals they hit with a pick-up truck. June seemed to me, even though she was being made into a public freak for it, to have torn off all the niceties by which the rest of us remained imprisoned. In that moment.

"She does whatever she wants," I remarked to Alexi. She swung her long legs off the couch to face me.

"You're joking, right, Mom?"

Of course, I knew this was crazy—and patronizing and politically incorrect as well as morally reprehensible. Alexi reminded me of all those things when I argued that I thought June was a kind of feminist.

Yet after Alexi gave up on me and left to exercise and meet Siobhan, I stayed in the living room with my laptop, pulling up archival episodes of *Honey Boo-Boo* and binge-watching them as if they were as sustaining as the recipe June made for her daughters to eat over and over: sketti, pasta with ketchup and butter melted in the microwave.

If the female protagonist of a show wasn't dead and naked, but morbidly obese and eating such a terrible diet that she was in danger of dying before my (and millions of other viewers') eyes, did that break my own TV rule? And what if her teenage daughters were putting melted butter on the floor and sliding across it on their bellies, a homemade, high-fat-content slip 'n slide? If I watched nine straight hours of *Honey Boo-Boo*, what purpose did my self-regulations (or life) serve?

Oh, Charles. Please come and talk to me. Forgive me, make me sane again. Was it always Charles who kept me sane? I wanted to tell him I'd made a mistake, had been sleeping with one of my students, that I was horribly, sickeningly sorry—but he wasn't home. I finally turned the television off after watching so many hours of *Honey Boo-Boo* that I realized it was how I'd spent most of the end of my life if I died soon.

But I tunneled deep into a well of online post-show analysis, only to find and read, my teeth literally chattering, numerous reports that June had dated a man who raped one of her daughters.

This revelation cost her more than my rabid, if short-lived, fandom; it had brought about the death of the series. Apparently even TLC, the network designed to celebrate and perpetuate freak shows (for which I was apparently among the target audience), wasn't willing to continue funding her stardom after the stories of June's romantic reunion with her child's rapist.

Again, I had an urge to discuss the finer points of this with Charles—maybe after the surgery, after the affair, after (if) he forgave me. Another network had picked June up, now a thousand pounds lighter, half her skin removed, her face trapped in the expression of someone on a hellish amusement park ride: teeth bared, skin stretched back. She and her rubber lips and newly tubular waist were the new stars of a new show, *From Not to Hot*.

After I was shuttled by the Internet from photos of June to still shots from a show called *My 600-lb Life*, I shut the computer. Please, God. I vowed never to watch anything about anyone else ever again. What was in those shows for me, consuming other people's naked miseries with my gloating, superior eyes? What terrible force drew me to stories of other people's ruined bodies? At least, I now believed there was a bottom rockier and further down than the one where I currently resided—and if that comfort weren't enough, I was rewarded for my asinine behavior and revelation because the first line of a poem came knocking into my mind, several sexy words at the door: *Our bodies move our minds, guide says climb, says don't look down.*

Yes! I fetched a notebook, a pen, my glasses, got stalacmites and -tites I'd never seen, got sinking, slipping, girls in danger. Bulbs and wound drains in my mind were words on the page now—which ones, I'd figure out. I got—from *Honey Boo-Boo* and *My 600-lb Life* and *From Hot to Not* and my own cancer diagnosis and appalling affair—the start of a poem! I sat until my body was a knot, sorting letters that covered a new page, made something. At the end of working, I felt like I'd entered a new romance with myself.

Straight Up
by Samantha Baxter, 11/10, draft

Spotlight strapped above the eyes
    head into blank space, tilt back until
        what hangs sharp from above is visible.
        Lean forward for what might rise.

        So said can be unsaid, turns out, done
    undone, recast. Cast about fast, flail alone.
Our bodies move our minds, guide says climb, says don't look down,
says fear makes girls slip off the edge, hold on

which girls are there
    scaling such hostile rocks in the dark, where
        is this cliff? Maybe there's no way, no me/her,
        night, no stars slicing a sheet of sky. Remember:

        remembering is falling. Vow to look down quick;
        in fact, take stock of what leads this way, that, up, back, stick
        this landing. I'm dying to climb out from each contradiction,
fix what can't be fixed, belay by way of impossible prediction—

So fine, fall. Get up, love a rope, a net,
    intent. Grab at whatever set
        of truths a fighting crowd of selves may make, all
        our holds along such a sheer, sleek wall.

CHAPTER THIRTEEN

OBVIOUSLY, YOU CAN BE JEAL-
ous of yourself. I knew that years ago, but somehow keep
re-realizing it. It felt fresh and revelatory just two weeks
ago, when I became scaldingly jealous of the person I was
who had never had cancer, who had breasts and thought
nothing of it. Jealous of the person who had a little baby
once. Jealous of the me who was sitting at the table only
sixteen hours ago, the Samantha Baxter who thought that
fucking poem I was writing—"Straight Up"—was brilliant.

Because today I had to be the me who got that it wasn't.
The me who woke up knowing that poem was a beer-gog-
gling, one-night stand of a writing exercise. The me who
was like Nicolas Cage in that movie *Adaptation*, where he
thinks his idea is fabulously, stunningly, amazingly awesome—remember? He tapes himself while he's thinking
of it, talking grandly into his mini-recorder, and then it
cuts straight to a close-up of his horrified face while he
listens to his own stupid idea later—the one he thought
was so great, mere hours ago. I am also the writer one day
and my own wrecking-ball critic the next.

And what if I hadn't become the other person, the
one who read that poem for real, no longer in visually
impaired love with it: *Our bodies move our minds, guide says
climb, says don't look down / says fear makes girls slip off the
edge, hold on*? Really, Sam?

It would be hot to stay blissfully oblivious, in love with my first drafts forever. I wished for that. And good health. And to be some other, earlier version of me, either a stupider one or a better one. I used to be well—used to be young! Used to be either a good writer or wearing good-enough blinders to *believe* I was a good writer, and given that I'd now written off what everyone else thought forever, I wasn't sure there was any difference between the two.

But after I realized I was this present-tense Sam, I had to sit with my coffee, festering with self-pity. Then, when I looked over, I saw that my phone was lit with notifications, including an email from Melody Ames, our pearl-clad chairwoman, whose tediousness was legendary.

I picked up the phone, read:

Dear Samantha,

I know it's almost the holiday, but I'm concerned about a few matters, and wonder if you'd be willing to stop by my office sometime today or tomorrow for a chat. Or if that doesn't work, please give me a call at your earliest convenience. Thanks, Samantha.

All best,
Melody

A tunnel hollowed out in my gut. I pitched myself backwards in my chair, as if by getting away from the screen I might escape the almost-content of her note. And maybe I could. Or maybe not. I considered what the few matters might be—the taste of Leah lingering on my lips, likely. Or was it the fact that I'd tried to torch our obligatory and normally euphemistic faculty meeting to the ground in such an uncharacteristic way?

Maybe I'd continue down that road, I thought suddenly, and do what I had never done when I was still in the business of earning the world's praise: not write back. Other people (men) did that all the time, ignored emails, "dropped the ball," didn't apologize. I wasn't going to write back.

The tunnel filled with bright, cheerful light. Fuck not just her and the department and my job and life, but the *entire enterprise* of emailing, of human interaction for any reason than one's most selfish and dire pleasures. Not responding to an email for the first time in my life! I was a true revolutionary. And if I died, she'd know why I slept with one of our students: because I'd been dying.

And if I didn't die and decided I wanted to rejoin the fabric of society, I could use my illness as an excuse, a get-out-of-jail-free card, temporary insanity. Or I'd just deny the thing with Leah. She said, she said. They'd believe me, right?

My mind filled with useful clichés. Okay, so I was a half-assed revolutionary.

I didn't write her back. I rolled up a printed-out copy of my new poem, collected my suit and goggles, and headed to the pool, wondering less about Melody's email and what it was going to mean than about how I would put a bathing suit on over metal breasts.

I listened to Prince on an underwater iPod Charles and Alexi got me years ago. The song "Cream" came on—the one about positions in a one-night stand, the lines about serving ribs to a fat fling he clocks that way. The lyrics suddenly sounded biblical to me. I remembered I wouldn't be allowed to swim for months after the surgery, because open wounds don't do well in bleachy water, maybe, or because I wouldn't be able to stretch my arms over my head. The water seemed to change then, as a result of the song or some chemical reaction between me and the song. The whole pool was suddenly warm and churning, too heavy for me to stay on top of, too much water. I thought about the ribs; she asks for ribs because she's trying to make herself something at his house, and she's apparently a person who asks for the actual thing she wants. He says, *LaToya, I don't serve ribs*, only to arrive a line later at, *Honey, them ribs is gone*. She asks for the thing she wants and gets it: ribs made by Prince on a one-night stand. In other words, Eden.

How do we learn to ask for what we need? To distinguish between what we want and what we need? And not to avoid want for so long that it becomes need? The light shifted on the water and I slowed, breast-stroked for a long time because freestyle took too much breath, required shifting more water than I had the strength to shift. I stayed under for as long as I could, only inhaled when I felt my lungs were about to explode. I tried to surface silently, gently, not to ripple or splash, thought again of my body next week, how it wouldn't be mobile, how my armpits might swell with what they called lymphedema, how that might make swimming forever different for me, if not impossible.

If I were in the Bible instead of my own small life or the community pool, maybe something could be made of the tissue they were taking, other than a mentally ill analysis of Prince lyrics by someone who once had her mind intact and/but had now lost it. What might God make of my chopped-up body? Another human? Out of breast tissue? It'd be like Eve coming from Adam, except a blob instead of a rib. You need bones, I think, to construct someone whole. Not just external flesh from my very large breasts.

I begged God or the world or anyone powerful who might be listening to let me swim back into my own past—push, kick, glide, push, kick, glide straight back in foggy goggles, regulating my breathing, to Alexi's baby days. Maybe what I could remember I could have, even if I couldn't live there.

Here: Alexi's rebellious curls are clipped back in a duck barrette, and she's swinging, laughing with her mouth open, two teeth coming up from her bottom gum. Drool. Alexi and I are back in the pool of my memory and longing, in those long and gauzy days of her babyhood. We are nursing, rocking, staring out the window at a firehouse, the old-age home next to it a distant mirage, something I thought would never touch me. I was so young. In my memory of that time now, I seem to be a baby, too. We are both rocking, rocking, like that creepy book about the guy who will always love his mom and so sneaks into her window at the end and rocks her in the Norman Bates rocking chair.

Remember that book? *I will always love you, forever my baby you'll be*? Why is unconditional love so often a horror movie?

I got out of the pool, put my clothes on, blow-dried my hair, spackled my lashes and lips with chemicals, and returned to Coffee Queen, hoping to reminisce about my bathroom escapade and maybe sit for a minute and revise my romantic poem to myself.

And then, behold! While I was waiting for my latte, I watched the barista run his hand down over his pants, describing—articulating, even—the shape of his cock. This changed the course of my daydreaming, and I knew I'd never manage to revise my poem now.

Because the thing is, he and I were having eye contact when he did it, and he was pulling a shot of espresso from the industrial espresso machine with his left hand. I didn't know whether it was obliviousness that allowed him to do these three things at once—meet my eyes, make coffee, and fondle himself—or something more sinister or belligerent. I didn't mind the gesture; in fact, it made me want a cock for myself. Not his, mind you, not someone else's—my own, attached to me, one I could describe with my hand in public and with words, too. One I could show people, both people who wanted to see it and those who didn't. Maybe I'd wave it around. How else would I use it?

This was something I had never pined for before, never had that famous envy; even the Rimbaud poem I'd translated in graduate school—this leg, this leg, and this leg left—had indicated something extra to me, appalling, even, the third limb in the line leaving me cold. But now, watching this man-boy feel his body in public, absentmindedly celebrating or shifting or rearranging, shot me through with a kind of selfish desire—envy, maybe, of his being him, or of some power I lacked.

I took my drink home, hoping to ponder, but took my

clothes off and considered disappearing—how my finger-prints would vanish, how my nakedness would be para-mount but no longer count. I reclined on our bed, naked, thinking about being naked: alive-naked and dead-na-ked. Some women walked naked in the locker room, so slowly they may as well have been underwater, nothing wrong with being completely naked—even if it was what I considered to be "bad naked," à la that *Seinfeld* episode about what you do and don't do naked. *Don't bend in front of people you don't know. Don't put a pantyliner in your under-pants standing at a locker, for God's sake. Don't walk, not even from your locker to the shower or the shower to the steam room. Don't sit naked on the slippery tiles of the steam room. Please, wear a towel while you get dressed.* Even if you are Leah, stunningly young, don't make a cheese sandwich naked. Don't stand at the counter naked.

Did this make me a woman-hater? Maybe, although clearly the same rules applied to men, maybe expo-nentially. So maybe it just made me a prude? Probably, although I was also a reinvigorated sex monster who backed my student up against the sink at Coffee Queen against her will and better judgment, so could I be both a prude and a pervert?

Of course! It was a common and popular Republican arrangement, wasn't it? I was just on my way to being a congressman, that was all.

I was happily organizing this justification in my mind when Charles found me sitting naked in our bed. He looked at me curiously, or hungrily, or angrily, or per-vertedly, I couldn't tell.

I pulled a pillow over myself. What a coquette!

"Sam?" he said. "We should probably leave in the next twenty minutes if we're going to be on time—do you want me to get you some clothes? Or make you a coffee, or—"

The mention of coffee sent my insides spinning, reeling back toward Leah at the sink. I didn't ask Charles why he was coming, or to what appointment—I had forgotten my appointment, the first time this had happened so far. I didn't ask anything at all, just said, "Okay, thank you," like a child, and he went into the closet, shuffled around, and came out with a sweater and jeans.

He turned away like a teenage boy while I dressed, and I felt such sorrow for him that I thought I might melt into the clothes like the Wicked Witch. There'd be nothing left of me but a pile of the clothes Charles had picked, skinny jeans he'd always liked and a sweater his mother had bought me: soft, pink, cashmere, the kind of present infused with her hope of my being someone other than myself.

"I'm going to go make you a coffee. Meet me in the driveway?"

I nodded. When I walked by the deck and saw the rail I'd hung from in the middle of the night, I felt an almost pathological urge to do it again, to feel that danger, the freedom of having made a choice that put me in peril. Please, God, not the doctor's office.

Charles was standing in the driveway, waiting and holding a thermos of hot coffee. He opened the door for me and squeezed my hand when I got in.

We drove mostly in silence, the turn signal clicking a frank pattern, punctuating our lack of conversation. Charles was like a trapped animal, his legs caught, his eyes darting, trying to find an escape, a way back or out. There was an uncharacteristic panic in his straight-backed posture, his hands shiny-tight on the wheel, ten and two. I wanted to rescue him—to tell him that it, whatever it had been, was over, that we were fine, that I'd had a momentary lapse of judgment but was back in town, within reach.

When we walked from the car to the elevator in the parking garage, Charles noticed he was rushing ahead of me, rushing for no reason—it was just hard-wired in him to be first, to win, to take the best spot, make it to the front of whatever boarding line, to push onto whatever subway car or bus came even if I was still miles away, coming down the stairs onto the platform, to shove up to life's various buffets and make sure he was first-served. I had asked him—sometimes serenely, other times sorrowfully, still others furiously—why he was so intent on saving ten seconds, why it was worth having me miss the train or falling down a flight of cement subway steps, but he found this line of questioning irritating. It seemed so obvious to him that efficiency was everything, that getting to the next and next rung was the whole goal. Why was I constantly slowing him down, making him miss the first bus to go by?

One reason was that I was a full foot shorter than he was, another was fuck him.

Maybe because he remembered that he was in no hurry and that *I* had to be there for the appointment to happen, he slowed and held the door of the elevator lobby open for me. I tried not to assign only the worst motives to him (a bad habit he'd pointed out that I had),

238

but I thought he was doing it to save face, that he'd been rushing ahead of me as he was wont to and then realized how pointless it was, so he'd stopped and pretended he'd been hurrying along to get the door.

I walked slowly. Punishing him? Maybe. Or tired, dazed as I had been since understanding what was inside of me. I walked past the lettered concrete pillars into the lobby. I could not bring myself to thank Charles for holding the door open. He shut it now and I pushed the elevator button, watched it turn red like a misspelled word, a mistake. Everything felt wrong. We had parked on the Frank Sinatra floor. No meaning for us. I thought of our wedding song, "We Belong Together" by Rickie Lee Jones, remembered a moment of heat in my heart when I saw Charles waiting for me in the front of the room, a flash of that day from underneath this one, the way Charles had just looked standing at the door.

We walked the sci-fi tunnel, which connected various hospital wings like some intricate map of veins, and were shunted to the cosmetic and reconstructive surgery suites. Women walked into these offices hoping to be rebuilt for too many reasons for me to number or even guess at, but in the interest of putting my breasts out of my mind, I thought of all the surgeries that were likely happening right now: turkey necks being tightened even as Thanksgiving turkeys were being trucked and trussed; "tummy tucks" sucking gallons of liquefied fat out of women's abdomens; some of it being injected back into lost breasts, some of it being dumped in what, buckets? How did they get rid of the sort of fat I'd now (accidentally, but still my fault) seen on *My 600-lb Life*?

Dr. B had said at my first appointment that they might do some "light fat grafting," but that I "wasn't a candidate" for using my own tissue to reconstruct because I didn't have an area of adequate concentration, meaning "not fat enough." Since hearing this, I had begun to look at other women jealously—to think, *she's a candidate*, because I preferred the idea of moving tissue around to that of deleting my flesh and replacing it with pieces of a bouncy house.

There were many candidates in the hallway, women waddling toward surgeries different from mine, but also, I reminded myself, with unknowable outcomes. Dr. B had told me that doing the tissue-swapping surgeries required what he considered to be "the much riskier work" of reconnecting tiny blood vessels. He twinkled his fingers when he said this, like tiny little squiggly creatures, maybe showing me how many wiggly vessels he would need to reconnect if he went that route.

"The risk of the grafted tissue becoming necrotic is also a concern, of course," he said.

"What?"

"Well, sometimes the blood supply doesn't work, so the tissue we move—say, from the abdomen or the buttocks—dies."

I sorted and resorted those words that day, and again now, waiting in the waiting room with Charles: abdomen, buttocks, supply, tissue, candidate, grafting, fat, dies. No matter how I worked them, they ended badly.

The nurse called my name. Charles looked up, his eyes so familiar and concerned that I thought I might shatter or turn to salt. "Do you want me to come with you?"

"No, but thank you," I said. "Could you wait here, though?'

"Of course," he said. "I wasn't thinking of leaving."

"Oh, right," I babbled, feeling confused. He had driven me here. But I wasn't thinking of logistics, was just on the question of who I'd be in half an hour or an hour when I walked out of Dr. B's office, having seen whatever objects he would put in the spaces underneath my skin—where my breasts had been—in twelve weeks.

"Are you sure you don't want me to come, in case we have questions?"

"That's okay," I said. "We'll have another appointment after the first surgery, when I have the expanders in. We can ask then."

Charles nodded and tipped his head down to look at his phone, the bald spot on his head especially vulnerable and pathetic. It occurred to me suddenly that he cared if I died too, that if I kicked it because of this, he would have to console Alexi and probably miss me, hideous though I was.

When Dr. B came in, I was sitting demurely on the squishy plastic table, trying not to crinkle its paper.

"Hello, Samantha, how are you feeling?" Dr. B asked.

"I'm hanging in there," I told him.

"I'm glad to hear it. Let's take a look." He walked purposefully to the metal sink and washed his hands, lathering, bubbling, scrubbing, rinsing. I bet he never once walked five feet in front of his wife. I wondered who she was— was she also an ambitious, meticulous doctor? Or a teacher, maybe? A housewife?

He put his hands on me, measured something.

241

"I want to show you a few samples we have, so you can begin thinking about what sort of implants you'd prefer. There are tear-shaped, rounder, and varying degrees of firmness." I hated what was ungrammatical in this list, but what was there to do? Correct Dr. B for listing mismatched parts of speech as he displayed a line of ludicrous Jell-O molds, encased in foggy plastic? I had to swallow the laughter rising in me. He felt it, though, and smiled at me non-comprehendingly—but accommodatingly, I thought.

"I want soft ones," I said, remembering the "cool mom" in *Mean Girls*, with her giant fake boobs stabbing the friends of her teenage daughter when she hugged them. I thought of Leah, and my breath caught in my throat.

I didn't tell Dr. B about swimming, or Leah, or today's Prince line in my mind—the one from *Batman* about Vicky Vale's body. *I'm going to bust that body right, oh yeah.*

Holding those gelatinous implants in my hands—as if there were some way to gauge which one I would want him to jam between the muscle and skin of my chest wall!—inspired in me a compulsive desire to alert Dr. B to the fact that I was a unique, individual human, not just a patient, not an inert slab of both removed and remaining tissue.

"I want the simplest ones," I said, "and I don't want them to be hard, or to be silicone, or to attract attention, or to explode and kill me."

"Well," he said, narrowing my lyrical list to its most tedious and reasonable possibility, "we no longer use saline, so it will have to be silicone. But I assure you, it's very safe these days, and we have some silicones that are almost liquid, so they feel more natural and softer. We'll probably want to avoid the tear-shaped ones, as those tend to be firmer."

I said, "Want to hear a poem?"

This snapped him securely out of his reality into mine. "Well, okay," he said. "Yes, fine."

So, I recited the Hopkins' poem "Pied Beauty," enunciating perfectly all its *rose moles* and *stipple, fickle, freckled*, riding along its choppy, fanatical meter with my mouth, imagining Dr. B's ear, Hopkins' words coming in in my voice, changing some kind of chemistry in Dr. B's body. Oh yes, *whose beauty is past change*, come to Dr. B and dare him to improve you. Dr. B, I reminded myself while reciting, had a body, too, was potentially subject to human misfortune. I didn't wish suffering, pain, or surgery on him, of course, but the thought of his flesh made me feel less alone. Not so singled-out.

When I finished, he didn't say anything, probably because—what could he possibly have said? I was more embarrassed by the silence than I had been by my own insane performance, which I guess was iconic of exactly who I was.

"Sorry," I said. "I guess I was just thinking that maybe it's important for a plastic surgeon to contemplate the loveliness of imperfection."

He was kind, humoring me again, because he said, "How impressive that you've memorized that. I was glad to hear it. I haven't read a poem in years."

"You're probably busy saving lives," I proposed, regretting suddenly that I was wasting his time when other women, as panicked as I was, were probably waiting in the line of identical exam rooms down this lime-green hall. But I was also patting myself on the back because I resisted my powerful, childish urge to tell him I had hundreds of poems in my arsenal. I didn't have to beg for compliments, it turned out, because he prostrated himself next.

"I'm a failed writer, actually," he said.

I paused, unsure now of my own footing, or of how far it was appropriate to take this. "Seriously?" I felt my paper robe slipping open.

He nodded. "Truly," he said. "I tried my hand at fiction when I was an undergraduate at Michigan, but I wasn't good enough."

"Well, that's fantastic," I said, recovering my dignity with a sprinkling of banter, "because I consider myself a failed surgeon. So how about you save my life and I'll write something for you?"

He laughed, and I remembered he was dressed and I was naked.

"Sounds fair," he said. "At our post-op appointment, I'll show you the implants I think you'll like most. They're called "Inspira" and they're a very soft silicone, very safe. And we'll try to get a size that's as close as possible to your natural size."

I tried not to cry.

He lowered his voice almost to a whisper and put his hand gently on my paper shoulder. "Samantha, I want to remind you that this is a very safe procedure. You've done a wise job choosing the least-risky way to approach this cancer and the reconstruction, and you're in good hands."

We both looked at his hands, and I let my eyes linger on them. There was nothing blunt about his hands; they were instruments of grace and precision. What might he look like losing control? Maybe his fingers would clench into fists. Or maybe he'd grab the sheets or the head-board. I remembered his gesture at the appointment where I learned I wasn't a candidate for using my own tissue, his blood vessel reconnection wiggle.

"I have hundreds of poems memorized, actually," I told him.

"I'm sure you do."

There was a brief, horrific silence.

"Do you think general anesthesia may dim the lights of my mind?" I asked, because I was scared it would. Because I wanted to pretend my telling him about all the poems I could whisper in his ear if he wanted was some-how related to the surgery we were talking about. I won-dered again who his wife was, what her syntax was like. It was impossible that he wasn't married, although he wore no ring—I assumed because it might fall off and stay inside someone else's body, and what kind of metaphor for marriage would that be? Or probably he wore gloves, I realized. Maybe he was divorced.

He looked me over carefully, keeping his eyes on my face as I rewrapped myself in the robe.

"There have been numerous studies on this question," he said, and I thought I saw him in his own mind, driving along, deciding on which of several routes to take and not choosing the one that led to him reporting on any actual findings. Rerouting, in other words. He sighed kindly. "I think for you," he proposed, "a brief unconsciousness will be restorative."

If he had been someone else, I might have liked this less. "Just wake me up when it's over, please," I said.

"That's our mandate." He smiled. I thought I saw his eyebrow flick up just slightly when he added, "And my pleasure."

Maybe he felt, as I did, that this had come out sexily, because then he cleared his throat and corrected his tone, said as he put himself outside of it and closed the door, "You'll do very well."

When Charles asked me how it had gone, I said I wanted him to come in with me next time. If he was willing. "Why wouldn't I be?" he asked, and I don't think he was being sarcastic. Maybe he had no idea what was happening, or maybe *I* didn't. How could one's point of view stay intact when the antagonist was inside the protagonist, squiggling its fingers, dividing cells into endless duplicates—killing me, killing myself?

I'd never considered cancer a "battle," never liked that idea because did it mean that those who were killed by cancer were weak-willed or lost some fight? But the story of my cancer felt suddenly like a badly written plot, a fight between two characters—and a mystery, since I had no idea who would be the victor.

CHAPTER FOURTEEN

ON NOVEMBER 14TH, THEY caught the guy who peeled the dead girl's skin off. Or they thought they'd caught him. The news was orgiastic—anchorpeople crowing, graphics flashing, a hunched figure with a sweatshirt over his head being dragged by a dozen cops. His mug shot: grizzled, ugly, subhuman—and yet also oddly bland. When the hood came off and everyone got to see the face of the person who had done this thing, it was just a face: watery eyes, smoked-out skin, a half-gone look.

His mother accepted an interview—incredibly, I thought, although maybe she just wanted to say what she said, that *he was human, too*, that *she was so sorry for the girl's family*, and that *her family*—his family—*was also heartbroken*. She used "and," not "but," a good choice. There was no question of his innocence; he had confessed—gloated, in fact—to a friend, the usual way. Now the screaming choruses on either side were at it, and he was walking through crowds picketing for and against his death, even those against it only arguing on principal.

What, I wondered, did it feel like to be him? Did he still have a driving hunger, pushing him to kill and peel more women? Was he sorry to have done it, hungover with murder? Or did he forgive his own past, knowing he couldn't resist then and maybe couldn't even resist now, if given a girl walking down an empty street, vulnerable to him? What did it feel like to peel someone's skin back, to mortify the flesh of another human?

The same day I heard this report, a sinkhole opened in Florida and swallowed some man's house with him in it. I was marveling over this when I arrived home, thinking that horrible mortal thought about how, well, it could be worse—I could already be dead, look, at least I was better off than this poor schlub the ground just devoured.

But then I bent to retrieve our *New Yorker*—really, *New Yorker*? Here again? Fuck! Had it already been a whole week? Stop reminding me of my inadequacy by piling up in a taunting mess, likely to fall over, unread, and crush me someday.

Just so I could feel I had at least "read" part of it, I snapped the pompous pages open—and incredibly, weirdly, arrived at an article about mollusks in lakes.

Oh, I thought, yes, this, because I saw a sentence in which the writer delightfully described a crackling carpet of calcium on the lake floor. So I stood in our doorway reading, thinking that this might take me away from peeled girls and sinkholes and maybe even myself, but then—not even ten sentences later—the story turned into a metaphor for metastatic breast cancer! The crackling mollusks were an extended metaphor about how we needed to know the mollusk and the lake—that is, the cancer and the body. It was an article about cancer! Literally. Oh, serpent's heart, hidden by a flowering face. If I'd known it was about cancer, I would have averted my eyes, of course, but I'd read enough to make me swoon against my own front door, surrounded by grocery bags, reading on to learn that maybe my body was a particularly warm and tempting Petri dish for more cancer, for it to come back no matter whether it was in my lymph nodes or not, no matter what toxins they pumped or didn't pump through me. How did people who'd had cancer sleep again, never knowing whether the twinges in their shoulders or lower backs were the first signs of the end of their own bones?

And could it be random that after weeks of not even peeling back the front cover of a single *New Yorker*, this one either arrived or blew open to that page? I was worried I'd become spiritual, begin to believe in something other than reading as the salve for mortality.

In case I wasn't in ragged-enough shape standing there, my phone rang—a university number. I picked it up.

"Samantha?"

Oh, shit. Melody Ames. "Yes, hi, Melody."

"How are you, Samantha?" My name twice, a bad sign.

"I'm okay, Melody. How are you?" I almost said *Melody* again after *how are you*, but that seemed like too much, even for me.

"I, um—I sent you an email three days ago, but I haven't heard back, so I was just calling to follow up. I—there has been some concern among faculty and students that you might be, um, having some trouble?"

I didn't rescue her. I wasn't going to name the trouble or supply possibilities. Why should I?

"Samantha? Are you sure everything is okay? There's

been a complaint, and, well—Karen found a note in room 308 that she thought might belong to you, might be a, uh—a, well, a cry for help."

"A note?" I asked, curious. My in-class writing assignment. X and Y. Fuck this and that. I used to give a shit, that list.

"Some things about maybe having inappropriate connections to our students?"

Connections! Melody was really struggling. I almost felt bad for her then, having to navigate this conversation with me. She'd never been a lover of the violently rocking boat, and yet here we were.

"Are you saying a formal complaint has been filed against me?" I asked.

"Well, it's not in writing yet, Samantha, but we've been hearing, well—some students have come to express their concern about your well-being."

"My well-being?"

"And some of us felt your behavior at the faculty meeting last week was—well, unusual."

"I appreciate your concern," I told her.

"Is there anything going on that I can be helpful with?"

I lowered my voice, as if someone might be listening in. "I think saying the things we all know are true—at faculty meetings, for example, but not exclusively—should be less unusual in our society."

"I understand that, Samantha, but what I'm really talking about here is what's happening in your classroom. With your students."

I looked over at a picture of Charles holding Alexi like

a basketball, smiling into the sun and out at me. I asked, "Do I need to involve my lawyer in this conversation?"

I expected Melody to say *no, of course not, we'll deal with this internally at the university, it hasn't reached that level,* etc. But she said, "That might not be a bad idea, because I'm afraid I'm going to have to ask you to take a brief leave of absence while we sort this out."

"It's a medical leave," I blurted out.

"Excuse me?" Melody asked, genuinely confused.

"I was going to ask you for a medical leave anyway, because I'm ill."

"You're having some psychological trouble, then?"

"I have cancer, actually, and am having surgery a week from today."

"What?"

"I thought I could teach through it, but that has turned out to be more difficult than I anticipated."

"Is this true, Samantha? Does this mean you won't be in to teach this week?"

"I've already rescheduled this week's workshop for after the break," I exaggerated. I had told them we weren't meeting, so this counted as true enough. "And yes, it's true," I added. "I'll send a doctor's note." I hung up.

Was this what getting fired felt like? Had I been fired? And if so, what did *fired* mean? It was so much more incoherent than I'd imagined, although I hadn't ever really imagined it—not even lately, when I probably should have been preparing some alternate plan.

I was a blown-glass poet, reshaped by the flame of my firing. Now I would just be a professional writer all the time! Was getting fired like ruining my marriage; would I never be married again? Would I never teach again? Or maybe these were "temporary conditions." Ha! My first book coming back to me, waiting to bookend my life as if that life were an artful novel.

I knew I should issue a press release to Leah and my other diligent, horrified workshoppers about how I was going to take some time with my family. I could showcase the disgraced politician at my core, tell everyone I was pursuing my hobbies—then maybe, if I survived the emotion and physical aspects of this, I could pursue my hobbies. Wait, did people with kids have hobbies? What even was a hobby? Bird-watching? Bee-keeping? Making your own beer? I hadn't had a hobby since I was twenty-two, other than making food, running around the wilderness like a deer about to be shot, writing mediocre drafts of poems, reading old love letters, and peeling my student naked like a piece of tantalizing fruit.

So maybe I wouldn't go into specifics in the press release—or maybe I'd write the truth in it, which was that the thing I was most afraid of was losing Alexi or causing Alexi to lose me. Her death was my worst fear, followed by Charles's if I was being honest with myself, and then my own. Since mine was the one that seemed most likely at the moment, I was focused on that, but losing one of the two of them would be intolerable—and would lead to my death, so in that sense, those were double threats.

Alexi liked to talk about death when she was two and three and three and a half. Once, she asked if when Charles and I died, our parents could be her parents.

252

I said what any sane person would in that situation: "We will always be your parents."

And she, practical to her core, looked up at me, her eyelashes casting spiderlike shadows on her plump cheeks, and responded, "But if you are dead, how can you make my snack?"

I am still terrified by that. Who is going to make Alexi's snack?

I DIDN'T DO anything for five days, didn't cook, write, think or answer calls, didn't see or sleep with Leah, didn't read the book I kept open in front of me (there so I wouldn't scare Alexi). I turned my mind off and waited, small self in the shadows, for surgery. I didn't tell Charles about maybe—probably—getting fired, because I guess I still cared what he thought of me, and I didn't want him to know that Leah was my student or that the department disapproved. He was home the night before my surgery, but he stayed hidden in his study, as usual, more and more Bartleby even in our house. In this way, I preserved myself and my energy, what lisping whisper of sanity remained in me, for the 21st—the amputating, implanting, recovering.

Alexi read on the couch with me every day. She was reading and I was pretending to read when my phone rang, the sound of its tone bringing the surgery upon me even faster, like something heavy and sudden, even though I'd lived an entire life these last few weeks. And the phone had nothing to do with the surgery, just suggested evidence of the world—the real world—in which the procedure would take place.

253

When I heard the ringtone, I had already been fasting for two hours and was starving, imagining a parade of sexy food twitching by me: caramel apples, smoked almonds, lemonade, champagne, good green olives, soup, any soup, coffee ice cream, anything. Whoever was calling was calling again. Ring, ring, ring, ring.

I saw the rings as if they were shapes, rather than—or in addition to being—sounds: donuts, gummy candy, pineapple, apple, crabapple. I wasn't normally hungry at night, so there was no reason to be so ravenous except that I knew there could be no relief or cure, and so I developed a rabid appetite—for whatever was forbidden, obviously. Reason, not the need.

Alexi and I were lying head-to-head on the couch, both of us reading—she, Claudia Rankine's *Citizen*, and I, Anna Akhmatova's collected poems. Neither of us was actually taking in any of the words for real.

I didn't pick the phone up, just silenced the sound so I wouldn't imagine each ring. But then it buzzed again so many times and so viciously on the arm of the couch that I felt Alexi craning to look at me. So I picked it up. What did I have to hide, after all?

It was a number I didn't recognize, so maybe it was a doctor or nurse or character from a Kafka story come alive to torture me with more logistics or paperwork or insurance. I stupidly picked up.

"Professor Baxter?"

Ah, her voice, her voice. I should have known. Calling from some other phone. The sound of her turned my blood to something that fizzed out and inside me, lit my skin and slayed me like a hair dryer in a bathtub. My arms and legs buzzed and hurt.

What did I want? I knew what I wanted. I would never have her again, and certainly didn't want to talk with her now. Or ever again, really.

We were back to Professor Baxter, all the way from "Sam," skipping the intermediate, gray-area "Samantha" I'd wished for that day in Leah's bath. Maybe she was angry about the Coffee Queen bathroom, or the last five days, hearing nothing from me. I might have been angry about those experiences myself, at twenty-four.

It was imperative that Alexi hear nothing out of the ordinary in my voice. "Yes, hello," I said professionally. "Who's this?"

"What? It's Leah," she said.

"Oh, hi. How are you?" I saw Alexi's eyes stop moving on the page. She was as suspicious as I had been when she'd mentioned her Iranian Literature professor. But while I'd been wrong and projecting and paranoid, she was right.

"H—hello? Hello? Can you hear me? I can't hear you!" I panicked and hung up.

"Who was that?" Alexi asked.

"One of my students," I told her.

"Calling your cell at night? The night before you're supposed to have surgery? Do they not know?"

"I haven't told them, no."

"Do they normally call your cell at night?"

I yawned performatively, and then became so tired and engaged in the yawn while I was faking it that I almost fell off the couch. Then I yawned again for real, uncontrollably.

"Jesus, Mom, go to bed already," Alexi said.

"I think I will."

I crept upstairs, not having answered her question about whether my students normally called my cellphone at night or not.

I couldn't imagine lying down to try to sleep, go figure. For one thing, I was starving. For another, I was excitedly justifying my behavior. I had done lots of good things in my life, right? So what if, at the last moment, I made a little mistake and hurt someone, or a few people? And lost my job and ruined my reputation and marriage?

I had turned out okay, even if I died tomorrow. What absolute bullshit! Americans love to tell each other that we "turned out fine," especially when we're facing death or happen to notice for some other reason that we've become either our own parents or ugly caricatures of ourselves. As soon as Alexi was born, the "I've turned out fine" trope popped up 200 times per conversation, or I started noticing it, anyway.

Spanking was the most obvious example, of course.

Person One: "My parents spanked the hell out of me, and I turned out fine. Just fine!"

Person Two (me): "Uh . . . yeah."

The "I turned out fine" clause invariably leads to the "I'm going to do exactly what my parents did" one, so that people who hated being spanked spank the hell out of their kids, and those who rebelled against Catholic school dispatch their children directly into the arms of nuns.

So which of my own mom's proclivities had I descended into during these last few weeks? Had my mother ever done anything this ugly? Maybe my father had, I suddenly thought. Who knew what atrocities he had committed after siring me? Who knew whether he even knew he'd had a child? I had promised myself never to become like him, the way kids who don't know their own parents sometimes do, but he was an absence, a shadow, so maybe I was like Oedipus, already exactly like my father, enacting a mysterious but ordained fate I never had hope of dodging.

When Charles and I were young and still a team, we once made a list together. I loved lists; they created the only kind of order I could tolerate long-term: word order. They made me feel sane, contained, okay. But now the one we made then made me laugh—and weep. It was a numbered account of all we promised never to do: never be late to pick Alexi up at school or at a birthday party or anywhere, lest she think we had died; never criticize her friends; never threaten to get rid of the cat; never embarrass her teenage boyfriends. We would also never disown her or any siblings she might later have (as Charles's grandparents had disowned Charles's uncle when he was arrested for embezzling. They should have stood by him, obviously. Maybe he needed the money, or in any case, once he was in jail for the crime and utterly humiliated as well as ruined professionally, he probably needed parents. Of course, James, whose parents these were, thought they did the right thing, that his brother "forfeited his right to have a family" by embarrassing them with his mistake).

So I tried again. I was mostly decent, had done reasonable work, and been an okay person, right?

On the other hand, who doesn't consider herself to be comfortably in the middle of life's important spectrums: happy (happy enough), romantic (when it's called for), successful (sort of), sexy (in secret), kind (mostly), etc.? Even the stuff of daily life offers a wide range of possibilities for how to live and judge yourself and others—cleanliness, diligence, discipline—so that if you have any friends at all, you're likely to feel that some of them (the ones who keep a cleaner house than you) are obsessive and overwrought, and others (those with lots of pet hair on their clothes and furniture, and old food in the corners of their rooms) are slobs. Of course, those same friends may be discussing either how anal, sloppy, rich, or poor *you* are, because most things (except morality, I think) are relative. Everyone is entitled to a personal set of ideas about how to live.

I didn't turn out fine.

I CALLED LEAH back and she picked up after one ring. She was breathing strangely, and I wondered if maybe she was crying. I didn't ask, not because I wanted to protect her from either her suffering or potential embarrassment, but because I wanted her crying not to be my problem. I thought about how I'd never let Alexi cry for even thirty seconds when she was a baby, and even now if she cried, I felt like I was going to cry too—and sometimes did.

"Hey Leah," I said, "Sorry about earlier. I was in the middle of something."

"It's finished, right?" she asked.

"What I was doing? It was—"

"No, I mean *this*. This is finished."

"Oh, you mean our—"

I waited for her to speak, to name the thing, thought she'd say *yes*, or *yeah*, or even just a mumble to rescue me from having to name it.

But she outlasted me and I spun like a bug pinned to a science fair project, still alive. Please someone, smother me with nail polish remover. Oh wait, that was happening tomorrow.

"Um—the affair," I said, changing "our" to "the" because that seemed better, somehow—and also hoping that my willingness to say *affair* out loud, not to avert my eyes, would be of some comfort to her.

"Yes," she said, upping the ante. "I mean our affair. The sex we've been having at my apartment, the love I thought we were in."

Ah! So she'd heard and noted my revision. Good for her. And good for me, too, because I'd taught her to pay attention to the small nuances of each line.

It was my turn to talk, I realized.

"Well," I said, feeling and trying to convey sorrow. "It's complicated, but I do think that should end now. I'm so sorry."

"No," she said, "you're not sorry. You're relieved."

I was surprised—not that she was perceptive enough to perceive something so obvious, but that she would put it so starkly, so angrily, and also that she, by doing so, would risk my confirming it. When I was in young romances, I tried not to ask questions that might lead to answers I hated or dreaded; I always felt that by putting

259

words into the world, I increased the chance of making them come true.

Impressed by her bravado, and also slightly irritated by it, I decided to raise her one. "Actually," I said, "I'm having a medical crisis and have to have some surgery tomorrow, so I've been a bit out of touch with everyone."

It worked. She gasped, recalibrated, slipped off the narrative platform she'd constructed for herself over the last week of my not coming by or picking up. "Sam! What's the crisis? Are you okay? Are you coming back to teach?"

Now I rescued her. I was off the hook, so why not?

"I'll be back to teach, I hope, but I don't know when yet. I'll know more about it after the surgery tomorrow." I didn't mention the call from Melody Ames, the fact that I'd probably lost my job over Leah.

"Oh my God, oh my God," she said. "Sam?"

"Don't worry. I'm going to be okay. I'll see you back in class. But in my free time, I'm going to have to focus on recovering. I'm sorry about that." I could hear her crying again, and I resisted acknowledging it still, even though now I was getting to pretend to be kind.

"I'll be sending love," Leah said carefully—craftily, I thought, with a lot of swallowing. In spite of my resolve, I couldn't help but hear the cricket noise she made in those other swallows, and at the thought of it, remember the soft feeling of her body, her lidded look.

"Thank you," I said, not wanting, no matter what other crimes I committed, to lie to her, to give her any more hope than sex itself suggested, either real or false.

IT WAS COLD outside, but I walked out anyway, straight out our front door. I didn't know if I closed it behind me or not. I could feel a mist of winter beginning to settle over the town, feel the colors leaving, the sky and branches going white as I walked. It was wet out, and the watery streetlights connected in damp lines—tracers, maybe, but I didn't think particular to my own vision.

I walked and walked, and as I went, I began to unbutton my cardigan. When it was open and I could feel the night on my blouse, I shed the sweater onto the ground behind me. Wind blew through my thin, silk shirt, and I unbuttoned that too, the one Leah ripped. I'd been wearing it under other things since. But now I tore it further and let it slip off my body and blow somewhere behind me. Who cared where?

I walked the sidewalk, passing everything: house, house, tree, tree, lit windows here, dark one there, people around tables, silhouettes, audio off, whole other lives transpiring everywhere, lives that would continue no matter whether mine did or not. No matter what. The world was relentless, but the air felt good on my freezing skin. I unhooked my bra.

"You're welcome," I said to my breasts. "I'm letting you out at night one last time."

I began to unbutton my pants. Why not? I opened them, felt the night air on my underpants, and began to skip—because I felt free to. Because that's how free I felt, here at night in my own cold neighborhood, in the dark alone, where bad-naked met good-naked, and alive-naked trumped—for a moment, anyway—dead-naked.

I hesitated before I peeled my pants off, because there was the difficult matter of my shoes; I didn't want to risk a splinter, but felt that taking my shoes off in order to allow for the possibility of shedding my pants—only to put my shoes back on—diminished the joy somehow, ruined the momentum of skipping naked through my own static neighborhood at night.

So I left my pants on. Shirtless was fine, I decided, socks too unsexy. Into my mind came Thomas Hardy's poem "Neutral Tones:" my MRI poem, the one I always recited to myself in machines where magnets banged in my ears and contrast dye poisoned my veins and lit the calcium in my breast:

We stood by a pond that winter day.
And the sun was white, as though chidden of God.

I stopped skipping and stood under a streetlamp, imagining the light warming me up a little, and said the rest of the poem out loud in my best voice:

And a few leaves lay on the starving sod;
—They had fallen from an ash, and were gray.

Your eyes on me were as eyes that rove
Over tedious riddles of years ago;
And some words played between us to and fro
On which lost the more by our love.

I used to think this was a breakup poem, but now it seemed to me to be a death poem. I sang some of it to my breasts, turning a slow, naked circle in the spotlight on Greenway.

The smile on your mouth was the deadest thing
Alive enough to have strength to die;
And a grin of bitterness swept thereby
Like an ominous bird a-wing...

Since then, keen lessons that love deceives,
And wrings with wrong, have shaped to me
Your face, and the God curst sun, and a tree,
And a pond edged with grayish leaves.

"Samantha?"

I finished my circle, stopped turning, exhaled after the last moment of the poem, half-expecting to see Thomas Hardy back from the dead, applauding my wonderful memorization of his poem. You're welcome, Thomas Hardy.

But actually, the person calling my topless name into the night was our neighbor, Sarah Eldridge, conservative octogenarian, board-member-of-every-board-extraordinaire, drinker of cocktails with Charles's mother. Right there, next to me.

"Hi, Sarah," I said. I started laughing as I had in my workshop, glad to be seen, to be real, but also to be losing it, whatever *it* ever was. I laughed with what I thought was going to be joy, but out came a shrill, cold noise: *hak, hak, hak, hak, hak.*

Sarah Eldridge took my naked elbow, a gesture I considered courageous and generous. Intimate, even. She did it firmly, like a principal, like a mother. "Let me walk you home, dear," she said. "Charles will be worried."

I said, "I've been having sex with one of my students," and she just nodded, busy as she was shedding her jacket and putting it over my shoulders.

"Let's get you home to Charles," she said.

I didn't object to this or to the jacket, which felt quite good given how my skin had started to burn from the cold.

We didn't look for my shirt. Sarah, to her reticent credit, didn't ask or say another thing, just guided me to my own front door, keeping her ideas about my behavior to herself. I reminded myself that she was old. No one gets to be old without seeing other people in awkward moments. She must have known that human nature contained such possibilities as me half-naked outside, at night.

I walked with her because I was cold. And afraid.

"Don't knock or ring, please," I had the wherewithal to say at the last moment, up the porch steps to my own house.

"Of course, dear," Sarah Eldridge said, "but I am going to have to wait to see you get in safely, Samantha." Ah, like a parent dropping off the babysitter, making sure she had her key and opened her parents' front door and closed it behind her.

I said, "Thank you, Mrs. Eldridge," and she looked at me curiously, nodding.

I pushed the door open and slid inside. From downstairs, I heard TV music and voices, guessed Alexi was watching something. But then she appeared in the foyer, so it must have been Charles, watching dead women on TV, the sort he could now enjoy forever without ever having to listen to me fuss about it.

"Mom!" Alexi was running toward me across the foyer, grabbing a coat from the closet, grabbing wildly as if there might be a latch available to her somewhere, a handle that could restore the planet, make whatever this was okay. "What the hell happened?"

I pulled the jacket Sarah had given me close as Alexi shrugged another coat from the closet over my shoulders.

And behind her, from the kitchen, emerged someone else.

It took me a moment to see who it was because my mind went to Siobhan, but in fact, this was some other young person. Who?

I squinted like an old crone from a Disney movie, hunched toward the figure standing between my kitchen and my foyer, standing behind my daughter like a shadow.

It was Leah.

Something drummed inside me: blood or words, the beat of a meter that might take me over.

"Oh—Leah. Well, hello," I said.

"Hi, Professor Baxter," she responded, squaring her shoulders. Was she ready to do battle? Take flight? Or maybe she was panicked and miserable and trying to hide it by looking courageous? "I'm sorry to disturb you and your family at home. I—I just stopped by with some deli. When I heard that you were, uh—um, having surgery, or—well, we all wanted to, you know, the others and

265

I wanted to send our good energy for tomorrow. But um, I'll be—"

Be what, Leah, going now? Traumatized forever? Should I tell her I was fasting and couldn't eat corned beef and coleslaw at the moment? How many nouns did I need to get this encounter over with? Leah had been so confident in the beginning. Had I destroyed or devoured something in her? Would she be able to get it back?

She had come to my house because she, like I, thought I might die. We were the only two. I looked at her face, thought about how this might be the last time I'd ever see her. She had come because we were alike, because she'd also thought this might be her last chance to see me.

Alexi's eyes looked dark, like marbles in an old teddy bear. Was that fury in them? Or fear?

"Mom, go shower. We'll wait for you down here," Alexi said, and her flat eyes landed back on Leah and lit. "Come, Leah, we can sit and finish our drinks while we wait for my mom."

I asked, "What are you drinking?"

Alexi grinned. "Whiskey," she said, and in spite of myself, I looked over at Leah again. I knew better than to say anything, but this time Leah met my gaze, and raised an eyebrow slightly, acknowledging, daring me maybe. If this was round two of our stare-down, she already had me beat.

Because was I going to argue? *But you don't drink. But you said when I was at your house, in your bed—you said*—would she need to reply that this was a special occasion, that she was seducing my daughter and needed not to embarrass Alexi by turning down a tumbler of liquor? Or that she had learned the youth-ending lesson that what we do actually has consequences? That I wasn't just a boundary to be traversed, but a dangerous human being, one with cancer and a daughter, one who could be broken, and also had the potential to break somebody else?

Or maybe she was just throwing caution for a moment, trained as she had been by me, her professor.

I looked away, obviously.

They had already been drinking, I now understood. Sitting. Talking. About what, I might never know. A Hitchcock crowd of flapping birds rose from my stomach to my chest and clogged my throat.

"Okay," Leah said to Alexi, and she smiled kindly at my daughter. Leah looked sweeter than anyone I'd ever seen, including Alexi, who was looking me over again. What was she looking for? What did she see?

"Leah's mom had breast cancer," Alexi said then, her voice unusually loud, and for some reason, my eyes cast helplessly back to Sarah Eldridge, who I'd just remembered was still standing in the doorway behind me. I stared at her as if she could decode this for me, fix the situation I'd created here, but now, having caught my eye, she turned to leave.

I said, "What?" But I was looking at Sarah, not Alexi or Leah.

"Good night, Samantha," Sarah said. "I hope you feel better. Alexi—is your father home?"

"Yes," Alexi said, "do you want me to go get him?"

"No, dear," Sarah said. "I'll just call him on my walk home and let him know your mom is safe and sound."

Alexi said, "Thanks," and she and Sarah Eldridge

nodded at each other like the actual adults in the room before Sarah slipped into the night.

"Leah's mom," Alexi told me, gesturing over toward Leah. Leah had not taken her work boots off, I now saw. They were tied with something thicker than laces—black ribbons, maybe. "Her mom had cancer, mom. Breast cancer."

Prepare the trophy, because I managed to look up from Leah's bootlaces then, right at Leah herself, and to say, "I'm so sorry to hear about your mother."

But it was Alexi who responded. "She's apparently doing fine, Mom. Just like Nana. Just like most people who get breast cancer. Leah's mom had it fifteen years ago, and she's totally fine." Suddenly embarrassed, Alexi turned to Leah. "I mean, that's right, right?"

Leah nodded. "Totally," she said, a word I'd never heard her use. "We were really scared when it happened, and the surgery and chemo were hard. But they did a good job and got it all and she's been cancer-free for fourteen years. She beat it."

"Oh," Alexi said. "Fourteen. I was rounding up."

They smiled at each other and the birds in my body died and fell and landed in a heap.

That was when Charles came in. He stood at the side of the room, as if watching potential jurors in a courtroom, a look of movie star-worthy focus on his face. I wondered if he had seen the birds die inside me, or if he could tell the kind of turmoil I was in. He would eliminate me from a jury pool, that was for sure.

"Hey, Dad," Alexi said. "This is Leah, one of Mom's students."

· Charles looked at me before he looked at Leah. He was nodding; there was something disturbing to me about the motion of it. "Nice to meet you, Leah," he said.

Her face was so hot I could feel the flames coming from it when she said, "Nice to meet you, sir."

Sir? We all died. I thought I could hear us swallowing, like in a seventh-grade filmstrip about anatomy. I saw inside our throats, all of us gulping air and spit, our pink windpipes contracting over words. Who would be first to cough?

No one coughed and I wished someone would.

Finally, I said, "That was so nice of you," the bland words pale as fish. I shuddered.

Silence.

"What, Mom?" Alexi was looking from Charles to me as if trying to understand something she knew she didn't want to understand. "What was nice?"

I pulled at the jacket she had put over me. "Just—it was kind of—um, Leah, to tell you about her mom. To tell us, I mean." Sirens. Sirens! If there had been a sound designer in my life, the emergency air raid noises would have blasted us all off our feet, that's how wildly I was careening from the sky, on fire. I mean, *um, Leah?* Was I pretending not to know her name? Had it left me for a moment for real? What was real at all? Was this actually happening, and where did it end?

Charles was squinting, and had crossed his arms over his chest. I thought about my chest. What would it feel like to cross my arms over it after tomorrow? Could I? There would be slices in my armpits, metal breasts where my VLB used to be. Had Leah's mother had expanders jammed beneath her skin? Had Leah seen her through that?

"Generous, I mean," I said. "It's generous of her—you—to share that anecdote. That's—well, it's—" All my words? Gone. Even the simplest pronouns. Was Leah third-person? Second? To Leah, she was first, of course. This was a story she was living too, in which I'd been what—her teacher fantasy, maybe, or someone she'd admired and desired. Someone who had turned out to be not only fatally flawed, but also tied to Charles and Alexi. Real people, with whole lives, who were their own first-person narrators. None of that could be said. I'd saved up words my entire life—maybe for this moment—but I lost track of them, felt them disintegrate into something granular somewhere underneath me, sand, glass, single letters, shards of something shattered. There was absolutely nothing left to say ever again.

"Mom, are you okay? Maybe you should go upstairs and warm up in the shower or something? I can make you some tea. Here," Alexi proposed, beginning to turn back toward the kitchen. Leah was electrocuted, staring at me. Charles was watching her. The twin notes of embarrassment and despair in Alexi's voice as she begged me to leave and offered me tea were maybe the worst part of this entire catastrophe. Well, until what happened next.

"Samantha?" Charles said.

The girls headed back toward the kitchen, either ready to rescue or destroy each other, but in any case, equally eager to get away from me. Alexi moved on her beautiful giraffe legs and I thought of the episode of *Planet Earth* where the giraffe is being chased by a lion and stomps the thing like it's an ant. I love underdog stories. I watched Alexi until she was almost to the kitchen.

"I love you," I said, and both girls turned. Hope streaked across Leah's face like an exhibitionist running across a football field, but I looked away fast and locked eyes with Alexi, who didn't speak, just nodded almost imperceptibly before they turned the corner and disappeared. At our table, they would now be young together, and kind to each other, and fall in love like in *The Graduate*. Maybe after discovering my worst secret, and either finding or not finding vocabulary to describe or cope with it. Leah would be much better off with Alexi than she would with me, obviously. Or maybe she'd continue to be kind, wouldn't tell Alexi anything horrible, wouldn't even intimate what had happened. Maybe she'd do what it seemed she had been doing since arriving at our house late the night before my surgery, which was comforting my daughter. With stories of her own mother.

Leah had a mother. Just like I had a daughter. I'd apparently been lobotomized not to have forced myself to consider that—I mean, really consider it—before.

"I love you, too," I thought I heard, but they were already in the kitchen, weren't they? So whose voice said she loved me? No one's, maybe. Or mine, or someone in the chorus of my mind. Maybe an Alexi from the last nineteen years. I saw her in her oink!baby pajamas with the small pig on the chest, the orange zipper, reaching up, *Mama*.

Or maybe Charles. Was it Charles who'd said it?

He followed me as I went upstairs to shower, thaw my skin, and put on actual clothes—followed close behind me on the stairs like a stalker, or an anchor. I thought for a strange second of the shirt I'd left on the street. Maybe it was blowing around now like a plastic bag in an art house film. Or maybe it was dirty and trampled, an already unrecognizable part of the pavement.

We arrived at our bedroom and I pushed the door open and walked in without saying anything. I headed past our closet, past our bed, toward the bathroom, resisted turning around, but Charles said, "Sam," and this stopped me. I looked forward, out the window at our deck, invisible in the night. How I longed to hang from its wet iron railing now. "Turn around."

I turned to face him, feeling suddenly stunned by every reality. I was forty-two years old. Charles and I had been together for nineteen years. This was our life. Even though I had tried to smash myself back in some kind of horror movie cut to a previous me, I was still here. Might still be here after tomorrow, and then what? I felt a singeing desire to wake up, to escape who I'd become and whatever he was about to say about it. If I could have, I would have chewed my way straight out of the lecture I knew awaited me, the trouble I was in.

But I turned, and Charles looked into my eyes with his familiar face, his unibrow, his gray eyes—so lovely, so close to Alexi's. His mouth made the straight line it made when he was disappointed by the world's idiocy. How could someone go from looking like Alexi to looking like Charles's father in under a single second, like a race car?

What his thin mouth whispered was, "What are you doing, Samantha? What's going on?"

"What?"

"Don't ask me what."

"I don't know which thing, I mean, don't know what you mean."

"I mean: what the fuck are you doing? What is happening? How am I supposed to help you through whatever this is, and what about Alexi? Talk to me, Sam." He was pleading, but *fuck* was unlike him. My cruelty was contagious.

"I was—I'm sorry about Sarah Eldridge, and the—did she call you?"

"Yes, she called me. But don't obfuscate. Just tell me whatever this actually is and then we can work from there." He lowered his voice then, to a register so deep he sounded like someone else. "Can you please give me the dignity of not lying to me, after—what—after—what is going on with the young woman in our kitchen? Are you—" He cut himself off, unwilling, as I had been and still was, to name what this was.

I was thinking, *obfuscate*?

Charles rerouted and asked, not unreasonably, "Why is one of your young students at our house in the middle of the night on the night before your surgery?"

I said, "I didn't ask her to come here—she just—I would never have—"

And he knew. His face looked like a wrecking ball had hit it, all the angles collapsing into a pile of jawbone and neck.

"So that is what this is. She's Alexi's age, Samantha. She's Alexi's age, for fuck's sake. And *your student*. What are we going to do? Where do we go from here?" He shuddered. Another *fuck*; he was losing his kindness, his advantage, maybe his calm. I felt for him. He was shaking, although whether with rage or misery I couldn't tell. I did not mention that Leah was five years older than Alexi.

But hold the applause, because I said, "I'm sorry. It's not a real thing, though," which we can all agree came out wrong.

Charles began shaking his head. He looked like he might be having a seizure.

"No," he said, but to me? To himself? "No. No. I'm not going to do this." He looked straight at me again, and I thought now that the shaking-his-head thing was intentional, instead of letting his body shake him. "I'm not doing this with you, Samantha. I'm not going to go into the worst-case scenario-land you sometimes create, just so you can live out every possible horror to its furthest and most damaging reaches. This is a real thing. I don't know what's going on with your student, but you're going to have to fix whatever in God's name is happening here, in our house. With me and with Alexi and with you. I'm not actually going to let you destroy us just to save us from grieving if you die—which, since there's no statistically meaningful chance of, seems to be an excuse you're employing. Why that is, I can't guess."

I swallowed a big, dark shape rising in my throat and started coughing, like I had in the dream where I spit my chicken insides into the kitchen sink. Charles did not ask whether I was okay. He just waited. There was so much waiting all the time now—sickening, dizzying waiting.

I finally spoke, and my voice sounded like the old me, the grown-up one who said sensible things to Charles, my partner. But what I said was so disingenuous that I hated myself more than Charles could have.

I said, "I think my student came over because she found out I'm sick and wanted to show her concern, but is young enough that she miscalibrated how to do that appropriately."

And Charles said, "Please don't patronize me with asinine deflections, Samantha. I am not one of your unsophisticated twenty-year-old students. I can't be hoodwinked. I'm an adult, Sam, with eyes. I could see what was happening downstairs. I just hope to God Alexi can't."

Asinine? *Hoodwinked*? Were we in some weird, terribly written, old-fashioned courtroom drama? But Charles's anger, stilted though it was, was unusual enough to make me feel flutters of real fear—at what outcome, I didn't know. Maybe that he would say what I was, what I had become, and I would have to hear it, face it for real, myself.

"I decided to take a medical leave from teaching," I blurted out.

This worked. He forgot he'd been ramping up to true fury, and descended instead into surprise. "What? When?"

"For the rest of the quarter. And maybe next quarter too. Depending on how I feel."

Charles took this in, became himself again. "Right, okay—I thought you had decided not to do that."

I stood still, hopeful that I had derailed him from the worst parts of this, especially the question of what Alexi was learning downstairs in our kitchen, what Leah might be saying. Had I wrecked the possibility of Alexi forgiving or loving me, whether I died or not?

"Samantha? Are you still conscious?"

I raised an eyebrow at the meanness, which surprised me, as much as I deserved it. "Don't ask me that. I changed my mind."

He said, "Indeed."

"Charles? Can I shower now? And put on my pajamas?"

He was still shaking his head, but he turned to leave the room then, and I felt eviscerated by relief and terror. I couldn't separate the two. Now there was nothing left between me and tomorrow. It would happen. What else could I do before it did? What would be the last thoughts I had before they cut the wiring in my brain, even if only for a few hours?

"Wait, Charles?"

He turned back toward me, resigned, his right eye twitching slightly. "Yes?"

"Did Sarah Eldridge say anything?" I had told her. Maybe he had already known about Leah when he came in. Maybe he hadn't been able to see it—whatever it was—in her, and maybe Alexi wouldn't, either. It hardly mattered, but I wanted him to stay. I wanted him to keep talking to me.

"Yes. She called to say that you were wandering in the neighborhood without your clothes on. For God knows how long before she found you."

I felt happier. Now we had something to discuss. "That's only partially true," I argued, still in my flat, sane voice. "I wasn't wandering. I was standing there, thinking about Thomas Hardy. Remember that poem, "Neutral

Tones?" I read it to you once at Walden, in that horrible cottage—it's about the grayish pond?"

He was scraping his hand through his hair and I thought he might tear a clump out. But he didn't, just kept combing his fingers and listening to me. Out of pity, I guessed, or deep obligation.

"Sarah Eldridge doesn't know this, of course, but the reason I took my shirt off was because it was the last time I would ever feel—I don't know. I don't know what it will be like to . . . I took my shirt off outside because I just wanted to feel free for one more minute, to feel air, or whatever, on my chest. Like taking a dog who's about to get euthanized for his last walk."

Charles turned away from me then, so I couldn't tell what he was doing or thinking—crying, rolling his eyes, or closing them, maybe, to escape me.

He spoke then in his low register, which I now understood was the result of restraint, of submerging what he wasn't willing to speak. And he was crying. I worried he might wake in the morning with debilitating back pain. What he managed to say was, "Tomorrow we will ask about psychiatric care for you when we're at the hospital, Samantha. Because you cannot romance your students, or invite them to our house at night, or walk naked—no matter how compelling your reason may be—around the neighborhood in thirty-five-degree weather. None of this is okay. Not for you, or for Alexi, or for me."

I didn't argue, just added, "Or Sarah Eldridge. For God's sake," and in spite of himself and the crying, Charles laughed with me for a minute before walking out, leaving me alone.

CHAPTER FIFTEEN

AT 4:20 A.M., WE ALL FOUND each other in the kitchen, and at 4:30 a knock on our hideous front door that I wanted to tear off the hinges revealed my mother, holding coffees for herself and Charles.

She kissed me on both cheeks and then on my mouth and forehead while I stood there like a teenager. "Okay, Mom, enough," I said, taking my face away from her.

"I'm so sorry you can't have coffee because you're fasting," she said. "I'll have one ready for you in the recovery room."

"They'll let me drink Starbucks in the recovery room?" I asked.

"This isn't shitty Starbucks, I beg your pardon," my mother said. "This is coffee I roasted and made myself. I just used paper cups left over from when Julie brought a cardboard Starbucks box of coffee to my house—imagine bringing that to someone's brunch!"

Alexi appeared at the bottom of the stairs then, looking like a skinny lion, her giant mane of tangled, blonde hair everywhere. I walked up to her and smothered her. She smelled faintly of lotion, shampoo, and teenage-girl sweat. I did not allow myself to be reminded by it of Leah.

"Go back to sleep, sweetheart. There's no reason for

you to come so early. You can join us later, when I'm awake."

"Are you kidding?" she asked. "I'm fucking coming with you guys. This is why I came home." I realized then, a slight clearing cutting into my daze, that I had, in fact, believed—in the vault of my cynical heart—that Alexi had come home to catch me with Leah, to figure out what sins I was committing, to know how horrid I was, maybe even to call me out on my betrayal of her father, to keep me in check.

But in fact, she'd come home because I had cancer and she was a good and decent person, a filial daughter who wanted to sit this surgery out with Charles, who thought I'd live through it and wanted to see me, her mother, recover.

"Of course," I said. "Of course you did. I know that—I— let's all get ready. I have to be there at five."

I had already brushed my teeth and washed my face. Now it was just a matter of taking off my rings and the studs I wore in my ears, putting on soft clothes, and trying to banish from my mind my almost-equivalent mortal fear and pathological longing for coffee.

I left my phone turned off in the nightstand drawer. I didn't want anyone other than my mother, Alexi, and Charles to be in touch with me—maybe ever again.

Even if I didn't die, I might willingly plunge myself off the face of my own life and never emerge again.

We all met back in the foyer. My mother looked like she'd been crying, but decided not to make it my business. I thought of Charles's grandparents, disowning his uncle over the legal troubles. What circumstances would make my mother disown me? I didn't think there were any. Even if I murdered someone, I could imagine her showing up at prison, carrying coffee she'd roasted herself. I remembered suddenly the kiln she'd had in her yard when she took a fleeting but intense interest in pottery. The exercise pool on her first floor, its single wave pushing her back over and over as she swam toward it. I'd found the pool too metaphorically horrific for words (let alone participation), but she swore by it, said it prevented arthritis, was the reason she was the only one among her cohort not to have any physical pain. She was very proud of this.

"You ready?" Charles asked. I looked up. He was talking to me. His hair was messy and he looked exhausted, even like he might have been crying, too. I felt a wildfire burn through my body and brain, melting them together, ruining all the work I'd been doing to keep them separate. Please, I thought, black me out, flames. Burn me senseless. Just like this. Please don't let me think or feel or do anything else at all. Was this the same as wishing to be dead?

"Ish," I said. We both noticed I was crying. I didn't care and didn't wipe my eyes.

Charles took my hand and held it on the way to the car.

We drove through the dark, wet morning, our headlights like my goggles in the pool, fogged, the streets empty and invisible.

"This is going to be okay, you know," Charles said in a quiet voice, and for the first time I understood clearly that he wasn't sure that was true, either—that the self-doubt

I'd wished upon him, the feeling familiar to everyone except Charles, I thought, of not being lucky, or blessed, or invulnerable, was upon him now. Was it poetic that he'd suffered it because of *my* body's failure?

I let myself imagine in the car what it would be like for Charles if I perished right after behaving like a lunatic and ruining our vows. I stopped crying. Would he be able to delete that penultimate chapter from his mind and the narrative? Or it would come to define me in the way such chapters can, the way his grandmother's late-life antics had ruined everyone's images of her, even though those images took decades to build and she was only crazy for the last few years? Poor Betty—ravaged by dementia at eighty-four after being a cheerful Pollyanna for all eighty-three years preceding that—was remembered finally by everyone as Mad Betty. Very unfair and yet, sometimes the last thing you do is the one for which people remember you.

That last workshop, where I laughed about the demon triangle in my student's poem. One of two things would happen: I'd return to teach and we'd smooth it over, or it would ruin me, be the last thing I ever taught—my own scorn.

The part in the email from Melody Ames, to which I had never responded, the one about my list of "I used to 'X' but now I 'Y'?" I would have to discuss *that* when I returned from my medical leave, right? Melody would probably be holding it, waving it like a flag. Evidence.

Maybe I would deny it, ownership, authorship, or just the truth of it, say it was someone else's or completely fictional. Or maybe I'd never have to explain that written part one way or the other because I'd be expelled without a hearing, on the basis of Leah telling them about my inappropriate relationship with her, a current student.

Hanging from our balcony—at least that one, I got away with! Also, the sleeping bag on the stairs.

The naked streaking on our cold street? I saw Alexi again, standing in the foyer, feral with alarm as I stumbled frozen and insane up the stairs. Leah behind her, coming out from the kitchen, a generous, fully rendered human being with agency, with her own feelings and ideas, who had been kind enough to tell Alexi that her mother had also had cancer and been okay. And kind enough, I thought and hoped, not to have mentioned my transgressions, to sit with my fearful daughter the night before my cancer surgery and console her, drink whiskey, stay even after I appeared, naked and crazy. Maybe she wouldn't like me anymore after that strange performance, and the whole situation would resolve itself without my having to do anything upstanding.

One of them had said, "I love you, too," when I said, "I love you." It had been Alexi, right?

I wondered whether Charles had hung up with Sarah Eldridge, told me he was sending me to a shrink the second I woke up, and then maybe stayed up all night consoling Alexi. If so, he had likely told her I was breaking a little under the stress but that after today, I'd be back to myself, would be okay. We would all be okay. You're okay, I'm okay. I wondered whether he believed—in a way I didn't—that I had a reliable or even consistent self, one to whom I could be returned. Is any of us ever okay, and if not, why can't we stop bullshitting each other constantly about it? Why not just say all the ways in which we aren't okay, and may never be okay, and let each other breathe?

Maybe Alexi was grown-up enough now to make her snacks, to fall in love and get married, to survive without me. And maybe she wouldn't have to. Maybe I would wake up after. They would clear it out, and I'd wave to this me from that shore. Fog, with a low green humming behind it, was now coming through.

Maybe machines, okay. Maybe lines, lights, faces. Maybe Alexi's face! Maybe I'd wake to see Alexi's face, blurry. I'd need my glasses—wait, here, my mother's face too.

Alexi and my mom would be floating over me like in movies and TV shows when women wake from comas, still naked, not dead. My mouth would be incredibly dry, my eyes blurry, or their faces blurry. Something. I'd want to say hi, try to reach out and touch either of them, but my arm would weigh too much.

"Sam?" My mother would be saying my name.

Maybe my daughter, my mother. Maybe thoughts would begin to line up in my mind behind words.

"You're awake!" Alexi would sing, the joy and relief in her voice so babyish I would get a glimpse of her toddling down a hallway toward me, arms up—to be lifted, snuggled, fed.

Charles would be behind her, an arm around her shoulder. I'd smile at him, maybe come back to life suddenly, see him. My vision would be sliding open. He would be looking at me, relief stripping across his face—why? Because he'd been afraid too.

Maybe he'd say, "Dr. A says she got it all. The reconstruction was fine, the expanders are in. And your lymph nodes look clean. They'll know for certain by Wednesday, but it's not in there. You're okay. This was it. Dr. A says they expect you not to need any additional treatment. It's over."

Maybe then I'd feel my mother's hand pulling a blanket up over thick, white bandages, feel the plastic drains shift as I moved to get a better view of Alexi.

Maybe I'd say two crisp words: "I'm awake."

Alexi would be reaching for something, which I would hope was water but which would turn out to be a small tube of lip gloss. She would unscrew the cap with her delicate, chewed-up fingers, and put gloss on my lips. "I know it's stupid," she'd say. "I just don't want your lips to hurt. They look very dry."

My mother, who always knew what I needed without my having to tell her because she was my mother, would come back in, carrying a Styrofoam cup. She'd hold it over me so I could look in, and I'd see ice chips, like the view of snowed mountains from a plane. She would ask if I was thirsty and even my arms would be made lighter by the possibility of the ice—my mouth would be rescued; she would fish freezing slivers out and drop them onto my tongue, where they'd melt immediately, numbing, erasing all the words I said leading up to this.

Maybe Alexi's voice would float over me. "Are you okay, Mom?"

I would make the sound of the many *m*'s that could mean yes and try to nod, while I set myself to receive mode, feel around with my mind for my body. On the

wall of the room, in a small, green space absent of medical equipment, a shadow would take the shape of a girl.
I wouldn't know then—as I didn't know now—whether I
was hallucinating, or even if what I saw when I was out
was more or less real than what I saw and knew when the
switches in me were on. That's what I'd have lost forever
after this, no matter what happened, no matter who I
became if I woke up again.

But maybe I would try to see the shape as clearly as I
could; it would look like Leah—or Alexi.

Or me—maybe it would look like me, on one leg, a bird
whose feathers I'd be able to make out along the lines of
what were clearly wings. Maybe.

ACTUALLY, DR. B came in with a headlamp and a blue
Sharpie.

"Are you going spelunking?" I asked. But his mood was
serious, for which I guess I should have been grateful. I
started to think of the MRI, its terrifying, banging mag-
net tubes, icy dye piping into my arm, each waiver I had
signed each time, promising if the contrast poisoned me
I wouldn't sue.

I remembered the feeling of the snow falling on my
shoulders, the cold light of the streetlamp last night, being
naked in the street, inside my own body, with at least
enough agency to have shed and lost my clothes on the
sidewalk. What might have happened if Sarah Eldridge
and her gentle voice and arm hadn't guided me home?
Would I have frozen like the guy in that middle-school
story about building a fire? The one where he tries his
best but the matches get wet? Would Charles and Alexi

have had to live forever with the final page of my story being the one in which I died reciting "Neutral Tones" under a streetlight, half-naked outside our house?

And even now that last night's romp in our neighborhood hadn't killed me, would it be my final gesture, the thing for which they remembered me best? Or were there more and worse revelations to come? How much had Leah told Alexi at our table, how much had Alexi guessed? Maybe Leah had said, "I'm your mother's girlfriend," and Alexi was waiting for me to be out of surgery before she asked me to explain myself—or worse, would pack the secret into herself without ever asking me anything. Or maybe Leah would confirm it for them after I vanished, come again to my door with her lips half-pink from gloss, half-blue from cold—and what? Read her snow poem about me out loud? She and Alexi would watch each other, knowing, the way girls do, that there was something unspeakable between them, something having to do with sex or outrage. *There's something you might want to know about your mother's life.*

If Alexi were thirty or forty, she might be able to feel some peace at learning I had derived strange joy at the end of my life. But now, what but absolute rage and betrayal (and disgust) could she possibly feel?

Dr. B took the Sharpie and drew lines: first at the tops of my breasts, then down my sides. I looked at the drawings; they made my breasts look like faces with sad expressions. I started to cry and was thinking about how I hadn't really cried very much at all in these hideous weeks when Dr. B took a tissue from the table next to the bed, delicately, waved it into my hand like a small, white flag, and waited. Who was surrendering to whom here? Who had been the king of Leah's and my sex, the queen, the master, the servant, the man? Maybe neither of us, maybe both. Not everything had to be so binary, right?

Dr. B stopped drawing while I tried to be okay. I had no power over anything at all. Never had. Dr. B's patience made my terror and self-pity more acute. But it also made me want to stop crying faster so I could get this nightmare show on and done.

Charles was suffering on the side of the bed, holding his hands as if each was something he'd just made of clay and now wanted to destroy.

I reached up for him, and he moved closer, bent down toward the bed to put his arm around my shoulders stiffly. He'd been right, of course; I had been crazy.

I had been crazy in Leah's hallway, living room, bathtub, life. Only three weeks ago, she had flung me onto her futon, torn my clothes off like we were in a soap bopper, like nothing meant anything—until it did, like it always does. Is it in *The Crucible* or *Sometimes a Great Notion* where he says, "There's a promise made in every bed?" I think it's *The Crucible*, but prose and dialogue have always been one melty mess in my mind.

There was a promise made, though, on every blanket with Leah in the park, in my hands moving over her skin, tongue tracing her teeth. Were those promises broken already, or just destined to be broken? And worse, not for her but for me, what if those experiences were the truth, the core of what I wanted and who I was? What if my entire, middle-class, bourgeois bubble life—leading

287

up to those few hours I spent with Leah—was the stupid artifice?

"Are you all right? Do you need a minute?" Dr. B asked.

"I'm fine," I said. "Thank you for the tissue. You can keep drawing." But he was done.

"Dr. A is on her way—we're going to start in ten minutes if you're ready. Do you have any questions for me or for the anesthesiologist?"

I turned to the anesthesiologist, a bald man with a Russian accent. "Have you ever lost anyone?"

He seemed unsurprised by this. "No," he said. "Not here."

He patted me awkwardly, and I wondered whether this kindness, and as a result Dr. B's too, were part of their training: *Be nice to the woman you're about to knock unconscious and saw up into parts. Don't let her be reminded of murder. Pat her. Wait while she cries for herself or the children she might orphan, at home watching* SpongeBob. *Offer your hand or a tissue. Human contact reminds patients of our shared humanity.*

He was patting my hand a lot, like Lenny, patting the girl to death in *Of Mice and Men*. I hadn't managed to stop crying, and Charles looked desperate, like he might despair or panic, neither of which I'd ever seen him do. But he hadn't slept in weeks, and such deprivation could break even the sanest among us. Was that why I had done so many disastrous things? To test or punish Charles for the ways in which we were different? Did I want to see him suffer, to see my own sorrow reflected in the person closest to me? And if so, had it worked?

He left then, because they only let one person stay

with me at a time and he and my mother had apparently made arrangements to take turns. My self-loathing rolled over my fear, and they combined into something so toxic I thought I might die before anything else competing for a chance to kill me prevailed.

I wished they would put me under right now. I couldn't stand to be with my own brain for another second. Unconsciousness? Bring it on.

"Can you please just put me to sleep now?" I asked the bald Russian anesthesiologist.

"Hi, darling," my mother said, appearing at the side of the bed. I let go of the freezing metal railing, which I hadn't noticed I was gripping, and let her hold my hand. Her hand felt warm and familiar, and I closed my eyes, breathed out.

Something cold came into my arm, something bluer than my vein, something intrusive, interrupting, freezing me, but contradicted by my mother's hand and voice.

Then something plastic, some edges maybe on or over or somewhere near my face. Upside down, inside-out, dreaming clouds.

"You're going to do brilliantly, Sam," my mother said. "I'm certain."

Someone, maybe me, or maybe someone outside me, a doctor or a nurse or Charles or Leah or my workshop students, someone I couldn't see or fully imagine or render began counting backwards: one hundred, ninety-nine, ninety-eight, ninety-seven, ninety-six.

I said, "Hi, Mom. I'm glad you're here. Please stay."

"Of course I'll stay."

"Close," I said. "Stay close."

She said, "Close, yes. I'll be right here. And Alexi and Charles are here, too, honey. We're all here. We'll see you when you wake up."

Then she leaned down and kissed me, in some kind of blue light. I could still hear the counting. Numbers moving down, down. November 21st. I was forty-two. There was some mathematical relationship between those, eleven, twenty-one, forty-two, right? But I couldn't assign meaning, couldn't think my way back to anywhere I'd been or what anything meant.

Numbers themselves had never been clear to me, but now, suddenly, the ones in my ears and mind became colorful and beautiful—became various voices, helium notes, floating until I lost track of them and myself. Here were a billion balloons, lovely words with double *o's*— *moons*, *zoos*, *taboos*, Leah's low, vowel-y *oohs*, Alexi's baby coos moving away from me.

I moved away from me too, a woman-shaped cloud shifting, changing, rising over, up, out.

ACKNOWLEDGMENTS

THE POLITICAL AND LITERARY solidarity I've experienced over the last three years have been essential and sustaining not only for my writing, but also for my life. I feel profound gratitude to those who helped me make and publish this novel:

Feminist powerhouse and inimitable editor Jennifer Baumgardner; warrior and ally in all, Jill Grinberg; and the army of fierce women I love, need, and trust most: Christine Jones, Julia Hollinger, Lara Phillips, Donna Eis, Erika Helms, Shanying Chen, Ally Sheedy, Rachel Cohen, Tamar Kotz, Olati Johnson; Nami Mun, Yvette Charboneau; Teri Boyd, Suzanne Buffam, Molly Smith-Metzler; Kirun Kapur; Emily Rapp-Black, and Cheryl Strayed. I could not survive, let alone write/revise without you. To my writers group, for years of support both moral and poetic: Gina Frangello, Thea Goodman; Dika Lam, Emily Tedrowe, Rebecca Makkai, and Zoe Zolbrod. My soulful, serious, and incredibly brilliant, generous colleagues and students; I am beyond grateful for all the imagining and work we do on literary empathy, rendering our opposites, and crafting bad heroines/good villains.

My literary family, who read this many times, forgiving its furious heroine and rageful syntax. Thank you for understanding what it means to imagine: my insanely fantastic parents, Kenneth and Judith; and my loving, radical in-laws, Bill Ayers and Bernardine Dohrn.

My daughters Dalin and Lightie make it impossible for me not to write about love, even when I'm trying to create a villainous heroine, even when resisting, even when enraged, even when. They are forever the best force of love, levity, and beauty in my life and mind.

Zayd, thank you most. You make everything better/ poetic/wild fun/right/complete.